feels like the FIRST TIME

Also by Marina Adair

Destiny Bay series

Last Kiss of Summer

Feels Like the First Time

Sequoia Lake series

It Started with a Kiss

The Eastons

Chasing I Do

Promise You Me

Crazy in Love

Sugar, Georgia, series

Sugar's Twice as Sweet

Sugar on Top

A Taste of Sugar

Heroes of St. Helena series

Need You for Keeps

Need You for Always

Need You for Mine

St. Helena Vineyard series

Kissing Under the Mistletoe

Summer in Napa

Autumn in the Vineyard

Be Mine Forever

From the Moment We Met

feels like the FIRST TIME

A DESTINY BAY NOVEL

MARINA ADAIR

FOREVER
New York Boston

Forever
Hachette Book Group
1290 Avenue of the Americas, New York, NY 10104
forever-romance.com
twitter.com/foreverromance

First Edition: April 2017

Forever is an imprint of Grand Central Publishing. The Forever name and logo are trademarks of Hachette Book Group, Inc.

The publisher is not responsible for websites (or their content) that are not owned by the publisher.

The Hachette Speakers Bureau provides a wide range of authors for speaking events. To find out more, go to www.hachettespeakersbureau.com or call (866) 376-6591.

ISBNs: 978-1-4555-6229-9 (mass market), 978-1-4555-6228-2 (ebook)

OPM

10 9 8 7 6 5 4 3 2 1

feels like the FIRST TIME

Chapter 1

Nothing pissed off Bradley Hawk quite like being played. Except being played while wearing nothing but boxers and an epic case of bedhead.

For a guy whose front door faced Main Street, grabbing his hockey stick, forgoing jeans, and rushing out the door was a bonehead move. But he'd heard the alarm sound, the one rigged to let him know if someone was tampering with his inventory, and he acted without thinking.

A trait he'd worked hard to overcome, with little success.

Over the past few weeks, several empty kegs had disappeared from his bar. Not enough to call the cops, but enough to make him think one of his employees was selling them on Craigslist.

It wasn't about the money. For Hawk, it came down to the fact that he was getting screwed over by someone he trusted. Because the Penalty Box wasn't just a sports bar and grill, it was his home. The employees, his family. And he refused to let his home be torn apart from the inside.

Not again.

So pants be damned, Hawk raced down the steps of his apartment, which sat above the bar. The wood planks were cold beneath his bare feet, slick from the fog that had rolled in off the Pacific Ocean.

It was late spring in Destiny Bay, and Mother Nature was acting as if she were menopausal, her mood fluctuating from hot flashes to freeze your nuts off. This morning's mood was the latter.

The sun was beginning to rise over the lush peaks of the Cascade Range, painting the sky a hazy mosaic of purples and blues. It was barely past dawn.

Meaning, it was too early for this shit.

Unfortunately, it wasn't too early for the Senior Steppers to be out. Dressed in their matching velour sweat suits, white walking shoes, and knit caps, the group was hitting their stride and passing Steel Magnolia's, the garden art shop next door, when Hawk hit the sidewalk.

A collection of shocked gasps filled the air. Two of the ladies even clasped their chests in a way that had Hawk skidding to a stop.

"Sorry if I scared you, ladies," Hawk apologized, dropping his hockey stick to a nonthreatening pose by his side. "Did you see anyone suspicious walking around the parking lot?"

"We were too busy staring at your stick to notice," Fiona Callahan, his best friend's grandmother said, her eyes dipping embarrassingly low. "About time, too. We started to feel left out, seeing as all of the other girls in town had their peek."

"Can I get a picture with me holding it?" Margret Collins, the senior center's Sunshine Girl, said pulling out her phone. "For Instagram. I'm trying to build my following. And me holding a Stanley Cup winner's stick would gain a lot of likes."

It would gain Hawk a never-ending supply of shit from his friends.

"Maybe later, I gotta go," he said, ignoring the giggles, and a catcall from the pastor's wife that would make even the most confident man blush. The camera flash that lit up the parking lot as he raced toward the loading dock behind the bar, *that* was hard to ignore.

Hawk reached the dock, saw the stack of empty kegs that he'd left out as bait, and nothing else. No prowler, no group of employees plotting how to take down the bar one keg at a time. He spun around, looking in all directions, his eyes expertly scanning the shadows for movement. Nope, Hawk was completely alone—and missing three kegs.

Crap.

He lowered his stick once again and considered accepting the loss. That way he could go back to bed and pass out until next week. A decent night's sleep would bring some perspective to the situation.

Ever since he and his best friend's company, Two Bad Apples Hard Cider, had taken off, Hawk was busting his ass to fulfill cider orders by day, and running his bar at night.

Today marked his first day off in three months, and he'd be damned if he was going to spend it in a dark parking lot, contemplating who was screwing with his stuff.

Determined not to waste another second, Hawk headed

for his apartment. He'd made it as far as the middle of the lot when a loud noise came from the back of the garden art shop next door.

Normally this wouldn't set off red flags, since the owner tended to work at the most infuriating hours—namely, the five hours Hawk actually got to sleep.

But this wasn't the normal power saw cutting through steel grating he'd come to know and loathe. This was more of a scraping of metal across the concrete.

Like someone dragging a keg through Steel Magnolia's back room.

Hawk closed his eyes and let out a slow breath, for the first time feeling sorry for the poor SOB who had the misfortune of trying to hide stolen property in Ali Marshal's work space. Ali didn't like people invading her space, and she might be small enough to pass for Tinkerbell, but she packed one hell of an attitude.

Not to mention she was lethal with the blowtorch.

"You might want to come out," Hawk said, crossing the parking lot and walking up to the back door of the repurposed firehouse. "You're safer facing the music and turning yourself in, trust me."

When he got no response in return, Hawk accepted his fate and pushed through the unlocked door. Only instead of finding one of his night staff huddled in the corner with his kegs, he found his thief standing over his missing metal canisters in a pair of combat boots, a welder's mask pulled low, and a blowtorch in hand.

A lit blowtorch.

"What the hell are you doing?" he hollered as the red flame closed in on one of the kegs.

Ali's head lifted in his direction, and from behind the

mask he could feel the narrowing of those intense green eyes. The blowtorch flickered twice in warning.

Hawk jumped back right before the heat would have singed his chest hairs—and other, more crucial, parts. But that wasn't what had him stepping back. Ali had spent the better part of the past decade threatening to roast his nuts, so that was nothing new. What was new, was the silky green strapless number that hugged her curves and showed off those toned legs that had his mind racing.

Ali either wore coveralls or denim, always black and always with a *Bite me* attitude that left men panting or praying for their lives. Men who weren't named Hawk, that is.

Not only had he known Ali when she was a pierced-nosed teen, but she was also his sister-in-law. Well, she had been before Hawk's wife, Bridget, traded him in for a newer, shinier model. He'd lost the ball when Bridget kept yanking his chain, but kept the kid sister.

Although she didn't look like a kid in that dress. Which in no way excused the sharp jolt of awareness that was anything but brotherly. Something else he'd been trying to overcome as of late.

"One mark on my keg and I'll post a photo of you in that dress on my timeline," Hawk said, folding his arms across his chest—making damn sure his eyes didn't stray below the chin.

The blowtorch flickered out and she flipped her mask up—and yup, those emerald eyes were skewering him. "*Your* kegs. Huh?" She set the blowtorch on the table and took off her work gloves. "Funny, since they were sitting on *my* side of the easement."

"You mean the easement that is on *my* property, giving

you and your customers access to your side of the parking lot?"

"My latest customer wanted a garden fountain made from kegs. How was I to know that those weren't for me?"

"I don't know, maybe by the Two Bad Apples logo on the side of each and every keg," he said, taking in the nearly finished fountain, confirming, first off, that Ali was one hell of an artist. And second, making it clear exactly where his other kegs had disappeared to. "If that wasn't clear enough, then the other ninety-seven sitting in my loading dock should have been a clue."

She smiled, all smugness and attitude. "Right. I guess I can see that now. Next time you might consider keeping them on your side of the easement to avoid any confusion. Or perhaps post a sign there for folks to see. Kind of like the PARKING FOR STEEL MAGNOLIA'S CUSTOMERS ONLY signs your bar patrons continue to ignore."

Ali took off her mask and set it on the work bench, leaving her in just her boots and that dress. Those chocolate brown curls of hers, once released, tumbled down to brush her bare shoulders and frame that expressive face.

God, she was stunning. How had he never noticed that before?

"Hawk?" she asked in that self-conscious tone that always got to him. So, when she crossed her arms in front of her, a clear sign she was picking up on vibes he'd tried to keep in check, he locked his focus on her face, even though he knew her current stance must be doing incredible things for her cleavage. "What are you staring at?"

"You're soldering in a dress." He waved his hand as if put out over having to explain the obvious. When, in fact, he couldn't stop staring at her in that dress. "I was just checking to make sure you hadn't burned yourself."

"It's just a dress," she said, acting coy, as if it were nothing out of the ordinary. But for whatever reason, Ali in that dress was extraordinary. It was also a sign that something was up. And unlike his patrons, he refused to ignore that sign.

"It's not just a dress, and you know it."

"Says the man breaking and entering in his skivvies," she snapped, confirming something was up. "And really, do you have to wave your stick around all the time? As your friend, it's my duty to tell you it's getting a little embarrassing. I mean, most of the town has already seen it."

She punctuated the word *friend*, yet strangely enough, she was looking at him as if he were a sculpture she couldn't wait to get her hands on. Or rip out his throat.

Either way, that look overrode the F-word he was coming to hate.

Hawk casually swung his hockey stick in his trademark *winning goal* motion, tightening his abs and flexing his biceps. "Some ladies out front were begging to hold it."

Ali rolled her eyes, but not before Hawk noticed her breath quicken. "Tell Fi she can buy a bigger one online for twenty bucks. Now if you don't mind, I have work to do."

"Have at it," Hawk said, and then, he had no idea what came over him. Maybe it was the uncertainty in her gaze, or maybe it was that sexy as hell dress. He snatched her cell off the workbench and, flipping it to camera mode, snapped a picture.

Ali's face went slack. She looked down at the light

green silk that would be the talk of the town, and launched around the workbench, grabbing for her phone. Which Hawk held over her head and out of reach.

"Give it back, Bradley," she said, jumping up to snatch it out of his hands. But her five-feet-nothing was no match for his six-feet-three-inches of badass hockey player moves. Her elbows, though, had some serious force behind them.

"Not until you tell me what the dress is about, *Aliana*," he said, purposely using her given name because he knew it irked her. When she didn't elaborate, just locked eyes with him, he added, "One swipe and it goes viral."

"Fine." She poked him in the peck. Hard. "One of my pieces might be in a magazine."

"You've had a dozen of your pieces in magazines. None of them inspired viridian green silk."

"What kind of guy uses the word *viridian*? Oh, wait, the same kind of guy who doesn't think selling hard cider is a pussy job."

"Cider is the next workingman's beer. The dress?" He lifted a brow.

"It's *Architectural Digest*," she said with a shyness Hawk wasn't used to witnessing from her.

Information, as the co-owner of the local watering hole that doubled as gossip central, Hawk was already privy to, but it was nice to hear her say it. Watch the smile hiding beneath the *play it cool* expression she always wore.

He knew how much this would mean to her. She'd been talking about that magazine since high school. Except there was that slight waver in her tone, one that she hadn't ever been able to hide from him. "And you were so elated, you decided to celebrate by wearing a dress at six in the morning?"

"There's a dinner tonight and I was breaking it in. You know, like a new pair of work boots. Now give it back." She jumped up to snatch it back, but if there was one thing that playing in the NHL for over a decade had taught Hawk, it was how to spot a deke. And Ali was using the magazine's prestige to fake him out, distract him from the real issue.

"A dinner?" he prodded, sliding an arm around her to keep her from ramming his shins with her steeled toes, which only managed to press her body flush with his. Noticing her gaze dropped right to his mouth, he let loose a grin. "A dinner that requires a dress like this is a dinner I'd hate to miss. So tell me, sunshine, who's the lucky guy?"

He didn't mention that whoever the guy was, he didn't deserve a woman like Ali. Or that his plan to mess with her had somehow backfired, because he couldn't seem to stop looking at her lips.

"Are you offering to be my date, Hawk?"

"Depends. Will that dress be joining us?"

"You have to come to find out." A totally cool, almost bored expression crossed her face as she casually rested a hand on his chest—her fingers gliding down his abs. "And Dad's grilling. I'm sure he'd love to see you." She looked up at him through her long, thick lashes. "So would Bridget."

It was as if a Washington winter snowstorm had blown through the shop—piercing his chest. "Bridget?"

"Oh, didn't I mention?" Ali said, snatching her phone back. "Bridget came home, just in time for my big night. You think she'll want to hold your stick?"

Chapter 2

One glance at Hawk's stupid stick should have been enough to quell the flutters in Ali's belly. She didn't do fluttery, didn't do beefed-up jocks, and she sure as hell didn't do stupid—no matter how impressive the stick.

She'd tried that once and ended up with a broken heart.

Which brought her to the next thing she didn't do—her sister's ex-husband. No matter how irritatingly irresistible she'd always found him.

Yet when she pulled up to her dad's house later that evening, they were still there—the residual flutters flitting around in her chest.

"Those are not flutters," she told herself. "It's heart-burn."

Nature's reminder to steer clear of things that were bad for her. And as good a guy as Bradley Hawk was, he was bad for her well-being.

It wasn't his two-hundred-and-twenty pounds of alpha-male badass, or even that he smelled like sex—something she'd gone way too long without. Nope, what had Ali feeling all feminine was the way he looked at her, touched her on occasion—as if she were all delicate and sexy.

After spending most of her life in her single dad's machine shop, Ali, vertically challenged or not, didn't have a delicate bone in her body. And unless a guy was turned on by steel-toed stylings and blowtorch skills, *sexy* wasn't a word she'd heard all that often with regard to herself.

Which was why the second Hawk had left, she'd ditched her dress for her usual Converse, ripped jeans, and offensive tank top. Tonight's was black with pink letters reading, THE ONLY THING SHORT ABOUT ME IS MY TEMPER. After all, informing people of her current state of mind was only polite.

Parking the car in front of the oceanfront bungalow, she grabbed two casseroles and a grocery bag off the passenger seat. The casseroles were to get her dad through one whole week without breaking his doctor's diet. And the grocery bag was just in case.

Marty Marshal walked out onto the stone porch holding a spatula. His hair was windblown, his boat shoes unlaced, and in his Bermuda shorts and Hawaiian shirt, he looked as if his life was a never-ending Jimmy Buffett song.

"Hey, sweet pea," her dad said. "I thought I heard you pull up. I was around back, getting ready to fire up the grill for the steak."

"You mean the fish and vegetable kabobs from the recipe I e-mailed you yesterday?" Ali said, giving her dad a kiss on the cheek.

Marty shrugged. "The cod didn't look fresh, so I went with the steak."

"Funny since the market advertises fresh cod caught daily. Right from there." Ali pointed over the steep cliffs that jutted out from behind her childhood home, to the ocean crashing below. "Can't get any fresher than that. And what about vegetables?"

"I got corn bread. The doctor said I can eat corn, and you girls love it with my special honey butter."

"Corn is a grain, not a vegetable, and when you bake it in a buttered skillet then smother it in liquid sugar, I don't think it meets the guidelines Dr. Cortes was going for."

Ignoring this, Marty took the bag from her hand and followed her inside. "Is this the pie?"

"No." Ali smiled. "That's my just-in-case-you-bought-something-else."

Marty peeked in the bag at the marinating kabobs and frowned. "What kind of man celebrates his daughter's big news with cod and zucchini on a stick?"

"A man who doesn't want to go into a diabetic coma," she said, walking into the kitchen, hiding her grin at the grumbles Marty was letting loose behind her. "And don't worry, Kennedy is bringing the pie with her."

Kennedy was also bringing a buffer—her fiancé, Luke Callahan. If Ali was to make it through an evening with her sister without losing it, then she needed a distraction. And nothing distracted Bridget quite like a handsome man.

Kennedy Sinclair wasn't just Destiny Bay's newest celebrity baker; as Ali's best friend, she also had her back. It had been a long while since someone had Ali's back—and it felt damn good.

"Coconut cream?" Marty asked, sounding like a kid at a candy store.

"Special order." Meaning it was high in yum factor—if one liked coconut, which Ali did not—and low in sugar for those glycemicly challenged. Marty would never know the difference. "But only men who eat their cod get dessert."

More grumbling ensued, but this time Ali ignored it and went right to the fridge, stacking the casseroles and pulling out all the ingredients needed to make a healthy garden salad.

"Where's Bridget?"

"Running a little behind."

Ali looked at the clock above the stove, then over her shoulder at Marty. "I thought you were going to take her out on *Chasing Destiny*?" Ali asked, referring to her dad's pride and joy—a forty-two-foot Catalina sailboat he'd spent the better part of the past decade rebuilding.

"Too windy. Bridget was afraid she'd get seasick," Marty said and Ali wanted to call bullshit. Yes, Bridget did suffer from the occasional motion sickness, but only when they were out in the open ocean. And since Marty had been restricted to sailing within a few miles of home, doctor's orders, Bridget would have been fine.

"I reminded her that I still have some pills left over from the last time she came up," Marty said.

"I don't think they make a pill for what Bridget suffers from," Ali joked, because it was the perfect day to go sailing. And the perfect day for Marty to spend time with his other daughter. The sun was bright, the sky clear, and there was a gentle breeze coming up from the south.

The only reason Bridget didn't want to go sailing was

because Ali was better at it. And everything in Bridget's world was a competition. Even father-daughter time.

Marty gave Ali a stern look, but his grin ruined the scolding. "I'd better check the corn bread."

"I'll get the corn bread," Ali said, choosing to let it go. "And I'll prep a nice green salad while I'm at it, so you can get the fish going on the grill."

"The casseroles, dessert? I'm supposed to be cooking *you* dinner," Marty objected.

"I don't mind cooking for you, Dad," she clarified.

Marty had been taking care of Ali her whole life, always going that extra step to show her that she was loved. After her parents divorced and split everything right down the middle—including the kids—Marty had done everything he could to ensure Ali had a happy childhood. So what if their roles were a little reversed now? It felt nice to pamper him for a change.

"But it's your big night," he said quietly. "You should be sipping a cold one on the porch and letting me take care of you."

"Just because they're shooting my work doesn't mean it will make it in the magazine."

The purpose of the article was to showcase the bold and innovative design of one of the Pacific Northwest's most renowned architects, Nolan Landon. Who had commissioned a piece of garden art from Ali, for his personal residence, last year.

"No sense in getting our hopes up until we know anything," Ali said, her hopes so high it was hard to contain herself. The issue focused on the art of repurposing, a high concept design with minimal environmental footprints—Ali's art in a nutshell. Making the cut would not only allow her to check off a major career goal, it would transform her career. "There are so many pieces in Nolan's house to choose from."

In fact, he had commissioned repurposed art from several different artists, Ali being the only unknown name. But, and this was what gave her the courage to hope, her work was the centerpiece of his property.

"I'd be thrilled to even be mentioned." Ali turned around to find Marty standing right behind her, an expression of embarrassment mixed with sincere pride that made Ali swallow. She eyed the two ice-cold beers in his hands and lifted a brow.

"Just a sip," he assured her, then handed her a beer, "to celebrate my daughter."

She was too focused on the elegantly set kitchen table to argue.

Made from distressed white wood, it had a blue and green table runner to match the nautical theme of the house, with glass tapers filled with sand and seashells. There were even flowers on the table, picked from the yard and haphazardly arranged—but they were flowers.

Twinkly lights twisted around the two paddles that hung above the wall of windows that looked out over the Pacific Ocean. When Ali had been little, she'd drag a sleeping bag out on the back porch and let the waves crashing against the cliffs lull her to sleep.

The sound was calming, hypnotic. Yet today, they didn't seem to help the building tension that came with seeing her sister. Or how many place settings there were.

Parties were supposed to be a compilation of the honoree's tastes and requests. Ali was the honoree, and had requested a small, cozy, casual dinner. Yet she couldn't help notice that Marty had brought in the extra table leaf from the garage. A leaf that took it to a party of seven.

"What's up with all the place settings?" she asked.

"Oh, your sister sent those ahead and told me how to decorate the table," Marty said. "Posted video instructions online and everything. She's got a good eye, that one."

"It looks great." Very elegant, very posh, very her sister. "But I meant, why so many? Who else is coming?"

"Whoever you put on that list," Marty said.

"There were four people on my list."

Marty's brows puckered in confusion. "Bridget told me to plan for seven."

"If we're being technical, Bridget was never invited, she's crashing."

"A girl can't crash a dinner in her own home."

Spending a mandatory two weeks a summer somewhere didn't make a place a home—one of the few things about their childhood Ali and Bridget could agree on. Whereas Destiny Bay would always be Ali's safe place, Bridget's had been a two-story McMansion in a gated community with their mother and stepdad number two in Seattle.

Ali gave a stern look. "Who else is coming, Dad?"

Marty lifted a hand in surrender. "I can't answer what I don't know. With you girls, I never know who's going to show. I just man the grill and hope for a good time."

"It will be a good time, no matter who comes," Ali said softly, not wanting her dad to be disappointed over cooking for a family, when the odds of Bridget actually coming through were slim.

Every Saturday, Marty hosted a family dinner, and every Saturday he invited Bridget to come. Until she'd married Hawk, she'd never once shown an interest. And since their divorce, she'd appeared only a handful of times. So even though this wasn't the ideal dinner for her sister to crash, for Marty's sake, Ali hoped Bridget came through.

"But just in case, maybe you should make up some extra of that special honey butter of yours. You know how Bridget loves it," Ali said.

"Bridget doesn't do honey butter or corn bread," a voice sweet enough to cause a glycemic overload said from behind. "She's gone Paleo."

"Since when?" Ali asked, turning to find her sister, Bridget, standing in the doorway. Her dress was couture, her shoes designer, and she had enough bling to accessorize the Kardashians for the Grammys. Her sister looked ready to walk the red carpet or have cocktails with the mayor. Not a family BBQ on the patio.

"Since I learned how important it is to only eat things that once had a soul," Bridget said, tossing her purse on the counter.

"Butter comes from cows and honey from bees. Both murdered souls," Ali pointed out.

"Great, then I will spread it over my steak." She crossed the room and gave Marty a kiss on the cheek. "Hey, Dad, sorry I missed our sail. I got caught up in a meeting."

She said it as if her meetings didn't include mimosas, a country club, and the latest "cause" of the moment.

"That's okay, we're all here now," Marty beamed, pulling Bridget into his arms. "All of us together again, and with so much to celebrate."

"That's why I brought the bubbly." Bridget pulled a

bottle of champagne from her purse. Correction, not champagne. Cristal.

"Isn't that nice," Marty said, giving Ali the same *Just go with it* look he'd given her every birthday when she opened her present from her sister and mom to find a doll or tutu or, the worst, a new dress.

Unless it was Jack and Coke, Ali wasn't all that big on drinks that fizzed. But her dad was right—the idea that her sister had thought to bring a present was kind of sweet. "Thanks, B."

"Are you kidding? This kind of news requires a toast. I was just excited that we could all make time to get together."

"Me too," Ali said, a little confused by her sister's genuine excitement. "Here, let me put that in the fridge so it gets cold."

"Thanks." Bridget handed over the bottle and took a seat at the counter. "I've been dying to post about it on Facebook, but we wanted to toast with you guys first."

Ali and her dad exchanged looks. "The pastor's wife, Bitsy, already told her quilting group about it, and that almost acts like a press release around here, so I don't care if you tell anyone. But speaking of we, who else is coming?"

"Mom, of course," Bridget said with a bright smile. "Oh, and perfect timing, she's here."

Ali's heart slammed against her chest, each pound bringing a clarity to the situation, and everything hit Ali at once. Marty's panicked expression, the way her heart pinched with insecurity, the reality that she was wearing Converse high-tops that said BALL BUSTERS on the toes, and that her mother was there. At her celebration.

And no one had warned Marty.

Gail never came with a warning. She came with a sweet smile, big dreams, and left with your heart. So Ali secured hers then turned to her sister.

"Why did you invite her?" she hissed.

Bridget rolled her eyes. "Because I knew she'd want to be here for this."

Somehow Ali doubted that. Gail was about as supportive of Ali's chosen field as she was about her fashion choices. When she'd gone off to art school, Gail had envisioned easels and watercolor landscapes, not abstract steel structures and welding equipment. "But it's Dad's house. You should have asked."

"Don't get mad at you sister," Gail said, walking through the front door as though she still lived there. "Proper dinner party etiquette states that everyone is allowed to bring a plus one. She was only invoking her right."

Forcing a happy smile, an emotion Ali had become a pro at faking, she turned around. "Mom? What a surprise."

"You say that like I'd miss this big moment," Gail said as she waltzed into the kitchen, a long scarf draping over her shoulders and billowing behind her.

Gail Marshal-Bowman-Stevens-Marshal-Goldstein-Fletcher looked like a cover model for *Serene and Sexy After Sixty*. Her hair was still fire red, her dress sleek and black and designed to cling, and her attitude was dialed to *cougar on the prowl*.

Fitting since husband number six was twenty-five years her junior.

"Hi, Marty, you're looking as rugged as ever," she said with an appreciative once-over.

And the way she looked at Marty, like he was tonight's prey, had Ali taking a protective step between them. But it was too late, Marty was already entrapped by the silky voice and copious amounts of cleavage on display. "Gail, glad you could make it. I'm sure Ali is over the moon. Aren't you, sweet pea?"

"I don't know, she seems put out," Gail teased. Then, as if Ali wasn't standing right there, looked at Marty with her heart in her eyes, "I would hate to think I ruined her plans. Did I ruin her plans?"

"No plans to be ruined, Mom. This was just a casual dinner to celebrate the news that I was in the running. The actual decision won't be for a few weeks. If a miracle happens, I'm sure my friends will throw a party in town. If that happens, I'll make sure you get an invitation," Ali said, wondering why she felt the need to explain herself, make sure her mom didn't feel left out.

"That would be wonderful, Aliana. Now let me take a look at you," Gail said, and Ali had the sudden urge to go wash up. "Oh, my! Is that a blister?"

"Nah, just a little burn," Ali said with a shy shrug, feeling all kinds of ridiculous.

"Little burn? That is going to leave a scar." Gail took Ali's arm and inspected it further, like a mother would do. And something about the concern in her voice made Ali want to cry.

Gail had been there two minutes and already Ali was being drawn into empty promises of milk mustaches and chocolate chip cookie afternoons. Gail had gone from Mrs. Robinson to Mrs. Cleaver so fluidly, everyone seemed to discount that she hated baking. She hadn't even hugged Ali yet, and already the woman had her swaying.

"Marty, the girl's going to scar. Get me some ice to put on this."

And as if two decades and a handful of divorces hadn't passed, Marty headed to the ice box to fetch a cube of ice and save the world from tiny scars. Or maybe he was running for the exit—either way, Ali wouldn't blame him.

Ali wasn't one to give in to dramatics. Filling Hawk's condom box up with lottery tickets or repurposing a few stolen cider kegs was about as dramatic as she got. But this whole doting mother moment was playing on all of her weak spots, making her want to give in to the fantasy.

But that's all it was. A fantasy created by a little girl who believed with all of her heart that her love could fix everything—even a broken family.

"It's fine." Ali shoved her hands in her pockets. "I'm fine." A state Ali had mastered—since it left little room for disappointment.

"It might fester. That alabaster skin of yours is just like your grandmother's."

"It won't fester, Mom."

"I have this lotion that might help," Bridget offered with a sweet grin. "My doctor gave it to me for the scars from the girls." She gave her *girls* a jiggle and smiled.

Ali smiled back, with a stealth finger scratch to the cheek. The middle one.

"Seriously, though," Bridget continued. "It is some kind of serum that promotes skin repair. A few weeks of using it and the scars practically disappeared. I can send you some if you want."

"I don't think it would help much. Scars come with the territory. One of the downfalls of working with metal."

Kind of like the blisters one got when thinking about an irritating man instead of how hot the metal had become.

"You're still working with metal, then? In Marty's shop? How nice," Gail said, sounding anything but nice.

"She had the grand opening last year. I posted a picture on Facebook. Didn't you see?" Marty asked, offering Gail a beer.

Gail waved it off. "I'll wait for the bubbly."

With a shrug, Marty took a hefty swallow. Ali didn't bother reprimanding him. Gail was going to kill them both long before the diabetes.

"Of course I saw it. I just didn't know if she'd found her own space, maybe moved to that gallery in town."

"Some of my work is in that gallery." Her work was in galleries all around the world. "And it's not like I'm squatting in Dad's shop. I bought it off of him last year when he decided to retire." A huge difference in her opinion.

An awkward silence filled the room at the word *retire*. Everyone there knew that Marty hadn't welcomed an endless supply of sailing time with open arms. His diabetes had been the leading factor in his decision to sell the shop.

And Ali had just been commissioned for her biggest project and needed the space. It had seemed a win-win all around. Only sitting idle, it seemed, was doing more damage to her dad's mental health than the diabetes.

Marty loved turning wrenches, fixing problems, chatting with the townsfolk. And being stuck this far out of town with nothing but his sailboat and Old Man Joe next door for company was wearing on him.

"You know, Ali made that big arch over the highway

when you came into town," Marty said, his voice thick with pride. "Her design was chosen over a dozen other artists."

"It's stunning, very unique," Gail said, walking over to take her seat at the table, in the same place she'd sat for the first eight years of Ali's life.

And there was something about seeing her there, in Ali's childhood home, finally claiming the seat Ali had been waiting a lifetime for her to claim, that sent a warm burst of hope into her chest. "Thank you."

"Is it similar to the one you sold Mr. Landon?" Bridget asked, referring to the piece that was to be showcased in *Architectural Digest*.

"Nolan wanted something more modern," Ali said about her biggest customer to date. He'd seen the town arch during his last visit to see Hawk and hired her on the spot. Her assignment had been to design an elaborate fifteen-hundred-square-foot pergola. "He wanted steel beams, stone, and local woods to match the feel of his house." Estate really. Fifty acres of manicured gardens and rugged woods with a view of the ocean that was worth the eight-figure price tag. "It's a structure actually, a piece of functional art where he can host gatherings."

"It took her six months to build," Gail said, and Marty snorted.

Ali was touched that her mom was so interested in her work, she really was, but to be honest, her mother didn't know a thing about her work—or Ali's life. If it hadn't been for the puff piece written up about Nolan in the *Seattle Times* last month, Gail wouldn't have even known about the biggest piece of her career.

Before the divorce was even final, Gail and Bridget

had moved to Seattle. Ali stayed with her dad in Destiny Bay, and her mom, too busy enjoying her green pastures being married to a plastic surgeon, didn't have the time for Ali.

They might as well have been nothing more than acquaintances, for as much interest as Gail took in Ali's life.

But she's here now, Ali told herself. Not allowing herself to be naïve didn't mean closing herself off to the potential of what the evening could mean.

"It took almost a year from beginning to end." It had also taken sixteen steel beams, thirty-four rods, shiplap from an old barn, and a roof made of stones and sea glass, but the result had been stunning.

The centerpiece for Ali's portfolio.

That one referral from Hawk had gained her access to a unique group of clientele. In fact, the client she was making the keg fountain for was a friend of Nolan and Hawk's.

"I bet you really got to know Nolan well, working with him that long. Maybe even became friends," Bridget said, in that singsong tone that always had Ali's ears bleeding.

"We're cool with each other, and yeah, he's a nice guy, but I wouldn't say we were friends." She paused, because the longer she talked, the bigger her sister's eyes got—and the worse Ali's headache grew. "Oh no. No way. I am not playing matchmaker and introducing you to Nolan!"

Been there, done that, still had the bridesmaid dress hanging in the closet.

"I'm not looking to date Nolan," Bridget said, sounding disgusted. "I already did the *local guy makes it big* thing. It wasn't for me."

It would have been nice if she'd figured that out before she married Hawk. Then again, Bridget always did have a hard time settling on which flavor of ice cream she wanted. She'd order strawberry and Ali would order pineapple sherbet, then Bridget would decide she'd wanted the pineapple sherbet. One lick in and she'd remember she hated pineapple anything.

But tossing a cone away and tossing a relationship away were two very different things. Bridget's inability to know her own mind had left a wake of disappointment and disillusionment in her past.

Gail claimed her older daughter was merely particular. Ali tended to think of her sister as lost. Someone who relied on other people's dreams, mainly men, to fill the emptiness and find validation. A series of drive-through dads could do that to a girl. And with the split-custody arrangement, she rarely saw Marty after the divorce. Which was why, even though Ali hadn't had a lot in terms of money growing up, she valued the importance of a father's love.

Understood how influential that kind of stable foundation was to a girl's self-worth.

"Well, good because dating Nolan would be"—she thought of Hawk and his friendship with Nolan—"awkward."

"I don't want to date him. I want to meet him." Bridget scooted to the end of her chair, and that was when Ali noticed that while Bridget and Gail sat at the family table, Marty and Ali were standing awkwardly in their own house. "So I can see if he'd be open to having an event there."

A thin strip of panic slowly coiled itself around Ali's

throat. "I already told you, my friends will have one in town, probably at Hawk's bar."

Speaking of friends, Ali looked at the door, wondering where her backup was.

"I'm talking about an event that needs a bigger venue. One that could host five hundred people."

The panic gave a sharp tug, making it really hard to breathe. "Five hundred people?"

It had taken Ali all week to be okay with the idea of a fun girls' night at the local watering hole. The only thing she disliked more than parties were parties for her.

Oh, and people.

Ali really, really didn't like people. Especially when they were gathered in big groups and smiling—at her. As if it were her duty to entertain them. Which, in Ali's opinion, was the stupidest expectation ever.

First, the only party trick she'd ever mastered was a one-handed keg stand, and this didn't seem like a keg stand kind of event. Second, the last time Gail threw Ali a party, it had been her sweet sixteen, she'd been forced to dress up like a dust ruffle, and no one from her school could make it.

Not a one.

Until Bridget showed up and started telling people it was going to be the party of the year. The draw of seeing what happened to "the other Marshal sister" was too much to resist. Or maybe it was that Bridget was the only girl on her cheer team who didn't have to stuff her bra. So while Bridget stunned and impressed childhood friends, Ali spent the night playing poker with the third-string hockey players.

Finally, and this was what had the oxygen leaving her

lungs in a big whoosh, Ali didn't want to spend her night watching Hawk watch Bridget. Sure, she said her mom and sister were on the invite list, but Ali had no intention of actually mailing out their invitations.

Normally Ali didn't mind being compared to her sister, but if she was forced to attend a party in her honor, and perhaps wear a dress, she didn't want to sit on the sidelines. Ali had polished a lot of steel over the years and finally it was her turn to shine. Only the brightest star in the Marshal family was on a direct collision course with her moment.

"I know, we originally thought seven hundred, but that number seemed a little indulgent," Bridget said. "Jamie and I want a small wedding. Just close friends and family."

And that was all it took for the disappointment of a lifetime to set in. "A wedding?"

"She's getting married," Gail proclaimed, that mother pride oozing out of every acid-treated pore. "Isn't that exciting?"

"I'm getting married!" Bridget held up her hand and wiggled her finger and—*holy shitballs*—Ali didn't understand how she had missed that boulder. In her defense, she'd been distracted by the copious amounts of glitter and flash Bridget had on, but still.

Whoa, a touch of heartburn pinched at her chest and suddenly Ali felt like she needed a seat.

Or a stronger drink. Her chest hurt and her head ached and—

Ali shook her head at her predictability. One small show of affection and it was as if Ali had been transported back to that eight-year-old girl, who thought that if she played the doting daughter just right, there was still that flicker of hope they could reclaim the relationship that had ended the day Gail walked out. But what if she put her best self out there and still couldn't make her stay? Then what?

Sadly, Ali knew that ending. Had lived it—twice. And nearly fell for it again.

"It's huge," Marty said, pointing to the ring, but his gaze flickering to Ali, saying with his eyes what he couldn't voice with the current company. That he was sorry, that he, too, had hoped for the best, that this was supposed to be her night.

"This Jamie is a..." Marty trailed off, his eyes big and imploring.

"Man, Dad," Bridget sighed. "Jamie is a man. He's Irish."

"Well, that's great." Marty paused. "Not that there would be anything wrong if Jamie was a she."

"She's a he," Bridget said. "And he is fabulous."

"Well, then, is he coming here to talk to me tonight?" Marty said, and even though Ali knew he was concerned for her feelings, he was tickled that Bridget was including him. "I'll be sure to go easy on him, while still making sure he knows my girl deserves to be treated right."

"He isn't coming to ask for my hand, Dad. I've already said yes," Bridget said. "And the wedding is a month from Saturday!"

"A month from Saturday," Marty said, his face going pale. "Well, that's doable, I guess. I mean five hundred guests is a lot to plan for and a lot to shoulder, I don't have much but—"

"I just need you to bring your dancing shoes, Dad.

Jamie has everything else covered," Bridget said with the confidence of a woman who could only be marrying up. With her first marriage ending in a seven-figure split, Ali could only imagine what this Jamie guy brought to the table.

"Well, what about the rehearsal dinner?"

"Covered."

"Oh," Marty said and so much was conveyed in that one word. That smile of his never faltered, even though Ali knew it took everything he had to keep it in place. "Well, I'm sure it will be a wonderful day."

Unlike Ali, Marty still clung to the fantasy that his love could bridge the years of heartache and separation. He charged into things flashing that smile as if he wasn't fighting a losing battle. And there was something about his unwavering belief in love and family that tugged at Ali's heart.

"How about an engagement shower," Ali asked, and when Bridget opened her mouth to probably say she'd already had sixteen different ones planned, she added, "Maybe a co-ed one."

"A co-ed shower? Jamie is pretty traditional."

"He's marrying a two-time bride. How traditional can he be?" Ali laughed. When no one else saw the humor, she changed tactics. "One of the girls at the gym had a baby last month and they threw her and the father a co-ed shower. It was nice," Ali lied.

It had given her hives. All the kissy poo love and baby talk made her nauseous. But everyone else had seemed to enjoy themselves. Plus, Marty looked about ready to book the Moose Lodge; he was just waiting for Bridget to give her blessing.

"Dad and Jamie can plan it together," Ali suggested brightly, her eyes pleading, *Let him feel like he is a part of this.*

To which Bridget gave a horrified, *Did you see the flowers on the table?*

Bitch isn't becoming on you.

"A co-ed shower sounds nice, Dad," Bridget said sweetly—too sweetly. "Something small and intimate. One of those hometown girl wins big-city man's heart themes. Jamie is a big commercial developer. High-tech campuses are his specialty." She turned to Ali, and proved that bitch was the new black. "You can invite your new friend, Nolan Landon."

"Oh, wouldn't that be nice," Gail said. "Jamie will be thrilled. He's been angling for a meeting with the famous designer. Oh"—her smile went mischievous—"he's bringing his brother to dinner. Stew is the best man and I bet he could help you out with what Jamie likes." Then to Ali, "He's handsome, a snappy dresser, successful, not as successful as Jamie, but quite charming."

"Every good shower needs a snappy dresser behind it," Ali joked.

"He's also single." Gail practically giggled. "I figured he would even out the partners."

"Partners?" Ali looked at the eight table settings and felt her right eye twitch. "So Bridget brought champagne to toast her engagement, and you brought me a blind date to my dinner. I don't know what to say."

She knew exactly what she wanted to say, but yelling would only make her head throb.

"When you told me your friends were coming, I figured it would be fun to couple up," Gail said, giving

Marty her best *Hello, big boy* bat of the lashes, and Ali threw up in her mouth a little.

Because by *couple up*, her mother seemed to mean that she was looking for a reunion of her own. One that involved cheap beer, bad decisions, and good old reliable Marty.

"What about Chad?"

"Chad and I broke up months ago. I am back in the saddle, ready to go for a ride." Gail gave an unconscious laugh that was free, full of life, and contained enough confident allure to tempt the Pope.

Poor Marty looked as horrified as he did helpless, because while Gail had married and divorced six times—twice to Marty—her father had never been interested in dating again.

He said he'd found his soul mate, married her twice, and both times she'd run off with the town doctor. The first was a podiatrist, the second a plastic surgeon, and he wasn't interested in nursing a third shattered heart.

Yet he couldn't take his eyes off his ex-wife.

"I'm not sure tonight was about coupling up," Ali said. "I think I'm able to manage coupling on my own. How about you, Dad?"

When Marty didn't answer, Ali elbowed him. "Ali's right. Tonight's about celebrating our amazing daughters."

"Oh, are you dating someone?" Gail asked Ali, but her question was directed at Marty. "I didn't realize."

"Yup, I'm dating," Ali jumped in, saving her father from having to admit to the woman who shattered his heart that, yes, he was indeed still single. "Pretty serious, too. He runs a business in town." And when it came to telling lies, Ali never knew when to stop shoveling, so she dug herself deeper. "Actually, he owns it. A big business guy. We met at the Destiny Bay Business Owners Association and now we go to meetings together every week."

"How...quaint," Gail said.

"Don't you go to the meetings with Andrew Sweeney?" Marty asked, clearly not comprehending his part in the diversion. Ali having a boyfriend would (a) give Gail something to focus on instead of Marty's dating status, and (b) save Ali from another one of her mother's matchmaking schemes. Because being a successful businesswoman paled in comparison to being a well-married woman in Gail's eyes.

"Andrew Sweeney?" Gail's brow furrowed and Ali sent her dad an *Are you being serious right now?* Because he'd named the only Andrew in town that Gail would remember. "Isn't he Dan and Susan's son?"

"He owns the realty company in town," Marty explained as the doorbell rang and Ali let loose a breath of relief.

"That's probably Kennedy and Luke," Ali said. "I'll be right back."

The doorbell rang again, confirming that her backup had indeed arrived. And just in time, too, because Gail's eyes twinkled with recognition and she snapped her fingers. "Isn't Andrew the gay son?"

"All relationships have obstacles," Ali said, then excused herself to answer the door.

She took a quick peek out the peephole, to make sure it wasn't her blind date, and when she saw the big red pie box blocking the view, she flung the door open.

"I could kiss you," she said.

"Well, if a pie was all it took to get on your sweet side, I would have bought out Sweetie Pies years ago."

"You?" Ali said, her heart doing this annoying flip in her chest. Because instead of a five-foot-nothing pie maker with a box full of pie, Ali was staring down a mountain of mouthwatering muscles and yummy man who had plagued her dreams since high school. Looking like a walking ad for sex in a pair of dark button-fly jeans and a cream Henley, Hawk had a large shoulder leaned against the doorjamb, and a wicked smile aimed right at Ali.

"Evening, sunshine," he said, all steel and velvet.

Ignoring the flutters that took flight, Ali crossed her arms. "What are you doing here?"

He looked at the Lexus in the driveway and grinned. "Apparently playing the hero. I didn't know Gail was coming to town, and from the frazzled look on your face, neither did you."

The frazzled look had little to do with Gail, and everything to do with watching the people she cared about get hurt. She'd barely salvaged her dad's night. Once Bridget realized that Hawk was there, she'd distract herself from the guilt of leaving him by either hanging on Hawk, or hanging all over Hubby 2.0. Which would leave Hawk the odd man out.

A position that he'd worked hard to convince everyone, including himself, no longer applied. He'd played the game well, and was now considered a legendary ladies' man around town. But Ali saw right through the *new day new girl* façade he'd created. He might drive her batshit crazy, but deep down Hawk was a stand-up guy. Hawk was a lot like Marty; he always saw the best in people. He was loyal, honest, and stupidly faithful. Refusing to give up on those he loved even when they didn't deserve his devotion.

And sadly, he was still devoted to Bridget. Who was about to pop the cork on her upcoming nuptials.

Hawk was bound to find out. But hearing the news and seeing the ring were two different kinds of hurt. And Ali didn't want her friend to hurt any more.

"You can't stay," she said.

He leaned a hip against the porch railing and hit her with a smile. "Two seconds ago you wanted to kiss me. Now you're telling me to go. You're sending off mixed signals, sunshine."

"Ali, who's at the door?" Bridget called from inside. Her heels clicking against the wooden floors, counting down the seconds until utter and complete devastation.

"Bridget is coming," she whispered.

"I know," Hawk said, his eyes warm with appreciation. "You told me, remember?"

"Ali?" her sister said, sounding even closer.

Ali walked out on the porch and shut the front door behind her. Voice still in a whisper, she asked, "Then why did you come?"

"Because Kennedy was swamped with orders, Luke is helping her, and you had a special pie that needed to be delivered." He lifted the lid to showcase the doctor-approved coconut cream pie.

"You came, knowing the evil stepsister was inside, to bring me a pie?"

Hawk was always cordial with Bridget, but that didn't mean that seeing her didn't hurt. In fact, it always managed to reopen healing wounds. Which was why, Ali was certain, Hawk did his best to steer clear of his ex. "I came *because* I knew she was in town and I didn't want her to take over your night." He pushed off the railing and stepped into her, his voice warm and masculine when he spoke. "There was also the dress."

Her heart skipped three whole beats, then those annoying butterflies took flight in her stomach. She had to work hard to sip in air. "I changed. It clashed with the boots."

He smiled. "I like the shirt, although after your night I bet you'll wish you'd worn the PETITE AND PACKING shirt you got for your birthday."

Ali laughed. She couldn't believe it. Bridget and her five-carat comet were two seconds from impact, and Gail was probably sweet-talking Marty into a disastrous walk down memory lane, and Ali was laughing.

Although it came out sounding horrifyingly close to a sob.

"That bad?"

"Bridget only eats food that once had a soul, Gail is single and apparently looking for her next adventure...with my dad, who is on his second beer of the hour, my shoes say Ball Buster, and I'm still sober."

"I can fix that." Hawk toed the case of hard cider that he'd set on the porch. "Or you can say fuck it, hop on the back of my bike, and we drive into town and break into the thirty-year-old bottle of Scotch I have hidden in the bar."

"Why would you do that?" she asked, hating how squishy he made her feel.

"Because even though you drive me crazy, you're still my friend, and I'd like to be yours if you'll let me," he said quietly. "And I've been saving that bottle since winning the Stanley Cup, and today seems like a pretty good reason to crack it open."

The game he'd finished on a blown-out knee. Hawk delivered the final goal that brought the trophy home and the crowd to its feet. His team had been celebrating what had been called The Comeback Win, as Hawk had been on his way to the hospital, learning that his career was over.

Alone.

Well, he'd learn about the end of this dream, too, but he wouldn't have to deal with it alone. Because he was right, while their relationship as of late might be as warm and fuzzy as sparring porcupines, there was a time, before Bridget, where they'd vowed to always have each other's back.

"Fine." Feeling suddenly protective, another annoying emotion that Hawk seemed to bring out in her, Ali headed toward his bike. "But I get to drive."

"The closest you'll get to the handlebars is sitting on them." Hawk grabbed her arm. "And since when do you run from a fight?"

"I'm not running." *Liar.* "I'm merely leaving it for another day."

Hawk studied her long and hard, and Ali resisted the urge to look away. "You're running. What gives?"

The door opened and she could see Bridget's perfect nose peek out. Followed by her long legs and blond Barbie locks. Her big green eyes widened when she took in Hawk's back, and then she gave an uncertain smile.

The same smile she got when she ordered strawberry and Ali ordered sherbet.

"Do you still love her?"

Hawk did a double take, then lowered his voice. "Do I still love Bridget? We were married for five years. What do you think, that she left and, poof, I stopped caring? Love doesn't work that way."

In Ali's world love did. But the way he said it, unashamed and so full of conviction, Ali found herself wanting to believe, too.

"Are you still *in* love with her?"

"*Pffft*...No."

"Oh God, you hesitated!"

"I didn't hesitate." But he hesitated again. "It's just that no one has ever asked me that question."

"Well, they should have." Ali heard the distinct sound of a Tesla pull into the drive, and the pressure grew heavy enough to constrict her breathing.

Then her sister was calling out, in that same alluring come-hither tone that had been passed on from Marshal mother to the older Marshal daughter, "Hawk? Oh my God. Hawk! I can't believe you're here."

Hawk went to turn his head and say hey to his ex, who he claimed he wasn't still hooked on, but hesitated in doing so, and Ali reached up and grabbed his face. A hard task when he had more than a foot of height on her.

"Focus on me," Ali said, looking him in the eye. "Are we friends?"

"Yes."

No hesitation, good. "Do you trust me?"

"You stole my kegs less than ten hours ago."

"Right." A car stopped a few feet behind her. Close enough that she could feel the heat from the grille push through her clothes. "But you trusted me enough to do right by the kegs and not call the cops."

He smiled. "I didn't call the cops because I trusted the kegs would be unrecognizable by the time they arrived. No sense in wasting good taxpayers' money."

"Ali, what are you doing?" Bridget whined, and stomped down the steps. "Stop accosting Hawk and get out of the driveway. You're blocking Jamie from parking."

She was also stopping Hawk from getting his heart run over. "Remember how you looked at me in that dress earlier."

His gaze tracked her body, leisurely but with purpose, until that grin became a full-on smirk—a bit wicked and full of something she'd never seen directed her way. Sexual curiosity. "Yeah, I remember."

Talk about potent. The man took flirting to an Olympic level.

"Good. Channel whatever that was," she whispered, fisting her hands in the front of his shirt and dragging him up against her. Because she wasn't so sure how "over" Bridget Hawk really was. But she knew, with a certainty, Bridget would use her engagement to test him—to torture him with how over him she was. And more than anything, Ali didn't want him to fail.

She also didn't want to examine too closely why it mattered to her, because she wasn't sure she'd like the conclusion she'd come to. Or why her pulse quickened at the mere thought of what she was about to do.

"And follow my lead."

Then Ali did the only thing she could think of to fix the situation. She went up on wobbly toes.

Chapter 3

Hawk never knew what to expect when it came to Ali. Today was no exception. Which was why, when she pulled him close, within fighting distance, he'd braced himself—for the knee to the nuts, a direct hit to his masculinity. But no amount of bracing could have prepared him for just how big a punch that mouth of hers could pack.

When smart and brassy, it was a force to be admired. When warm and soft, and shyly pressed against his—it was damn lethal. So lethal it nearly short-circuited every wire in his brain.

But then he remembered that this wasn't some puck bunny who had strolled into his bar looking for a good time. This was Ali—and her idea of a good time was being a never-ending pain in his ass.

So even though the feeling of her mouth on his was

even more fan-fucking-tastic than he'd fantasized, he reminded himself that when it came to Ali, nothing was ever what it seemed.

Which was the only excuse he had for what he did next. Well, that and the fact that Hawk considered himself a damn fine player—on and off the ice. It was his ability to commit himself fully that made him such a formidable opponent. And the second those thick lashes fluttered shut, and Ali's lips touched his—he was fully committed to whatever crazy challenge she was throwing his way this time.

Committed and determined to be the victorious one.

So when he felt her start to pull back, Hawk changed tactics, going from defensive to a fully offensive position. His hands slid around her back and held her to him, so tight that all of those soft girly parts she kept hidden under her tough girl attire were pressed firm against all of his hard manly ones. Then he held that kiss until he felt her start to squirm.

Nothing overtly outrageous, keeping it clean enough that to an outsider looking on it would appear to be two old friends sharing a chaste kiss.

Hawk was more than aware that his ex was standing a few yards away on the front porch where he'd first met her, courted her, got down on one knee, and offered her everything he had to give. The same front porch they'd shared their first kiss—and their last.

She was probably wearing one of her slinky dresses and complicated up-dos that drove him crazy, looking as gorgeous and out of his league as ever. Even when they'd been married, he'd always felt as if he was just a visitor in her world. Not an uncommon place for him to be, since

Hawk didn't belong in his own family, but a position he was determined to overcome.

Which was why he'd come home to Destiny Bay, and paid a fortune to ensure it remained Bridget-free. Because moving forward with a new life was impossible when the life he'd lost was teasing him at every turn.

Bridget loved Seattle and Hawk still loved Bridget, so when she asked for a divorce, he knew he'd need space that didn't smell of failure and lost dreams. She'd get the cars, the house, the 401K, and an epic settlement.

He'd get Destiny Bay.

Only now she was back and he had his ex-sister-in-law in his arms. And that friendly peck she'd planted on him was inspiring a whole other kind of problem.

"What are you doing?" Ali whispered against his lips.

"What you told me to do." He slowly opened his eyes—to find hers shooting daggers.

"I said follow my lead, not grab my ass," she hissed, with a smile that was big and bold and so manufactured he wanted to laugh.

"Sunshine, my hands aren't anywhere near your ass," he said, noticing that maybe they'd slid a wee bit farther south than planned—but still within the realm of appropriate. "And since following your lead usually winds up with you kneeing me in the nuts, or a Sunday drive in the back of the sheriff's car, I decided your lead, while always fun, is a little too unpredictable for my preference today."

"I didn't ask you what your preference was," she said quietly, smacking his chest—moving him back a whole inch. "And I didn't ask you to show up unannounced with a pie. But you're here and so is she, and—"

A horn honked and Ali jumped.

"Shoot. Now Jamie's here and is going to toot his horn all night. So here's to you being over Bridget, because if not, shit is about to get real." Ali looked over her shoulder at a pearl white Tesla and blew out a tight breath. "And the stench is going to be epic."

Before he could ask how much more real things could possibly get, the asshat in the princess mobile spun his wheels before jamming it in Park—stopping inches from Ali's legs.

"Watch out," he said, taking her hands and easing her to the side. Then when the polo shirt with the loafers climbed out of the car, Hawk approached him, chin up, chest out.

"What the hell was that, Asshat?" he asked the prick whose name probably wasn't Asshole, because based on the car and big-city shoes it was more likely Pierce or Kenneth, but Hawk didn't give a shit. "One more inch and you would have hit her."

"Sorry about that," Asshat said, resting his arms on the hood of his car. "I wasn't sure you knew I was there and I didn't want to be late." He shrugged. "I did honk."

"You're not late," he heard Bridget say from the porch, moments before a soft scent of jasmine and vanilla blew past him and right into Asshat's arms. "In fact, your timing couldn't be any more perfect than if we planned it this way."

"Besides missing the boating trip with my dad, you're right on time," Ali deadpanned, then crossed her arms in greeting.

Hawk wanted to smile at how fiercely she protected those she loved, but he was too busy trying to hold it together. Waiting for the sucker punch that always came with seeing his ex.

"That's my sister, Aliana." Bridget turned to face them. "And this is Bradley. Guys, this is *my* Jamie."

The added emphasis on ownership was a hard word to swallow, because Hawk had once been hers. And even though he knew it was over, it still burned. Just like he knew the polite thing to do would be to stick his hand out in welcome but he couldn't seem to move.

Slinky, sophisticated, and heart-stoppingly gorgeous didn't even cover it. Even the small smile she gave him brought on a tsunami of emotions that were as complicated as ever. Some were familiar, others were painful, and some just created a dull throbbing beneath his ribs.

The irritation at her appearance, that was new, but combined, they all made for a painful knot that twisted in his gut.

Divorced or not, Bridget was still the girl he fell for, the woman he'd vowed to love for eternity, and the partner he'd dreamed of sharing a family with. And she'd left him for another man. Oddly, not the man whose hand she was clinging to as if he was her soulmate.

Hawk wanted to tell the smug fucker not to get too comfortable, because she'd clung to him that way once. And all it took was one tiny imperfection to send her running. And guys like Jamie might look polished and shiny on the outside, but inside was a slew of imperfections waiting to be discovered. And Bridget would find them—and eventually move on. It was what she'd done her entire life.

A part of Hawk, the really stupid part that was desperate to believe love wasn't a fleeting emotion, needed her to find someone who made her so happy she'd stop running. And although Hawk had come to terms with not being that guy for her, the betrayed lover in him hoped she'd find that special someone, perhaps, in Europe.

Not that Asshat was the *someone* for Bridget, but he was obviously special enough to bring home to meet Marty. And if Marty had been telling the truth, Hawk had been the only boyfriend of Bridget's he'd ever met. One of the few memories he didn't have to share with another man.

Until tonight.

Hawk never considered himself a jealous man—hell, Bridget had been sleeping with another man before Hawk had even known she wanted a divorce—but the idea of sharing this house, Marty and Ali, and Friday night barbeques with another man didn't settle right.

Hawk felt a strong, unwavering hand slip into his and give a squeeze. One of those *I've got you, bro* signals he'd come to count on when it came to Ali. But instead of taking out Jamie at the knees with her steel toes, Ali did the most un-Ali-like thing he'd ever witnessed. And that was a lot to say coming on the heels of her kissing him.

She linked both of her hands with his, then snuggled into his side, and in a tone that was all sunshine and sorority girl said, "It's nice to meet you, Jamie. You can call me Ali. And this here is Hawk." There went those lashes again, fluttering up at him in a way that could only mean trouble. "My boyfriend."

"Did you just say he's your boyfriend?" Bridget laughed.

"Did I stutter?" Ali leaned in toward her sister. "Boy. Friend."

"You're saying *boyfriend* with a pause, as in a friend who is a boy."

"Maybe this will clear things up. Hawk is my boyfriend and this is a date." She said it so serious, it dried up all of Bridget's laughter. In fact, it sucked all of the oxygen out of the immediate area and Hawk damn near choked on his own breath.

"A date?" Hawk said at the same time as Bridget snapped, "Boyfriend? As in one word?"

"Yup." Ali just stood there, fluttering her lashes and swaying as if she'd just spoken the gospel.

Asshat, completely unaware that Ali's prank was bringing Bridget deathly close to DEFCON 1, smiled and said, "Congrats."

"Thanks," Ali said, not even a splinter in her façade. She was so convincing, if it weren't for the fact that he was the boyfriend in question, Hawk would have believed her.

"Don't mind my sister," Bridget said, those cat-shaped eyes of hers slitting dangerously. "She thinks she's being funny, when really she's being awkward. Ali has a talent for making things awkward. On everyone."

Ali, bless her keg-stealing, lying little heart, only smiled bigger and held on tighter. "I'm actually just trying to make tonight easy on everyone. What do you say, can we all leave smelling of rainbows and unicorn farts?"

Bridget shrugged. "As long as it includes champagne toasts, jubilation, and you dropping whatever prank you think you have going."

"No prank," Ali said smoothly, a challenging air circulating between the sisters.

Hawk was skilled in female nonverbal communication.

He'd seen enough of it pass between the two sisters over the years to be considered fluent in lady-speak. But he had not a clue as to what was going on between them tonight.

"I know it might feel weird, us just springing this on you without giving you time to prepare, but this is kind of new, so we haven't really told anyone yet. You know how that goes, right, Bridge?"

"Drop the act. Hawk's not yours, he's mine," Bridget stated in that possessive tone that used to turn Hawk on—until he realized she was only possessive over what was hers when somebody else wanted a piece. "Now stop trying to ruin my special night."

The words settled over the group like a bathtub full of cement, and Hawk stood in disbelieving shock of his ex-wife. No one had the power to silence a room quite like Bridget when she was ticked. But this went beyond anything he'd ever seen from her.

She wasn't even ten minutes into her visit and already Soulmate 3.0 was starting to question his sustainability. Ali looked ready to throw up, but was doing a hell of a job keeping herself rooted in the moment when he knew on the inside she wanted to bolt.

"Man, how I love these Friday night dinners. Always leaves me wondering why I don't try harder to get you here every week," Ali said and, with a one-fingered salute, turned to Hawk. "Thanks for dropping off the pie, I owe you."

All that bravado tucked into such a tiny package was impressive, but Hawk saw the apology in her eyes mixed with a shit-ton of uncertainty. Knew that she was terrified of going back inside the party alone.

"For the record, I'm your ex," Hawk said, holding up

his naked finger and giving it a wiggle. He considered wiggling another finger Jamie's way, but was more concerned with the way Ali's lips were slightly trembling—and the strange fury growing inside him. "And this isn't your night, it's Ali's. Which is why I came. Now, if you'll excuse us for a moment."

Chuckling, Hawk slipped his hand inside Ali's, holding tighter when she flinched—as if she were holding hands with Ted Bundy.

"What are you doing?" she whispered.

"Something I'm certain I'll come to regret," he said as he tugged Ali around the side of the house, and away from prying eyes.

In the past, this was the part when Hawk would smooth down some of Bridget's ruffled feathers, coax Ali into talking it out until the sisters made nice. In his more recent past, he'd distract himself with work or some blond co-ed until the town's quota of Marshal females dropped back down to a manageable level. But strangely a blond distraction didn't interest him much.

And that made him nervous.

When they'd reached the steps on the side of the porch, he placed the pie on the railing and Ali on the first step.

"First, congratulations on the cover. I know how hard you worked on that piece, and no matter what Bridget says or does in there, this is your night. Not hers. So remember that," he said, not surprised when her cheeks went pink. If there was one way to disarm the town's tough girl, it was with soft words. "Because if I hear tomorrow that you let her walk all over your night, just like you let her scare you out of wearing that dress, then I will post that picture of you in said dress, sunshine."

Ali didn't flinch. His threat only seemed to make her eyes narrow in challenge. "Bridget had no impact on my wardrobe, and since when do you care about what I wear?"

"Since you kissed me in front of Bridget, then told her we were dating."

"You are my friend, and that was a friendly kiss," she corrected, unflinchingly direct.

"There was nothing friendly about that kiss, sunshine. Admit it." He stepped closer, and closer still, until her heels hit the back of the step and he heard her breath catch.

Gotcha, he thought, but didn't let up. He held her gaze, challenged that stubborn set to her chin with a slight twitch of his lips. Light enough to piss off her competitive side, but with enough heat to make her think he was picturing her in that dress. Which he most certainly was.

And when picturing that dress suddenly led to him thinking about her *not* wearing that dress, he knew he was in trouble.

"I told her you were my date, not that we were dating, big difference."

He chuckled. "Seriously? That's the best defense you got?"

"By your own admission, you came here for me, *and* you brought my favorite dessert. That sounds pretty close to a date."

"What kind of assholes have you been dating?" He held up a hand. He didn't want to know. Every time he saw her around town with some yahoo sporting a neck tattoo, it set him off. And he was already primed.

"Until my sister leaves, just one." Then she let go one

of those big smiles of hers and he found himself wanting to sit down. "You."

Yup, he needed a seat, and since he wasn't all that choosy at the moment, he plopped on the bottom step and tried to ignore the sweat that broke out on his forehead at the thought of Bridget staying. Even worse was the way his chest pinched over the realization that Ali had kissed him to stick it to her sister.

"And how long will that be?"

"If we play this right, I think she'll leave right after dinner."

"That's the thing, Ali. I'm not a part of this game. I'm the pawn." Something he should have been used to by now when it came to Bridget. But never Ali. Sure she gave him a hard time, and they had their own odd way of showing affection. But she'd never used him in one of her ridiculous family feuds before.

"Look, you're the one who decided to show up uninvited," she accused. "I didn't ask you to come. In fact, I told you not to. But you couldn't resist the chance to throw on your superhero cape and save the day. Or maybe it was just an excuse to see Bridget."

"I came to bring you that." He pointed to the pie box and he watched the guilt light her eyes. "Yeah, and to make sure you were all right. But I can see that you're as crazy as the rest of the women in your family, so I'll leave you guys to it."

He stood to leave and she grabbed his hand. "I'm sorry, I was just trying to help."

"By kissing me?"

"I know, it wasn't a very well thought out plan, but with the time constraints and the pressure of Bridget standing right there, it was the only one I could come up with."

"Even though you knew you'd be dragging me back into all of this?"

"That wasn't the plan, and I'm sorry," she said and Hawk heard the truth in her apology. Ali, in all of her brazen glory, really had been looking out for him. Ali might be tough and appear to have quills, but beneath it all was a huge heart—that cared too much to purposefully hurt someone.

"Don't be sorry, just be honest with me." Sensing that this was a *have a seat* kind of conversation, he sat back down. This time he took her hands and pulled her onto the step with him. "You knew she was coming so what's with the theatrics?"

Ali let loose a big breath and met his gaze. "Bridget showed up with champagne and my mom. They were talking decorations and venues, and how I'd need a date. They were moments away from discussing the pros and cons of silk versus lace when you showed up with the damn pie, and I couldn't let her...not again."

Without a word, Hawk shifted closer. He didn't pat her back or offer her his shoulder, Ali would have been offended. But he sat close enough so that she could feel his strength. "I didn't know Gail was coming."

She sent him a sidelong glance. "You know her, she loves surprises."

She was also relentless when it came to Ali. Her choice in career, men, lifestyle. Why she'd never left Marty to go and live with her. It was as if Ali's insistence on living life against the grain somehow reflected poorly on Gail.

Funny, since Hawk had always considered it one of Ali's strongest attributes. But Gail was determined to rid her of her rebellious side. And when she was reminded that it was a losing battle, she'd disappear on Ali—and break her heart a little more.

"I also know you," he said, softly bumping her shoulder with his. "You hate surprises and blind dates. Not to mention, Jamie isn't your type. Not nearly enough tattoos and I bet he doesn't even have a police record."

"Jamie wasn't my date, but you already knew that." Yeah he did. But it didn't stop the squirrelly feeling taking over his gut. "His friend Stew was supposed to be my date, but I guess he's a no-show."

"So what? I'm your beard."

She turned fully to face him. "No. I'm offering to be yours."

He laughed, but it came out sounding hollow. Because Ali always rooted for the underdog, and if she was looking at him with the same pity in her eyes as she'd had the day she visited him in the hospital to tell him Bridget was filing for divorce, then he was in for one hell of a night. "She's engaged, isn't she?"

"They're announcing it tonight," she said so softly Hawk barely heard her over the pounding of his heart. "And my dad is throwing a shower for her, here in Destiny Bay. He's really excited to be able to be a part of the wedding plans this time around."

"Shit." Hawk stood. When that didn't help, he paced until he felt as if he was going to explode. He'd done everything she'd asked of him, and all he'd asked is that she leave him alone. Then again, he was the genius who told Luke not to worry, that he'd deliver the pie.

Luke had given him the same worried look that Ali had when she'd opened the front door and saw it was him. As if he was about to go back down the rabbit hole he'd finally escaped. He'd meant it when he said he'd come to bring Ali the pie. But now, with his heart in his throat, choking the hell out of him, he wondered if he'd been lying to himself.

Maybe he had come here to catch a glimpse of Bridget, to prove to himself that he was over her. Or maybe he'd come here to see the girl who he'd promised never to give up on.

"She doesn't even want a fucking party here. This is just another one of her games."

"I know," Ali said, even though she knew he was talking more to himself than her.

Bridget had done a number on him, letting him go only to reel him back in when he'd start to move on—or she found herself feeling lonely. Only Hawk could no longer stomach being pulled back into this yo-yo of a relationship. Was desperate to cut the string, ached for some finality on the situation. And maybe this was what he needed to hear, that she was no longer available.

No longer his to fight for. Not that it would deter Bridget from spewing her marital bliss all over Destiny Bay until there wasn't a place Hawk could go without being reminded that his ex-wife had officially left him for greener pastures.

"Look, I know you were trying to help, but I'm fine," he said, assuring himself that since he hadn't punched anyone or anything, he was acting completely within the realm of fine, after hearing about Bridget's engagement.

"And I don't need to pretend that we're a thing to prove that I've moved on."

Ali said nothing, just kept staring at him with those big eyes of hers.

"I don't," he said, feeling tired. The kind of tired that went soul deep and cast a shadow so broad it made seeing the light difficult.

"Okay, you don't." She raised her hands. "Forget I even brought it up. It was a stupid idea. I'll just go tell Bridget that I was kidding, and chalk the last few minutes up to one of my jokes. You leave, life goes back to normal."

Hawk wasn't even sure what normal felt like anymore. Only that if he ever planned to get back there, he had to start doing things differently. That kiss with Ali had felt different—and in a way that should have him burning rubber back to town.

Yet there he stood, still able to taste Ali on his lips, and watching her intently when he asked, "Why are you doing this?"

She smiled. "Because I'm the only one who gets to ruin your day."

This time when he laughed, it felt warm and full. Ali wasn't trying to hurt her sister, she was trying to protect him. And it had been a long time since anyone had gone so far as to look out for his well-being.

"Well, we both know that Bridget won't let this rest, ever, if I sell you out. So, I say we go with your plan and pretend we're newly dating. I came because what boyfriend would miss your big dinner? Bridget will be so thrown by the situation, she'll make up some excuse to leave before dinner is even ready."

"Nah, my dad would be crushed if Bridget left, which she would if you stayed. And he is so excited about throwing this shower and spending time with her doing all the dad stuff he never gets a chance to do."

"He does dad stuff with you."

"Building engines and fishing." She looked at him, and the resignation there broke his heart. "We both know it's not the same."

"And what about you?" he asked, knowing that what Ali was suggesting would ruin any hope she had for salvaging her celebratory family dinner. "What about your night?"

She looked out at the cypress trees, bent and bare on one side from the harsh coastal winds with a look of pure resignation, as if any notions she'd had about the evening's events had been destroyed. "I got pie, so there's that."

"It's coconut cream; you don't even like coconut."

"Marty does."

"Plus, it's sugar-free," he said, then took her hand. Because Ali needed a little sweet in her life, and Hawk needed to do something drastic to prove to Bridget—and himself—that he'd moved on. He was tired of avoiding Marty's place when Bridget came to town, or holing up in his bar until she left town. If playing along with Ali's plan for a night got him one step closer, then he was game.

Marty had slipped into a twenty-year holding pattern when Gail left, and he hadn't even recognized it. Hawk would be damned if that was to be his own future.

"Where are we going?"

"To wish Bridget and Asshat the best on their upcoming nuptials, then I'm going to walk my girlfriend to the door, give her a big congratulatory kiss that has enough heat to imply the party will continue later at my place, before I head off to work and leave you to your family dinner." He stopped. "Why do you look so horrified? This was your idea, remember?"

"Yeah, but I never thought you'd go along with it."

He lifted a brow. "So then the kiss? That was, what? For fun?"

"The kiss was to make it look real, nothing more. You're the one who got handsy and took it to a weird place."

He grinned, because weird or not, it had been hot, and she knew it.

"Which makes me question your motives." She dug her hands into her curvy hips and looked up at him. Stern and solid. "You didn't know what was going on, so why did you kiss me back?"

Good question. One he could worry for hours over and never come up with a good answer for it. *It just happened*, was something he'd used back when he'd been a young gun on the ice and didn't care. But Hawk cared now, so that didn't apply. Neither did, *You kissed me first.* And since he was pretty sure the real motives would land him in the penalty box for a good, long time, he settled for, "I was just being friendly."

She glared at him. "Liar. And no second kiss. One was enough to last a lifetime, thank you."

'Tude dialed to "*hands off*," she walked away. Not that he was complaining, he had a great view of her 'tude as it swished back and forth in those jeans she favored.

"Now who's lying?" he laughed, racing up to catch her and throwing his arm over her shoulder. "And we could spend the rest of the thirty seconds we have arguing about who did what, or you could use it to prepare." He leaned down to whisper, "And if I were you, I'd take the time to prepare."

"For what?" She tried to shrug off his arm, but he let it slide obscenely low on her waist, then pulled her in to him.

"For my A-game."

She snorted. "Your A-game? What's that? A bottle of sparkling cider and showing me your stick?"

"You seem to be really focused on my stick, sunshine. Is there something you want to talk about?" A bony elbow shanked him in the kidney, but he didn't let go. "Is that any way to treat your boyfriend?"

She slid him a hard look, but beneath it she was smiling. He could see it in her eyes. "My *fake* boyfriend. And as long as your A-game is comprised of a quick hug and an even quicker departure, your stick will live to charm another puck bunny."

"You like it fast with no lip service. Not a problem," he said as they rounded the porch to find not just the couple of the hour, but also Gail and Marty. "I'm more of a hands guy anyway." He lowered his voice. "And sunshine, everyone knows I'm an ass man."

She looked up right as he grabbed a solid palm-full of that heart-shaped gift she was always swishing his way, then announced to the group, "I hear congratulations are in order!"

Chapter 4

The only thing Ali hated more than being wrong, was Hawk being right. And damn it, he was so right that three days later she could still feel the aftershocks from his touch. He hadn't kissed her, hadn't stayed longer than necessary, hadn't done much more than wrap his arm around her and hold her tight as he said his goodbyes.

It hadn't mattered.

Two minutes of Hawk's A-game ignited enough heat to melt a truck full of the steel kegs. Two minutes as his girlfriend, pretend or not, had felt too good to be anything but a warning to keep her distance.

Ali figured the best way to do that was to keep busy. When she wasn't checking in on her dad, she buried herself in a new project for one of the local orchards, a vintage-inspired produce stand to work as a welcome center. The steel was scheduled to arrive later that morning, so Ali had headed out with the sun to find some driftwood for the piece.

She'd spent a solid five hours at Sunrise Cove, a remote strip of rugged coastline that sat at the bottom of a fifty-foot drop of eroded cliffside and thick forest. The trek down was so difficult it was rarely traveled, making it a collector's trove for sea glass and driftwood. It was the trips back up, with eighty pounds of sea-sculpted spruce, that had been the challenge.

She arrived home cold and exhausted, surprised to find that, in her absence, a good samaritan had stacked all of the steel beams in her shop.

Hawk had not only brought in her shipment, he'd put each piece in its respective slot, saving her tired body another hour of heavy lifting. And sitting on her desk, next to the pile of preliminary sketches, was a small pink box.

She opened the box to find a single slice of pie. Chocolate, her favorite. And a note, which said simply: *Congratulations, sunshine.*

Ali stood in her shop, shivering from the ocean water clinging to her jeans, and smiled. Wondering how it was that the one person she couldn't have, seemed to be the only one who got her. And the only one who got *to* her?

Tucking the pie box under her arm, Ali locked the shop and headed up the back staircase that led to the studio above. The place was small, drafty, and smelled faintly of machine oil and mothballs. But it had plenty of natural light, running water, a commute that let her walk to work in her pj's unnoticed—and Ali liked the smell of mothballs.

It reminded her of childhood summers spent in her dad's shop.

She flipped on the lights and eyed the piles of mail

stacked neatly on her kitchen table. Bills were on one side, junk mail on the other. Next to them sat the newest edition of *Architectural Digest*. It was opened to the middle section and had a smudge of Stripper Pole Red lipstick on the corner, a sticky substance, most likely from the half-eaten bowl of Lucky Charms, pasting two of the pages together.

With a long sigh, Ali cleaned up the mess, grabbed a fork from the kitchen, a seat on her counter, and whipped out her phone.

She dialed the post office and waited. Eleven rings later, the postmaster answered. "Destiny Bay Post Office, this is Loraine, how can I help you?"

Ali could hear Loraine running her nails along the PO boxes in the background.

"You know you can just leave the package on my front stoop, like they teach you to do in postmen school."

"Now what kind of service would that be?" Loraine said, as if they'd never had this talk before.

Loraine wasn't just the postmaster; she was also the delivery man, a stamp philatelist, and the town's biggest busybody. If it happened in Destiny Bay, Loraine was the first to know—and the first to blab.

"Plus, I didn't get a chance to finish looking at the new Victoria's Secret before I had to get the mail delivered. There's a pretty pink lace bra and pantie set I marked on page seven that would go lovely with your skin tone. And it's guaranteed to bring the boys to your yard, or your money back."

Ali flipped to page seven and rolled her eyes. The only boy she wanted in her yard would burst out laughing if she showed up wearing pink anything.

"I'm not really a pink girl," Ali said. "And next time keep the magazine if it means avoiding B and E."

"Then how would I have separated the bills from the junk mail," the older woman asked as if Ali were the unreasonable one. "Or know to tell you that your aunt Sue sent you a card. It's to congratulate you on getting in the magazine. She sent you a twenty-dollar gift card to the Coffee Hut. Last time she sent thirty; I wonder if she's having financial troubles."

"Sue is fine," Ali said, closing her eyes against the growing headache.

"Good to hear. After that business with your uncle and that showgirl, we were all concerned."

"And would you please stop telling everyone I got in the magazine? I haven't gotten in anything yet," Ali said. "I am just one of many they are considering."

"You'll get it, honey," Loraine said. "Oh!" Loraine snapped her fingers. "There was a package for your dad. I set it by the fridge so you'd see it. It's next to my note about needing more milk."

Ali hopped off the counter and walked over to the white shipping box. It was from Seattle, stamped EXPRESS MAIL, and had a signature-required space on the label, with a really badly forged *Marty Marshal* scrawled across it. "Why did you drop it off here?"

"Your dad opened it, took one look, and started mumbling about fishing and his boat, saying he was going to take a sail up the coast. He was so upset he forgot the box."

"What's in it?"

"How would I know? Opening your dad's package would be unethical." Loraine lowered her voice, as if she were imparting a national secret. "I did peek at the letter inside, though, and saw that it's from your sister."

"This can't be good."

"When Marty starts mumbling about sailing up the coast, it's never good, honey."

Didn't Ali know it. When her mom left, Marty took Ali out for an afternoon sail—which lasted three days. When the divorce papers came in, he took Ali out on a semester at sea. And when Ali went off to art school, he sailed solo around the tip of South America.

Twice.

Bottom line, when things got complicated in Marty's world, he stocked up the boat with Corona and Jimmy Buffett tunes, and went in search of Gilligan's Island. Only, the Buffett lifestyle wasn't conducive to daily sugar logs and insulin therapy—so Marty couldn't just pick up and sail off into the sunset anymore.

"Since I wasn't sure if he was taking a day sail, or going to Mexico, I brought it to you."

"Thanks, Loraine," Ali said, emptying the box on the counter.

"My pleasure, honey. And next time you go to the market, can you get one percent milk? You got in another movie from Netflix, the new Bond film I've been dying to watch. But Single and Ready to Mingle is this weekend at the senior center, and I need to watch my waistline."

Ali would have told her she was changing the locks, but she was too busy staring at the contents of the envelope. "One percent. Got it."

Ali hung up and immediately called the one person who would know what to do with all of the frilly shit staring back at her.

"Glad to know you're done avoiding me," Kennedy said in greeting.

"I wasn't avoiding you." Ali pushed the collection of magazines cutouts aside and picked up a bubblegum pink silk with her thumb and forefinger. "I've just been busy."

"Busy avoiding me. I haven't heard from you since I made that special pie for your dinner." Kennedy gasped. "It was the pie, wasn't it? Sugar-free isn't in my vocabulary."

"The pie was amazing," Ali assured her. "Marty gobbled down two slices and didn't even suspect a thing. And Bridget was so impressed she asked if you did Paleo wedding cakes."

"I haven't done a wedding cake since college, and I have been tampering with coconut and almond flour—wait. Your sister's getting married?"

"I'm looking at swatches for bridesmaid dresses and tablecloths right now." Ali saw an itemized list titled, HOW TO THROW A POSH AND PROPER ENGAGEMENT SHOWER, and dropped the fabric. "She wants us to wear fascinators, and play Pin the Fascinator on the Bride." She thumbed through the clippings. "There's a list of foods I can't even pronounce, with recipes and instructions and— oh God!" Ali took a huge step back, her stomach churning with nerves. "There's a note to my dad, thanking him for throwing her the best engagement shower ever. My dad can't even throw a dinner that doesn't include a grill and the Margarator. Why would she send him all of this?"

"Maybe because she wants to include him in her big day," Kennedy said softly.

"No, this is her getting back at me for the other night. She knows that Dad will do anything to make her happy, but that he can't handle putting something this elaborate together, which means I will have to make this perfect or my dad will be crushed."

"What happened the other night?"

Ali pressed her lips together. She was already stressed out over this party; there was no way she could talk about her and Hawk right then.

"Okay, this deserves an emergency chocolate fix. Friends don't let friends have a freak-out on an empty stomach. Come over, I just pulled a batch of chocolate-filled croissants out of the oven. And I know everything there is to know about throwing a shower," Kennedy said.

"You do?"

"Well, no, but I know my way around a kitchen, and I know the best way to a solution is through chocolate."

"I already have pie."

"One can never have too much chocolate in these kinds of situations. Get your butt over here." Kennedy ended the call before Ali could argue.

Not that she would have. Kennedy was a great sounding board, and Ali's closest friend. The two had met last year when Kennedy had first moved to Destiny Bay. They had immediately bonded over a common love of sweets and loathing for the two owners of Two Bad Apples Hard Cider.

And there they were, a year later—Kennedy was engaged to one of the owners, while Ali had engaged in a two-minute fauxmance with the other. And now she was about to host his ex-wife's engagement shower.

Ali put the pie in her fridge and hopped in the shower. Five minutes later, she locked up her shop and, sure to look both ways for good Samaritans, scurried down the sidewalk, past the Penalty Box, and through the front door of Sweetie Pies.

Even though the morning pastry rush had already ended, the bakery was still a hive of activity, with a lively coupon bingo game taking up most of the front of the shop, while a line of late-wakers wound their way past the display case, seeing what was left to sample.

"I was about to send out a search party," her friend said, coming out from behind the counter.

Kennedy wore a light blue cardigan with a coordinating sundress, pearl buttons, shoes fit for a stripper, and what looked like a glob of chocolate on her butt that matched the tray of treats in her hand. A tray that came with five delectable selections, two forks, a mountain of whipped cream, and extra hot fudge on the side—just in case.

"I thought I was here for breakfast," Ali said. "That looks like a tasting to me."

"Just a few ideas for a high-society cocktail party. And enough sugar to make the impossible seem possible." Kennedy set the plate down at the far end of the counter and pulled up a stool. "Dig in, but I warn you, Destiny Bay's Bible group has labeled my chocolate truffle cake one of the seven deadly sins."

"Death by chocolate doesn't sound all that bad right now." Ali took a forkful, keeping a careful eye on Bitsy Cunningham, the pastor's wife, just in case she had her handbag ready to swing. She took a bite and the rich chocolate and bitter hints of espresso exploded in her mouth, making her moan—loudly. "Sinful indeed."

"Are you serving some of your gateway treats, Miss Sinclair?" Bitsy said, her voice half condemnation and half envy.

"No, Ms. Cunningham. I'm doing a tasting for Ali."

"Is it for her big reveal party? I heard about that; the town's been talking of nothing else since it was posted in the paper."

Ali had been so caught up in Bridget's drama, she'd completely forgot about her own party. A party like Bridget's, which would consist of close friends and family.

Unlike Bridget's, though, Ali's gathering would be a cozy party of seven—thirteen if she included the old farts from the welding club.

"No, it's for my sister," Ali said, forcing a smile. "She's getting married."

"Again?" Bitsy eyed the plate one last time. "Well, then you might want to skip the two pieces on the right, since you're already on the weekly prayer circle for tangling with Hawk and his stick."

"What?" Ali inhaled and some of the chocolate powder stuck to the back of her throat, choking her. She reminded herself that all of the witnesses to their kiss were in Seattle or out on their sailboat playing skipper, but it did nothing to tame the thundering in her chest. "I didn't go anywhere near his stick!"

"That's not what I heard from the Senior Steppers," Bitsy said. "According to Fi, Hawk came out swinging with purpose last week right before he stormed into your shop. Gave everyone a good scare." Ali wanted to argue that he'd given them a good show, but was still working to dislodge the cake—and panic—from her throat. "He said something about stolen merchandise."

Ali relaxed. "It was a simple easement issue. All resolved now."

Kennedy snickered and Bitsy didn't look convinced.

Thankfully Ms. Collins started screaming bingo and waving her card in Fi's face, so Bitsy had to drop the inquisition and go into mediator mode.

"And Friday night," Kennedy asked with a laugh. "Was that an easement issue, too? Because from what I heard, you had your hands all over Hawk's property."

"I kept my hands to myself," Ali pointed out. "And where did you hear that?"

"Judy Baker was bird-watching through her binoculars again, and saw the whole thing."

"She also says Larry at the Gas and Go looks just like Channing Tatum."

Judy was nearsighted, nosy, and lived across the street from Marty. She ran the local chapter of Single and Ready to Mingle, and the only place she ever aimed those binoculars was through Marty's bathroom window—right at shower time.

Kennedy rested her palms on the counter and leaned in. "And what about your lips, did you keep those to yourself?"

"Are you always this nosy?"

"Only with my friends."

"This is why I don't have many friends," Ali mumbled.

"You love me, and I love you, which is why..." Kennedy's smile faded and she lowered her voice. "I wanted to make sure that you didn't—"

"Make it into something more than it is?" Ali said on a sigh. "Don't worry, I won't."

She loved turning discarded materials into something beautiful and meaningful. And yes, she might have given in to a daydream or two over Hawk. But Ali was a realist, and there was no reality where she and Hawk could ever be more than they were.

Friends.

No matter how great that kiss had been.

Kennedy was looking at her strangely. "I was going to say, you didn't let Bridget get between you and Hawk."

Ali rolled her eyes. "The only thing between me and Hawk is an unlikely friendship based on irritation, distrust, and childish pranks."

"Huh, I've been watching you two circle each other since I moved here, and I've always thought it was chemistry that was one admission from combustion. And according to June, that kiss was more of a mauling."

"The kiss was pretend." Ali let out a breath, but it didn't help. She had made a rash decision, then let things get out of hand.

Not intentionally, but a huge miscalculation all the same. That kiss, which she was sure had been a joke to him, scorched her so hot she could still feel the burn. Everywhere. Which was why she should have never instigated it. Hawk loved a challenge, Ali was pretty sure she might still love Hawk a teensy bit, and both of them loved Bridget.

Queen of her own world aside, she was still Ali's sister—and the one person Hawk couldn't manage to get over losing.

"Bridget was about to drop the marriage bomb and I knew how much it would hurt Hawk, so I panicked—"

"And kissed him?"

"I know, it wasn't the best idea, but it distracted Bridget enough to make the announcement and then leave the topic of how in love she is with her new life and new man alone."

Kennedy's smile was back. "And what if it backfired and now Hawk won't leave you alone?"

Ali laughed. "The only reason Hawk went along with the stupid plan was because I backed him into a corner."

Kennedy lifted a brow. "Then why did Hawk buy a single slice of your favorite pie this morning?"

"Because he felt bad that my dinner turned into an episode of *Bridezilla*." He'd also wanted to make her know that, in the whirlwind that was Bridget and Gail, he was proud of her.

"It's been three days and she managed to assemble and send me this." Ali opened her backpack and pulled out a swatch book, the dreaded How To list, and enough clippings to equal six wedding magazines.

"Her ideas are actually pretty impressive."

"Bridget has always known how to pretty up a room."

"Maybe so, but these lamp decorations are creative and stunning. If she was going to be in town next summer, I'd hire her to plan Luke's and my wedding," Kennedy said, flipping through the clippings.

"She's been planning weddings since she was five. Barbie always had the most elaborate receptions."

"I bet." Kennedy stopped halfway through, and met Ali's gaze. "Wow, she's invited half the town. Who is she looking to outdo? Princess Kate?"

"Herself," Ali said, knowing that Bridget needed this time to be bigger and better than the last. The more elaborate the party, the more right her decision would feel. Until it was all over.

And then her sister would feel lost and empty. And start looking for the next high. Bridget was in love with the idea of love. But she didn't know a thing about creating lasting relationships.

Sadly, neither of them did. Which brought Ali to the

most important reason why that kiss could never go anywhere. Life had taught her that, for whatever reason, she wasn't the kind of person who inspired lasting love.

Her friendship with Hawk was too important. She wouldn't dare risk asking for more, only to wind up with nothing. She'd been there, done that song and dance before. Wasn't interested in a repeat.

Just like she wasn't interested in a repeat of how broken up her dad was when Bridget invited him to her first wedding—as merely a guest.

"You know you can count on me to help," Kennedy offered, and Ali felt a strange pinching in her chest. "I suck at decorating and themes, but I can make that menu with my eyes closed."

"Thanks," Ali said, putting the papers back in the envelope. "But first I need to find out exactly what my sister's intentions are." With her dad—and with Hawk.

Because his name was at the top of Bridget's guest list.

* * *

A few hours later, Ali pulled up to her sister's house. It was a three-story colonial that was all rose-covered lattices and Burberry drapes. So polished and showy, it was more George Washington than Washington State—and hard to believe Hawk ever lived there. But he had; for five years he and Bridget had spent the off-season in that house.

Together.

Ali sighed at the reminder, then walked up the front steps, where she could see her sister inside—entertaining a group of suits. Ali glanced down at her faded jeans and BITE ME tee and considered leaving and coming back another time. But it seemed that she'd used up all of her stealth moves on Hawk, because Bridget looked right at her through the window and motioned for her to come to the door.

The front door opened and Bridget stood there looking like a model from one of the magazine clippings Ali had in her hand. She also looked genuinely excited to see Ali.

"Thank God you're here," she said, slipping out on the porch and closing the door. "Jamie's colleague Stew was trying to explain to me how he was the reason that Y2K never happened."

"Stew, the not-as-handsome-as-Jamie guy you were trying to set me up with?"

"Mom tried to set you up with," Bridget said, then looked behind her again at the crowd inside.

"I didn't know you were having an announcement party or I would have just called."

Bridget waved a hand. "This isn't for the wedding, it's just Jamie's monthly mingle night for his clients. They talk tech, trends, and—"

"Croquet?"

"I was going to say zoning laws."

Three things Ali couldn't see Bridget being interested in. "Sounds thrilling. I won't keep you."

"Don't worry, he won't even notice I'm gone," Bridget said as if that wasn't another reason to kick the pecker to the curb. "Are you here to tell me that you talked to Nolan Landon?"

"I built him a glorified pergola; I don't go to Sunday dinners at his house." Ali snorted. "So no, I have not and will not ever talk to Nolan Landon about having my sister's wedding at his place. Plus, with your ex being a good friend of his, it might be awkward. For everyone."

"Marriages end every day, Ali. It doesn't mean people have to take sides."

"I'm not taking sides. I'm telling you it's not a fit. His place is a few hours from Seattle."

"But only thirty minutes from here."

Ali stopped short at that. Bridget was considering getting married in Destiny Bay, the place she used to bemoan visiting?

"What's up? You and I both know that getting married *here*, in an estate in the woods, is not your style," Ali said, thinking of the exposed steel beams, concrete floors, and glass and stone walls. Not a single pastel in the color scheme.

Bridget walked over to the edge of the porch and leaned against the railing. "I have less than a month to plan a wedding before Jamie starts in on some big project. So unless I want to wait a year, or have it at Jamie's parents' summer house in Palm Beach, I need to make it work. Somehow, the idea of plastic flamingos and ninety-eight percent humidity have opened me up to out-of-the-box ideas."

"Why not wait then?" Ali asked, going to stand next to Bridget, and for a moment it felt as if they were kids again, hanging out on the porch, while other people controlled their world. "Take the year and plan the wedding you really want."

Bridget blew out a breath. "I want to start my life with Jamie now. I'm tired of waiting."

"And you have to get married to do that?" Ali honestly asked, because as far as she was concerned, life started without a partner.

"Yes," her sister said, and Ali found herself equally surprised and saddened by her sister's admission.

"And before you judge me..."

"I'm not judging you," she said quietly.

"Yes, you are. That little pucker you get in your forehead when you're about to say something judgy is fetching." She pressed her pointer hard against Ali's forehead and pulled it up. "And while I get that this all sounds silly to a person like you who isn't afraid to go it alone, I'm not you. And I don't know how to be alone." Bridget slid her a sad look.

And *that* was one of the realest things Bridget had said to Ali since they were kids and snuck out onto the sailboat to watch the sunrise, and Bridget said she was making a memory because after the sun was wide awake, nothing would ever be the same.

"I'm not afraid of going it alone, but that doesn't mean it wouldn't be nice to have someone I love by my side," Ali said and the two of them stood quietly, watching the sun slowly sink beneath the skyline of Seattle.

When the sun went from blue to orange, and streaks of pink started to bleed in, Ali turned to her sister. "I'm not saying yes, but how does Jamie feel about tying the knot at his wife's ex-husband's friend's house?"

"It was his idea," Bridget said with such a fragile smile, Ali knew she was about as excited at the prospect of having the wedding there as Nolan would be hosting it. "He's trying to build a new campus for a big environmental tech in Seattle and wants to get Nolan on board as the architect."

"Then Jamie should ask Siri for the number to Landon Designs." Ali nudged her sister's elbow with her own. "You can tell him that she will even dial for him."

That earned her a small chuckle.

"He's already tried, and Nolan hasn't returned his call." This time when her sister faced her, there was nothing but desperation in her eyes. "I'm not asking for your kidney or even for you to lie and say you like Jamie. All I am asking for is a simple phone call to establish a connection."

"You're willing to use your wedding and my relationship with a client, my professional relationship, to get Jamie that connection?" Ali asked.

"Yup," she said, sounding suspiciously shrill, the way she sounded when she was trying hard to be selfless. "An opportunity is an opportunity."

Ali was shocked. Not that Bridget would try to leverage Ali's connection to further herself, or her fiancé's career. When her sister was in a new relationship, it was all about melding into the man's world, proving to be an asset in his life—and into his industry. She'd done the same thing for Hawk, going from hockey-hater to the best wife-ager in the NHL, orchestrating and maintaining the celebrity rise of Hawk's career.

Until there was no career to maintain.

But no matter how much of a catch this new guy was, Ali never dreamed that Bridget would agree to let her future wedding double as a business opportunity. Weddings were what she lived for. She'd already planned her first five by the time she was thirteen.

"And what happens if your opportunity creates waves and messes up my opportunity?" Nolan had so many unique pieces to photograph, and while it wasn't up to him which ones made the spread, he had some influence over the final layout.

"It won't," Bridget promised.

Ali drew in a deep breath and decided to go for honest. "Fine, next time I talk to him, I will mention Jamie's project, not the wedding, just the project. But in return, I need to know if you really want this engagement party?" She held up the file. "Or is it your way of getting back at me?"

"Everything isn't about you, Aliana." Bridget lifted her wineglass to her lips and took a sip, her eyes amused. "And what would I be getting you back for anyway?"

"I don't know, telling the groomer you wanted a lion cut on your cat when you asked for a line cut, wearing combat boots to your wedding, telling Jamie you have a weird fetish for loafers with tassels."

Bridget swirled her wine. "Pretending you and Hawk are a thing?"

Ali ignored this, instead focusing on the real issue, and the reason she'd driven three hours to confront her sister. "Look, if you're pissed at me, fine. But don't take it out on Dad. He will do anything to make you happy, and you and I both know that there is no way he can pull this off and not feel like he disappointed you. You're setting him up to fail and it's going to break his heart."

"I didn't know I was being such a pest to him. I mean, he was the one who said he wanted it to be the party of my dreams," Bridget argued. "I told him something small and quaint."

"Then what's all this?" Ali held up the binder.

"That is the engagement party of my dreams, which he had Mom send to him when I reiterated small and quaint."

Shame and a bit of guilt welled up, because Ali had come here under the assumption that it was Bridget setting her dad up. In reality, it had been Gail's doing. And Ali couldn't come up with a single reason why her mom would do that to Marty. Unless…

"Is she using this to spend time with Dad?"

Bridget's face fell, as did all her earlier posturing. "Is it so hard to believe that I regret not having Dad more involved last time?" she said with so much hurt in her voice, it sliced through Ali. "I never expected him to be into all the wedding stuff, but when he seemed so excited at dinner, I figured maybe this was a chance for him and me to connect on something that interests me. Something other than fishing and sailing."

And here Ali thought that she was the sister who was misunderstood and overlooked. "So you want to plan this with Dad?"

"Planning my own party would be weird." She wrinkled her nose. "But helping him from the sidelines might be fun."

Ali saw the genuine longing in her sister's eyes. It matched Ali's when she'd been younger and was still optimistic that one day Gail would realize she couldn't live without Ali and come home. She would never get that with her mom, but Marty and Bridget still had a chance.

"It will take more than you being on the sidelines for Dad to pull this off," Ali said, gentle warning in her voice, a long-forgotten protectiveness settling in her chest. Not just for Marty, but also for Bridget.

Bridget smiled. "Which is why I was hoping my maid of honor would help him. Dad thinks she and I could also use some quality connecting."

Ali's palms started to sweat. "So the bubblegum pink

satin, that was your way of asking me to be your maid of honor?"

"Nope." Bridget opened the door and turned to walk back into the party, pausing at the threshold. "I was going to call you tomorrow and ask. The fuchsia silk, that's payback. Tell Hawk I say hi."

Chapter 5

It was Double Tap Tuesday at the Penalty Box. Drinks were two for one, the San Jose Sharks were on the big screen playing Hawk's old team, the Chicago Blackhawks, and there wasn't a person in town who hadn't dropped by for part of the festivities.

Except Ali.

She'd been avoiding him since Friday, and Hawk had played his part in their little game. He'd pretended not to notice her sneaking past his bar to go talk to Kennedy next door. And when she'd done a cute little duck and cover maneuver behind the cantaloupe selection at Kline's Fine Foods, Hawk didn't ask if he could sample the melons. He'd even pretended not to stare at her ass while she unloaded the driftwood from her car as if she knew he was watching.

But he was tired of playing pretend and wanted to engage in a new game. One that included some more face-to-face time. Because it was becoming harder and harder to pretend he didn't miss seeing her at his bar. So when his best friend, and business partner, Luke, walked through the door, he had a hard time not looking to see if Luke was alone.

"Where have you been?" Hawk asked, pouring a mug of their new Spring Cider and setting it on the bar.

Luke plopped down on one of the few empty bar stools. "Delivering a new shipment of apples to Kennedy."

"That's what you were doing this morning when you left me to stock the storage room. Alone."

"Her apples take some finessing," Luke said with a grin that had that *just been laid* smugness to it.

"Yeah yeah," Hawk said, snatching Luke's cider back because while Hawk had been running their business, Luke had been playing house with his lady friend.

With a shrug, Luke reached over the counter and filled up his own mug. "You're just pissy because Bridget came back to town and you were cock-blocked."

"Trust me, when it comes to Bridget, there is no blocking necessary." Not anymore.

Sure, once upon a time, Hawk would have given his left testicle for a chance with Bridget again. But that dream had sailed the second she left to find her happiness somewhere else, and no matter how much he wished he could go back and change things, he knew it could never be the same. That's what happened when people walked out; they could never really go back. No, Hawk knew all too well that everything changed the second love came into question.

"Glad to hear it." Luke patted him on the shoulder. "But I was talking about how you finally got the balls to make a move on Ali and Bridget shows up so she dumps you. Tough break, man."

"She didn't dump me, we're just friends. And I didn't make a move. Ali was being, well...Ali." Spontaneous, big-hearted, and a never-ending pain in his ass. Which, sick bastard that he was, Hawk was growing to enjoy. "Thankfully, Bridget is gone, I have my town back, I mean, she's here now but it's only temporary, and in a few months I won't have to pay alimony anymore."

"There's that," Luke said, taking a swig. "So tell me, what does one get their ex-wife for a wedding present?"

"How the hell would I know?"

"I mean, are you going strictly by the registry or maybe something a little more out of the box?" Hawk sent Luke a look. "What? It's proper party etiquette to show up with a gift, and between the engagement shower, the wedding shower, the wedding itself... You don't want to show up empty-handed."

"I'm not going to any shower and I doubt I'll make the wedding guest list." And if he did, he'd be conveniently busy that weekend. It was one thing to wish his ex well in her future. He wasn't about to go have his past shoved down his throat. "And since when do you care about party etiquette?"

"Since we've been talking about renting out the bar for private events," Luke said and Hawk grimaced.

He was a bar owner and a brewmaster, not some fucking caterer. He liked that locals knew they could drop by and grab a cold one, catch a game, and shoot the shit. That's why Hawk had opened a bar in the first place. He'd added food to the menu because he was there so much, he needed to eat, too.

So he'd hired a cook to serve up all of his favorite foods.

Only now, their small town of Destiny Bay was having some growing pains. Besides the Moose Lodge, the Penalty Box was the largest venue in town. And the only one with a license to serve liquor. Several businesses in the area, including Kline's Fine Foods, had approached them about hosting private events.

Cosmo Kline wanted to hire the Penalty Box to host his yearly Fine Food Enforcers retreat, in which a group of independent retail food store owners got together to fish, eat, and talk shop.

Destiny Bay had some of the best coastal fishing spots in the Pacific Northwest, and it was also surrounded by incredible views. The FFE was comprised of the exact kind of people Hawk and Luke needed to network with if they wanted to expand Two Bad Apples Hard Cider into more stores.

It seemed like a perfect opportunity.

Until Luke decided that they needed to do a trial run first. Something low-key, which if they screwed up, wouldn't hurt business. And even though Hawk hated the idea of private parties, he begrudgingly saw his point. This was a great opportunity, and sure, they'd had plenty of parties there for their own cider label, but hosting an event for grocery store owners was a different ball game.

Cosmo, a supporter of local businesses, was on board. Unfortunately, there was another fishing spot up the coast that some of the other FFE members favored—and it was up to Two Bad Apples to get them to commit to Destiny Bay.

"I put a call in to the local university's hockey coach, offering to hold their end-of-season party here," Hawk said. Because if he was going to cater a freaking event, it would be with a bunch of guys who expected hot wings, sports on the flat screen, and knew how to throw one back.

"That's still a few months out, so I found us a better offer," Luke said with a smile.

"As long as it doesn't include someone messing with my menu, my decor, or bringing outside liquor, I'm open."

"Great." Luke polished off his cider and set the mug down. "Marty wants to reserve the bar for a party next weekend."

"Marty?" Hawk felt his shoulders relax and a grin take hold. The only reason he'd want to rent the bar would be for Ali's *Architectural Digest* party he'd heard was in the works—but still hadn't received an invite to.

If the party was here—at his place—then he wouldn't need an invite. And she couldn't avoid him forever. Not that he expected Ali to hide out much longer; Destiny Bay was too small a place to stay hidden.

"Does Ali know that Marty asked?"

Luke didn't answer; instead he stood and said, "I told Marty you'd call to get the details."

Hawk handed Luke his bar towel and walked into his office. Even though it was a converted storage room, Hawk had spared nothing when designing his office. Plush leather couch, two flat screens, a custom-made desk for giants—or someone Hawk's size. It was dark, lush, and had all the comforts of a masculine home.

After the divorce, he'd spent a lot of time in there, planning his business and his new life, making sure to surround himself with things that made him happy. Made him focus on his successes and not his biggest failure. In the beginning, he often favored sleeping on the couch rather than his lonely apartment upstairs.

Hawk sat behind his desk and picked up the phone, dialing Marty. He stretched his long legs out, resting his feet on the desk and leaning back in the chair.

"I hear you're looking to throw a party," Hawk said when Marty answered.

"I am, and before you say no, hear me out," Marty said. "I need this to go perfectly, and I don't want to stress out Ali, so I haven't told her yet, but with the kind of crowd we're talking about, my place is just too small. I already asked the Moose Lodge, but a celebration needs a toast, I've been told, so that won't do. Your bar is the only place in town that will work."

"Why would I say no?" Hawk asked, picturing the look on Ali's face when she learned that he'd managed to get his invite after all. "We're like family, Marty. I'd be honored to help out."

"Well, I just assumed after the other night, you wouldn't be open to the idea," Marty finally said.

"Not only am I open to it, I'm giving you my personal promise that it will be the perfect party."

After dinner the other night, Ali deserved that much. Sure, she would be uncomfortable at first; she'd hate having the attention on her. But Hawk knew what she liked, really thought he was the guy to find a nice balance between letting her feel celebrated and letting her feel understood. But mostly he thought about that kiss.

Shit.

"You always were a stand-up guy, Hawk," Marty said

and Hawk wanted to laugh. "And if it were up to me, I'd be toasting you at the party instead of that Silicon Valley smarm."

Hawk froze. "You're inviting Bridget and Assha—um, Jamie to the party?"

Hawk didn't know how Ali would feel about that. But he had a feeling her response would be similar to his. A hard, *Fuck no!*

"I know, seems odd inviting the groom to a shower, but Bridget told me that co-ed is what she wants, and what do I know about showers?" Marty laughed, but Hawk could hear the uncertainty in his friend's voice. "I'm not sure if she'll ask me to walk her down the aisle, or have one of her stepdads do the honor again, but I feel damn lucky that she asked me to throw her an engagement shower. Here in Destiny Bay."

Understanding wrapped around Hawk's neck like a noose, holding him hostage, and knowing that it would only pull tighter and tighter as the event closed in. Because watching Bridget and Asshat sharing secret smiles, and stealing private kisses, was going to leave a mark.

"Does Ali know about the shower?"

"Oh, sure. She offered to help me plan it," Marty said, and suddenly Ali's determination to avoid him took a painful turn. She hadn't been avoiding him because of the kiss. She'd been avoiding him because of Bridget.

And something about that felt too familiar to swallow.

"Well, then, I guess I'd better get with her to hammer out the details of this arrangement."

* * *

It was well past dinner by the time Ali stumbled up her stairs and toward her studio. She'd spent the afternoon sampling menu options, learning the difference between appetizers and hors d'oeuvres, and deciding that anything excluding wings and poppers was just plain crazy.

Balancing her grocery bag in one hand, she reached for the doorknob with the other and froze. The light was on inside, and the door was unlocked. Two things that were different than how she'd left them.

Sticking her keys between her fingers, and dialing her tone to *Dirty Harry*, she walked into the apartment.

"Loraine?" she ventured. "I hate to break up the party, but I only have full-fat milk."

"Good thing I brought pie then," a sexy and surprising voice said from inside. "Can't have pie without milk."

Ali peeked into the studio to find Hawk on her couch. His long legs stretched out, feet on the coffee table, making himself right at home—reading a magazine.

Ali dropped the groceries in the fridge, reached over the pie box, and grabbed herself a beer. She popped the top off and took a pull. "I'd offer you one, but then you'd think it was an invitation to stay."

"You say that like you want me to go," he said, his eyes never leaving the magazine.

"I do want you to go." She knocked his feet off her coffee table then sat next to him on the couch—and pointed with a jerk of her chin. "There's the door."

"I see. You know, you really should beef up your security." He slid her an amused glance.

"I'll talk to management." She took a swig of beer. "Now, leave."

"Can't. It seems I have a party to plan, and my assistant's been holding out on me."

"Your assistant? Luke would be offended if he heard you call him that."

"Not Luke." His eyes looked over the magazine and met hers. "You, sunshine."

She snorted. "In your dreams."

Hawk gave her a slow once-over, pausing at her lips, her throat, grinning right before he reached her cleavage. Which thanks to modern lingerie technology, she could pass for an almost C rather than her barely there B's. "In my dreams you're wearing that dress." His gaze locked on hers. "What am I wearing in yours?"

"My boot print, on your ass."

He wiggled a brow. "Kinky, but a bit risqué for this kind of event. Don't you think?"

Hawk flipped the magazine around to show her a photo of an elegantly dressed couple dancing under twinkle light filled mason jars, which hung from an old oak tree.

Ali choked on her beer. "Is that a wedding magazine?"

"I bought it for the articles." His grin vanished. "There's a great one on how to throw the perfect *She said Yes* party. It's all about the signature cocktail. Which comes in a fancy glass and not from the tap."

"Why do you care what kind of glasses it comes in?"

"Because I have to, A, order those fancy glasses from a rental company; B, break my one standing rule, everything good comes from the tap; and C, be in attendance for another one of Bridget's famous parties. One of the few things in the divorce that I actually didn't mind saying good-bye to."

Ah, so Bridget did the unthinkable and invited Hawk.

"You don't have to go to the party," Ali said, a ping of unease at the thought of walking into that party knowing Hawk wouldn't be there. "I'm sure she just put you on the list because there is some etiquette book that claims inviting ex-spouses to upcoming nuptials helps in the healing process or some BS."

"Oh, I'm not going as a guest," he said. "She's bringing the party to my place. The Penalty Box to be exact. I'll be pouring drinks for her and the man of her dreams."

Ali could have assured him that Bridget would never agree to have her party held in a place that plastered their I'D TAP THAT tagline in bright neon across the wall and on every souvenir.

By the irritated look on Hawk's face, that would have been the sweet thing to do.

Only Ali was never crowned Home Town Sweetheart—that sash belonged to Bridget. Which was all right with her, since sashes were a hazard around a blowtorch. Not to mention a sweet girl wouldn't let Hawk squirm—and Ali loved to watch Hawk squirm.

There was something about the NHL's biggest badass looking as if he were about to eat the ice that made her day. If fact, it had become one of her favorite pastimes. Yet she couldn't manage to muster up even an ounce of joy over his discomfort.

"Bridget wants a party to impress all of her hoity-toity friends," Ali said, suddenly wondering if that was really what her sister wanted. She'd believed Bridget when she'd said she'd be happy with small and quaint. "And I don't think that includes flat screens and beer pong."

"Then you might want to tell your dad that since he

called me tonight and booked the entire bar for a private event."

That caught her completely off guard, so when Hawk went for her beer again, she let him have it. "Please tell me you said no."

"How could I say no to Marty?" he asked.

"Easy, you say no. N. O. Or how about, 'Hey, I am sorry, Marty, but you're going to have to hold my ex-wife's engagement party somewhere else, because holding it in my bar is wrong on so many levels.' "

Too many to count. Although Ali came up with seventeen on the fly, without even trying. What was her family thinking?

That normal boundaries didn't apply. Not when it had to do with a wedding. Which was why she'd wisely been too busy to call Nolan Landon.

"Where else should I tell him to go? The Moose Lodge? The senior center? Neither of those places is big enough for what he wants to host. Not to mention I have the only liquor license in town." Ali went to argue that they could have it at the park, a nice and sophisticated BYOB affair, but he cut her off. "If she remarries, it's finally over, Ali."

The ache in Hawk's eyes reached out to her, reminded her how painful it was to be stuck in limbo with someone you loved. How impossible it was to love fully when you weren't sure where you stood.

"No more alimony, no more whispers, no more wondering." Hawk let out a breath. "No more ties. It will finally be over and we both get to move on."

Ali wondered if she was part of the ties he wanted to sever, and she knew she'd never move on from Hawk.

She'd tried, and now was back—about to be stuck between him and his relationship with Bridget. Again.

"I'm not saying she can't have her party here in Destiny Bay. But your bar? You can't really think this will work out?"

"It has to," he said. "Because what would people say if I told my girlfriend's sister no?"

Ali opened her mouth to argue, then closed it because there was that. Who knew one kiss could lead to such a mess? Leaning her head against the back of the couch, she muttered a miserable, "Fuck me."

"That's not generally the attitude I go for. You'd need some kind of adjustment before we got there," Hawk said, and she felt him scooch a little closer on the couch. "Maybe we can work on that during foreplay."

His hand, big and strong, rested on her thigh and gave a little squeeze. Ali opened one eye and slid him a look that was cold enough to freeze his nuts off.

"What? If you jump every time I touch you, people are going to figure out we're faking it."

Ali wanted to say that the only thing she was feigning at the moment was immunity to his touch. He was so handsome it was haunting, the memory of their kiss sneaking up on her at the worst times. Like now.

"We were faking it." She swallowed that half lie, the reality of it clogging her throat and burning her chest as it went. Hawk had been faking it, but she'd embarrassingly been all in the second their lips touched.

"Were we?" he asked, leaning back and rolling his head toward her, until they were nose to nose and she couldn't feel his breath skate over her lips—feel her need collide with the confusion churning inside her. "Because

I'm pretty good at knowing when a woman is into it or not, and you seemed to be pretty into it."

Ali fought hard not to lick her lips. Or worse, lick his. "Maybe I'm just better at pretending than you are at reading women."

"Maybe." His eyes dropped to her mouth and he grinned. "I guess I'd need more time to assess..."

His gaze lingered, long and hot, until her lips heated as if he were kissing her. As if she were kissing him back. She told herself to move, but her body didn't seem to want to listen. It was too interested in the way Hawk was moving closer, her breath coming shorter.

His hand reached out to touch her cheek, and she didn't flinch, didn't want to. And that more than anything worried her. But when his mouth closed in, instead of the soft flutters she experienced the other day, her heart pounded violently.

What was she doing?

She'd dreamed about this moment for over a decade, yet now that it was about to happen, she couldn't help wondering why. Why now? Was it because the kiss had opened his eyes to the possibilities? Or was it because Bridget was getting remarried?

She wanted Hawk, but not if she was merely the fill-in for the real thing. There wasn't a world in which Ali could replace Bridget; the two sisters couldn't be more different. And Hawk had a type—and it wasn't Ali.

Terrified that she was making a mistake that could ruin everything, she reached for the only thing she knew for certain.

"This isn't right," she said and watched as his eyes fluttered open.

"It's hard to get it right when you're talking," he said.

"No." She placed a hand between their mouths. "Last time, I kissed you as a spur-of-the-moment solution, to what could have been an awful moment. But the more I think about this, the more I realize it was a mistake."

Hawk's face went carefully blank and he sat back, on the opposite side of the couch. "Funny, I'd call it eye-opening."

"Hawk, every woman is eye-opening to you, which is why you burn hot and fast. Add that to my history with men and we're destined to go off like a firecracker."

"Fireworks, because there would be lights, sunshine."

Ali gave a small roll of the eyes. "We both know there's nothing more than friendship between us," she admitted, the lie burning as it came out. "And I don't want to lose that. Even for..."

He studied her for a moment, his expression impossible to read. "I don't want to lose that either," he finally said.

Ali felt light with relief, but her heart was heavy with the understanding that he was agreeing. Confirming what she knew to be true: whatever it was between them wasn't strong enough to withstand more.

"Good, because you're my friend," she admitted quietly. "And I don't have too many of those in my life."

"Me either," he whispered, and Ali wanted to laugh.

Not only was he respected around town, but he was revered for his warmth, humor, and loyalty. If there was an Everyone's Best Friend Award in town, Hawk would be the lifetime recipient.

"You're right," he said with that laid-back grin of his. "You are good at pretending. Just stick with that dreamy look you have going on and no one will question that you're hot for me."

Ali laughed, surprised at how he could lighten the moment.

"You might want to work on that." He pointed to her smile. "Anyone sees *that* and they'll know it was a lie and I'm going to look like the asshole who was using his sister-in-law to get back at his ex. And then every time we're seen together, people are going to whisper."

Ali sobered because there was the flaw in her self-preservation plan. Preserving their friendship—and her heart—meant calling off the charade. But the charade was the only thing saving Hawk from another year of people thinking he was still hung up on Bridget.

"How do we fix this?" she heard herself ask.

"Like we always do," Hawk said, putting his arm around her shoulders and pulling her in. It was a comfortable position they'd sat in a thousand times over the years. That it still felt safe gave her hope. "You pretend that my attention annoys you, and I keep flirting with you. Only this time you get to flirt back. And at Friday night dinners, instead of bringing you cider, which I know you hate, I will bring you Scotch."

"Yes on the no more cider, and maybe we should hold off on the family dinner nights until Bridget leaves. I don't want to make it harder on my dad, and the last time you showed up, shit went south—fast."

"Funny, I thought it was finally starting to get good," he said, and Ali elbowed him.

"Fine," he said, blaming the sharp pain in his side on bony elbows, and not disappointment. "But that means you owe me a dinner night once a week." He held up a hand. "Don't hug me yet, I know you're excited, but there's more. I will cook you those dinners at the bar, and you will bring pie for dessert. Instead of *barmaid* or *pansy ass*, you'll need to find a sweeter endearment for me, such as *babe* or *boo*."

She looked up at him. "Boo?"

"Just a suggestion. You can use *sex god* if you prefer. And I get to pamper you, and you don't have to pretend you hate it anymore."

"That's a lot of rules."

"Rules are important," he whispered.

"And what do you get out of this arrangement?"

His smile went wicked. "To see you in that dress."

Chapter 6

Hawk jerked awake. He was hot, sweaty, his head was pounding, and his right arm felt as if he'd gone a round with the sexy blowtorch wielder next door. Which would have hurt less than the fire searing through the right side of his body.

But it was neither his shoulder nor his fiery neighbor that had awoken him. Nope, that honor went to the club music blaring from the front of the bar.

Hawk sat up, his skin squeaking against the sticky leather as he carefully rotated his shoulder, like the doctor had shown him, hoping to stretch out the muscles before his entire upper back cramped—and nearly passing out as a jolt of jaw-biting pain shot from his shoulder all the way down to his lower back.

He adjusted his hold, took a deep breath, and held it there for the count of ten, focusing on his breathing.

Okay, he made it to *four* when Bruno Mars started in

with one of those high notes Hawk hated, and for *five*, *six*, and *seven*, all he could concentrate on was how he'd pummel whoever had that music playing.

By *eight*, he was giving one last roll of the neck. *Nine*, he was headed down the hallway toward the bar. After spending his nights wondering what the hell he'd gotten himself into, and his days wondering just how explosive those fireworks would be, he'd needed a refresher.

Yet he'd achieved exactly forty-three minutes of sleep, a kinked shoulder, and enough pillow marks on his cheek to double as Cosmo Kline's twin. Even worse, it was the best rest he'd achieved since several days ago when he found out Bridget was having her engagement party at his bar.

Tonight!

By the time he hit *ten*, he entered the bar through the swinging back door and muttered a "What the fuck?" Because what the fuck was going on?

The bar had been transformed into some sort of *sport coat required* tasting room. The hand-carved redwood tables were now draped with tablecloths. Some cream and others light pink, but all were dressed with a silver vase and votive, and moved to the outer rim of the room, leaving the center empty as if for—dancing. The canister lights, originally made from hanging cider barrels, were wrapped in some kind of silver mesh netting and secured with cream fabric. And his bar…

Jesus, his bar.

It was covered with glasses. Strike that: stemware. Wine, goblets, champagne, martini. Every kind of GNO glass was represented—except the kind meant to go with a tap-only bar. And at least a dozen women were flitting around, hanging twinkle lights over his bar, stacking wine bottles under it, and debating the merits of finding the right color palette.

Luke stood behind the bar, wearing dark slacks and a button-up, uncorking a wine bottle as if this were a fucking tasting room, and he was Robert Mondavi, the famous winemaker. In front of him sat Bridget, wearing a tiny white dress, a sparkly tiara, and a diamond big enough to cut through glass. She was flanked by a group of women: all lean, blond, and each one wearing a cream dress—one shorter than the next.

Her bridal party, he assumed by the matching silver heels they all wore. Well, all of them except the petite brunette on the far end. Two seats away and eating a burger that had clearly not come from his kitchen, Ali was dressed in a lacy cream top, a denim skirt, and black boots. The boots hit above her knee, the skirt mid-thigh, leaving a nice sliver of silky skin exposed.

Unlike the other day, her hair hung loose, in tousled chocolate brown waves that slid over her shoulders and down her back. Her lips were wet with wine, reminding him of how sweet she'd tasted when they'd kissed—or just how sexy she was when she was bold.

She wasn't bold right then. She was nervous, sitting on the outside of the inner circle, doing her best to fit in. For Bridget. For Marty.

For herself.

"About time you showed up," Luke said from behind the bar, uncorking another bottle.

Ali turned in Hawk's direction and hesitated, finally sending him a smile that was a heart-stopping mix of bravado and uncertainty—leaving him wanting things that were definitely not approved decorum for friends. Even friends who were pretending to be dating.

So he gave his double-barreled smile, the one that had graced the cover of *Sports Illustrated*, and headed her way. "Had someone told me my bar was going to be turned into a sorority house during pledge week, I would have shown up earlier."

"You're here now," Bridget said, bringing his attention to the fact that Ali wasn't the only Marshal woman who had zeroed in on him. Like a heat-seeking missile, Bridget was off her chair and walking his way before he could change directions.

Her hips swishing for his benefit, her lips pursed in a practiced smile. She was wearing her game face. He'd expected to see her, prepared himself so he could get through the event, but his chest ached all the same.

"Thanks," she said, rising up to give him a kiss. Had she moved a centimeter to the right, it would have been more lip than cheek. "For agreeing to have my party here. You didn't have to do that."

Hawk wanted to laugh. She knew damn well that saying no to a man who'd treated him like a son, even after their divorce, was impossible. Hawk hadn't had a lot of experience with unconditional love growing up, but Marty had always been there for him. Even before he'd married Bridget—and after their marriage had crumbled. So there wasn't much Hawk wouldn't do for the old man.

"Right," she said, as if reading his mind. "Well, I wouldn't have blamed you if you'd said no."

"It's one night," Hawk said.

Which wasn't exactly the truth—and they both knew it.

This party was the compilation of seven years of history and family, a true test of his vow to always love her. It didn't matter that she'd walked out on their marriage, Hawk had promised Bridget, and Marty, that he'd make her happy. And that promise didn't end when Bridget filed for divorce.

It just became more complicated. And that complication, which had colored the past few years, was finally coming to an end.

Hawk was determined to live up to his promise—right up until the moment she vowed her love and life to another man. Then it would be up to someone else to ensure her happiness. And maybe, then, Hawk would be free to find his own.

"Does that mean you are coming tomorrow night?"

Hawk looked around the bar and cringed. "Is that your way of telling me my bar is going to look like this until then?"

Bridget laughed. "No, it's my way of telling you that I want you to be there. To be a part of my special night."

It was his turn to laugh. "I'm working the party, so yeah, I'll be the guy behind the counter pouring overpriced wine in fancy flutes."

"I meant, I want you to come as a guest." She rested a hand on his chest and he was certain she could feel it pounding. "I can't imagine you not being a part of my day."

Hawk took a step back, a big one to clear his head—the confusion pumping through his veins. She'd denied him the right to be a part of her tomorrow two years ago. So while serving drinks was going to be uncomfortable enough, there was still the bar separating him from the emotions of the event. But mingling with her friends, being in the fray with a bunch of people who had known Bridget was leaving him before he did? Actually toasting the happy couple? Not going to happen.

"That might be a little awkward," he said.

"It doesn't have to be." She looked up at him with those big green eyes he could never deny. "We were friends first, then lovers. There is no reason we can't go back to being friends, and why you shouldn't be a part of the celebration."

There were a million reasons why he shouldn't—and wouldn't—but all Bridget was thinking about was her night. How having him there, toasting her, supporting her would mean that she was free from the guilt. That she was forgiven.

That if things went bad, she had him to turn to and lean on.

"You were my friend, then my lover, then my everything, Bridge," Hawk said, a sour taste in his mouth. "I get that we're over, and I'm even okay with it." Surprisingly, he was. Six months ago it would have been a different story.

Something shifted the moment he'd seen Ali in that dress. Oh, he'd been over Bridget long before that, he just hadn't admitted it. But seeing her welding in that dress, the vulnerable excitement he'd seen in her eyes when she told him about *Architectural Digest*, confirmed it.

Just like it confirmed that the feeling he'd had for Ali had become something much more than friends.

The kiss? Hot damn. That told him he was not only over the divorce, but ready to move on.

"But that doesn't mean I want a front-row seat to the

big event," he said quietly. "Or that I can just pretend we're nothing but old friends."

And that's when Hawk got it, what Ali was so afraid of. Because there was no way he could go back to being friends with Bridget, at least not the way they'd been before. He'd forgiven her, could even wish her happiness in her marriage. But he couldn't forget the pain she'd caused him.

Friendships, like all relationships, were based on trust and the ability to be vulnerable without the fear of being taken for a ride. And Bridget had taken him on so many rides over the years, he wasn't interested in adding another stamp in his passport.

"Then what are we?" she asked, her heart in her eyes.

Hawk wasn't sure what the right answer was. Bridget would always be a part of his life. Hell, she was some of the best parts of his past. Some of the worst parts, too. But no matter how much he'd wished it at times, that kind of history didn't just go away. Especially when he loved her family as much as he did—maybe more.

"We're friends with a complicated past," he finally said. "And you should focus on the guy who's going to be your future. I'm focusing on mine."

The color in Bridget's face rose. "You mean Ali?" Then she laughed, one of those laughs that was uniquely Bridget. It was sexy, serene, and condescending all at the same time. "I know Ali, she wouldn't ruin your friendship for a fling. Outside of my dad, she's incapable of long term—in any capacity."

"If what you say is true, then it would be one of the few things you have in common," he said and watched her face fall. "But I also know Ali. Have for the last fifteen years. And while she might not make a bestie out of everybody she comes across, she is one hell of a loyal and caring friend to those people special enough to be a part of her life."

Bridget lifted her chin. "Maybe, but I know you. And she's not your type."

"If you really knew me, then you never would have left," he said, because she'd know that he wasn't the kind of person to give up when love got hard. He was a fighter, and would have fought for what they had. "You'd also know that, once down, it doesn't mean I stay down." He studied her shocked expression, as if she had no idea who she was talking to. "Are you upset about me and Ali? Or are you upset because I'm no longer waiting for you to take me off the shelf and play with me until you get bored again?"

"I never meant to make you feel that way." The sad part was she really believed what she was saying. "I'd start missing you and wondered what if I made a mistake..." She shrugged. "But in the end I knew it wasn't right, and I just wanted us to be happy."

Hawk wanted to tell her she made the biggest fucking mistake of her life, because he would have stopped at nothing to make their dream family a reality. All he ever wanted was to make her happy, but in the end she'd brought him more pain than his dad ever had.

"Ali makes me happy." When Bridget's shoulders sank, he almost admitted the truth. But then realized that everything he'd just said *was* God's honest truth.

Ali made him laugh, she made him frustrated as hell, and here was the kicker, she made him a better man. No, Ali wasn't the typical beauty queen he'd gone for in the past. But that didn't mean she wasn't beautiful. Ali radiated a confidence that was as magnetic as it was sexy.

Hawk cleared his throat and looked around the bar. "Speaking of happiness, where's the fiancé?"

Bridget squared her shoulders, twisted into her most appealing stance, and plastered on one of those manufactured cool-as-a-cucumber expressions she wore for the world. An expression she'd never worn for him. Until now.

"Oh, Jamie?" She gave an affected laugh. "He had a business meeting in Silicon Valley. He won't be back until tomorrow."

"In time for the party?"

"Of course." Bridget smoothed down her dress. "He wouldn't miss it, and since he doesn't really care about color palettes and wine tastings, he said he trusted my judgment."

"You always were great at throwing a party."

She smiled. "I like to think I have a touch with creating ambience, but I have to give credit to my dad and sister. They put this together, well, with the help of my friends." She waved a hand around the bar. "What do you think?"

He held her gaze. "What do *you* think?"

Bridget dropped her hand to her side and gave a small shrug. More than fluent in nonverbal-lady-speak, Hawk understood that she wanted his approval. Which made no sense. She hadn't given a rat's ass about his opinions since the divorce, but he could tell she needed it now.

"I think it is very you," he said honestly. The Martha Stewart decor, the couture wedding, even the starched and sophisticated jet-setting fiancé. It was everything Bridget had always wanted. And nothing that Hawk could relate to.

"You said the same thing when I decorated our house," she said with a soft laugh. "You hated everything about it."

Now it was his turn to shrug. "You loved it more than I hated it." *And I loved you more than anything.*

Bridget studied him for a long moment, her eyes going soft, reminding him of the woman he'd known when they'd been alone. In love. "You're one of the good guys, Hawk." She looked over at Ali, who was sucking down a beer from a goblet, then back to him. "Don't forget that."

"And you're one step from having everything you always wanted, so don't forget that you need to let it go."

Let me go.

Hawk gave a parting smile and headed toward the bar. He grabbed a bottle of whiskey, the one he kept stashed for moments like this, and poured himself two fingers.

"You okay?" Ali asked, taking a bite of her burger.

"As okay as a guy would be to watch his man cave turned into a tea room."

"Your 'man cave' is used by the Destiny Bay Ladies Choir for *The Bachelor* viewing parties," she reminded him around bits of fry.

He crossed his arms. "Fine. Maybe it's because you're eating in my bar."

Ali looked over her shoulder and pointed to the sign above the door. "'Bar and Grill' means people are welcome to pull up a seat and enjoy a burger and beer."

"Not when the burger isn't from my kitchen."

"I like Burger Barn's fries better. They've got the right crisp to grease ratio." Ali sopped up some ketchup with her fry and offered it to him. "Taste for yourself."

Why the hell not, Hawk thought. His ex was ten feet away, his pretend girlfriend was ten inches from his face, and he could use a little taste of sunshine.

Resting his elbows on the counter, he slowly leaned in and took the fry—with his teeth. His lips brushed the tips of Ali's fingers and she snatched them back and skewered him with a look.

But not before he watched her eyes dilate. Heard her breath catch.

"You're right," he said, licking his lips. "Perfect combination."

She waved a hand at his mouth and whispered, "We agreed, no touching."

"And I thought we agreed to keep this simple," he said, looking around his bar at the matchy-matchy theme and realizing the only thing that didn't match was him. "At no point do I remember agreeing to a wedding magazine spread in my bar."

"You should be thanking me," she said. "I saved you from hours of talk about tulle and proper wick management for candles and which fork to use with shrimp."

"Why hear about tulle when having it draped all over my bar is so much better."

"Trust me, this is pretty tame," she said, dousing another fry.

He thought back on the dozens of parties Bridget had thrown during their marriage. The floating candles in their pool, the rose petal walkways, the food with names he couldn't pronounce. The way he'd always felt like the odd man out. Even a designer tux and a six-figure Rolex couldn't make him comfortable in her world.

"Point taken." He snatched the fry out of her hand and ate it. "Some kind of warning would have been nice, though."

"When the first bolt of fabric arrived, I came into your office to tell you, but you were sleeping," she said, then studied her lunch as if it held the answers to life. "I didn't want to wake you because I knew you'd insist on hanging the fabric and lifting the boxes and well…being Superhero Hawk. And I knew it would only make it"—she pointed a fry at his shoulder—"worse."

She looked up and lowered her voice. "Are you okay?"

Honestly, he was. Sure, he was holding his shoulder, and his breath, because a strange feeling filled his chest. But he was feeling relaxed, content. There Ali sat, in the middle of her own personal hell, and instead of dumping his mistake on him, she'd handled it. So he could sleep.

"Are you looking out for me, sunshine?" he asked, sending her a wink.

"No. Just curious." She took a bite of her burger. "Fi's got a poll going on Facebook about what excuse you'll use to bail on going to the party. If you're using your shoulder, I can double my money."

"I'm not bailing on the party." Hawk rubbed his temple and noticed that some of the patrons in the bar were watching his every movement. "And some might say you're asking because you care."

"Nope." She inhaled the last bite and wiped her mouth off with a napkin. She picked up a bag from the chair next to her and set it on the bar top. The smell of hot grease and a Burger Barn double cheddar jalapeño special seeped into the air.

"What's that?" he asked.

"In case you were hungry."

He was hungry, but he was also touched. "Wow, sunshine, did you bring me lunch?" He opened the bag and took in a deep breath, then met her gaze. "That's a very girlfriend-like thing, you know. Some might call it a sweet gesture."

"It's plan B." She tossed her napkin on the bar and stood, that skirt not going any lower from the gravity. "In case the shoulder doesn't pan out, I had Chester add extra peppers and cheese. Lactose and spice on a girly stomach like yours is a pretty potent combination."

Hawk leaned in, resting his elbows on the counter. "Not as potent as that dress of yours."

Chapter 7

Ali never considered herself a crier. She'd learned that tears could blur reality for a time, but when they vanished, they only made the truth that much clearer. Yet she was one dress away from bursting into tears. Or punching someone.

Hawk would do, since he was the one who'd gotten her into this mess. Unfortunately, he wasn't around, and since punching Kennedy would be like kicking a puppy, Ali settled on flapping her hands to the side and groaning. She'd seen Bridget and her mom do it a thousand times, but it just didn't bring the same satisfaction as slamming her fist into something.

"I have the red dress from Fi's Holiday Hot Buttered Rum-Run Party," Kennedy said from the bed, where she was sprawled out like they were at some kind of slumber party—and not the most miserable night of Ali's life. "It would look great with your complexion."

Ali pulled the excess fabric of her new dress out to the sides and swayed. "Unless I grew six inches and two cup sizes, it would just look…"

"Like you're playing dress-up?"

Ali spun to face her friend and glared. "I was going to say, it looks a little big."

Kennedy bit her lip. "More like, pastor's wife."

Ali looked down at herself and gave a little twirl. "It's not that bad."

"You could hide another person under the skirt. And that cut?" Kennedy made a dramatic gagging sound. "I swear Ms. Bitsy has a hat that would look lovely with it. She wore it to Easter Sunday service."

"It's the best one so far," Ali said, looking at herself in the mirror. The dress was practical, pressed, and perfect for a night of working the bar. "Plus, it's black, so it will match my boots, hide any food stains I might attract, and piss off Bridget. What more could you ask for in a dress?"

"I don't know, one that shows off your figure, makes men think about sex."

Ali plopped on the bed and fell back with a huff. "I could wear pasties and dental floss, but the second Bridget walks in the room, no one will notice I'm there."

"And by no one, you mean Hawk?" Kennedy guessed.

"Hawk is my beard, nothing more." Kennedy gave a noise that translated into *bullshit.* "I'm serious."

"Okay, then why won't you wear the pretty green dress in the back of your closet? The one you got on our last girls' weekend to Seattle that says, *Let's get serious… at my place*?"

Because she was afraid that the one man who she'd want to take her up on the offer was still in love with another woman.

Ali covered her eyes with her hands and groaned.

God, when had she become *that* girl? To be fair, she'd been that girl since the moment she'd heard her dad call Bridget "Daddy's little princess." Ali, on the other hand, had always been "Daddy's little helper." Not a bad position, since she'd much rather hold a soldering iron than a curling iron, and blending lipstick wasn't nearly as much fun as blending metal alloys.

But just once it would feel nice to step out of the shadows and enjoy the sun on her skin. Enjoy the attention of a man, knowing that there was no one else he'd rather be with. That she was the first choice.

Not the runner-up.

There had been a moment in the bar yesterday when Hawk had looked at her with something other than friendship. Something that had crackled and sparked and felt so real Ali almost let herself give in to the fantasy.

Then suddenly, Bridget was there. Tall and regal and everything Ali could never be—and reality had crept in. Ali went from being the object of his affection to the amusing little sister with one well-placed bat of Bridget's long lashes.

"God, why did I agree to this?"

"Because you care about Hawk," Kennedy said softly. A warm hand covered Ali's and pulled it away from her face. So Ali closed her eyes. "And he cares about you, too, Ali."

"I know." Problem was, she cared more. And Ali knew all too well just what happened when the equation for love was skewed too far in one direction. "He cares for a lot of people."

"You mean Bridget?" Kennedy guessed.

"Bridget, the blond co-ed from Portland, the bikini model with the fake accent and even faker boobs." She slowly rolled her head to the side and met her friend's gaze. "Hawk likes women. Period. I'd just be filling an empty spot in his calendar."

"Maybe. Maybe not. But you won't know unless you give it a shot." Kennedy sat up and crossed her legs on the bed. "Women come and go, but have you ever wondered why you're the only one special enough to keep around?"

Hawk went out of his way to do nice things for Ali. Small things to let her know how special she was to him. The problem with being special was one could only shine so bright before a shinier star came along. And even though guys like Hawk saw the good in everyone, they were still drawn to the light.

"He lives next door, I'm too difficult to escape."

Kennedy didn't look convinced. "Is that you talking or Bridget?"

Ali sat up, too. "Bridget hasn't said one word about it." Not since the other night.

"Seriously? Nothing?" Kennedy asked, and Ali shook her head. "Well, that's a relief."

"Oh no, silence is bad." *Very bad.* "Bridget only goes silent when she's scheming." And she was definitely up to no good. At least as far as Ali was concerned.

She hadn't brought up Hawk and Ali's relationship once over the past week. No questions, comments, or even petty jabs. "She's been all wedding all the time. Easing me into believing that this is really about spending time together. Waiting until I drop my shield so she can catch me."

"Or maybe she is just really happy and in love and wants you to be happy, too."

Ali snorted. "Tell me if you think the same thing *after* seeing her in action tonight." The doorbell rang and Ali stood. "And after you've met Jamie."

Ali walked over a pile of clothes and through her studio, the material of her dress tangling around her legs as she opened the door. And sucked in a breath.

"Hawk, what are you doing here?"

And why did he have to be so damn good looking? And big.

He towered over her, his shoulders blocking the setting sun, his arms, which were tucked behind his back, nearly busting out of the crisp white button-up he wore. It was expensive and custom fitted, she could tell, just like his slacks, which were a dark gray and hugged his thighs and—she imagined—his butt to perfection.

His dark hair was styled in thick waves, his stubble gone, showing off those dimples he used to melt the hearts—and panties—of ladies everywhere. But it was his smile that got her, kick-started her heart. It was warm and a little crooked. And as if there just for her.

If the man was devastating in jeans and a jersey, then he was lethal in a suit. And she was wearing a dress fit for the pastor's wife.

"I'm picking up my date for the party," he said in a smooth, deep rumble that rolled down her spine to her toes.

Ali peeked around him at the bar below. The parking

lot was filling up, the twinkle lights were flashing inside, and people already lined the counter. She looked up at him. "I live next door. I can walk myself to the party."

Humor tugged at the corner of his lips, his eyes sparkling with mischief. "I'm your boyfriend, remember? Protocol says I pick you up."

"Fake boyfriend, so protocol doesn't count in this situation. So you can leave."

"Fake boyfriend or not, I'm walking you to that party." He leaned a shoulder against the door frame, rooting himself in place.

She looked around, and when she found that no one was looking back, confusion puckered her brow. "No one is watching. I think we're good."

"Jesus," he laughed. "What kind of assholes have you been dating?"

Well, that stung.

Ali crossed her arms. "Assholes who know I'm capable of walking myself across a parking lot to a party."

Still smiling, he said, "There's a difference between being capable and being pampered." He pulled a long box out from behind his back. It was black and narrow and tied with a silver bow. "And sunshine, I'm going to pamper you so hard, you won't even remember how to walk come morning."

Ali swallowed—hard—unsure how to respond to *that*. Her nipples, though, were responding with party blowers and confetti cannons. Then there was the box. Glossy and mysterious and incredibly nerve-wracking.

Men didn't bring girls like Ali boxes with bows. And they didn't wear suits with ties and cuff links.

"What's that?" she asked.

"Pull the tie and find out." Hawk moved the box back and forth in front of her, tempting her. Challenging her.

She made a big deal about rolling her eyes, in hopes of covering up the rolling over her heart was doing. With the silky ribbon between her fingers, she slowly tugged, watching his expression for a clue as to how to react. "Be warned, if anything jumps out at me, my reflexes are honed to go for the boys."

"Depends on what reflexes you're talking about, but it could be fun." Before she could react, he popped the top off and—

Oh my God. Ali froze. And so did her lungs. It was like one of those movies where the heroine was transported into somebody else's incredible life. Only this was Ali's life, and the moment was pretty incredible. "You brought me shoes?"

"Not just any shoes," he said and Ali had to agree.

They were sexy, slinky, and sleek, with enough angles to be considered edgy without being mistaken for harsh. They were feminine and classy, and yet somehow still her.

"These have the power to make a woman strut and a man stumble at her feet with a single step." He knelt down on one knee and gently took her bare foot, caressing her ankle in his sure, capable hands. "When I saw them in the window, I thought of you."

"They're silver," Ali said breathlessly. She never considered herself a silver girl. Black, yes, steel-toed, absolutely. But slinky, sexy, and silver? Never.

The way Hawk was looking at her foot as he slid the heel on, gently fastening the strap around her ankle, said he disagreed.

"They match your dress perfectly," he said, and she looked down at her drab black dress. "Not that dress, sunshine. The green one that makes you look like an angel."

She gave a self-conscious flap of the hand. "It's a little too much since we're going to be working the bar all night."

Hawk looked up at her and, with his hand still on her ankle, said, "Oh, I'm not working tonight, Luke took my shift. I'm on the guest list and I'm bringing the prettiest girl in town as my date."

* * *

"I need a drink," Ali said, desperate to get away from the prying eyes.

"How about one of the signature cocktails," Gail suggested, as someone walked by with a tray of martini glasses rimmed with pink sugar. "They're fantastic. So elegant and swanky. The perfect statement for Bridget's wedding."

"My thoughts exactly," Ali said with a big smile. "Which was why I was going to grab something from the bar. Something that doesn't come in a sugar-rimmed glass or from a bottle with bubbles."

Okay, that was a lie. At this point anything that could get her three sheets to the wind would work. But she wanted to hide behind the bar, like a big fat chicken. She was surprised she hadn't sprouted wings.

She wasn't sure what she'd expected to happen tonight, but the strange fluttering in her belly was starting to give her concern. She'd prepared herself ahead of time, was ready for the fauxmance to continue, and then Hawk had to go and do something sweet, like make her feel girly, and muck everything up.

Even worse, the entire time he'd been right there for her, making her feel as if she had a partner to get her through tonight. Instead of focusing on the fact that this was his ex's engagement party, which most people would, he'd focused all of that intense concern and care on her. Offering a comforting hand on her back when she welcomed her mom, steering Marty away from the dessert table and toward the veggie trays, even stepping behind the bar when Bridget complained that the signature cocktail was too sweet.

Never once had he complained. And that made it so much worse.

Ali knew how to deal with friend Hawk, knew how to handle tough situations, like her demanding family or Hawk's undivided attention, when wearing her steel-toed boots. But in this dress and these heels she felt soft, delicate.

Vulnerable.

And then he'd squeezed her hand and said he'd be right back, asked if she'd be okay alone while he grabbed something from the storage pantry. And her heart had fluttered. So had her lady land. A sure sign that it had been too long since she'd had an orgasm with someone else in the room.

"Be careful not to get red wine," Gail said, and Ali held tight to her smile, even though she knew what was coming. "The stains are impossible to remove and would stand out like lint on Velcro with Ali's dress color."

"Couldn't look any more ridiculous than that bride trying to pull off white," Loraine said to Ali, her red lips puckering in horror. "That's why I didn't bring a present. I figured she could rewrap the last one I gave her. You don't get a second set of corncob plates just because you made an oopsie."

"Ali was always a dribbler," Gail went on as if she'd heard not a word. "Too busy to sit still, always in motion, especially at meals. I'd spend half the time trying to get her to sit still, and the other half in that laundry room, scrubbing away stains."

Even though her mother was talking to Loraine, all eyes went to Ali. She felt her cheeks heat, and her chest tighten until she couldn't breathe. It was like she was ten again, with her mother in tears because Ali had spilled apple juice down the front of her flower girl dress.

"Girl was always a class act, if you ask me," Loraine said with a wink. "All those meals on the boat she'd help prepare. Marty would man the grill and little Ali would be inside shucking peas or making a salad."

"We had a lot of fun eating out on the sailboat," Marty said to Ali with a warm smile. "We were too busy having fun to worry about stains. Huh, kiddo?"

Ali's chest got tighter, but this time it wasn't from being misunderstood or disappointed, it was from love. Her dad's love.

"Oh, I didn't mean..." Gail looked helplessly at Marty, then gave her an apologetic smile. "It's just you look lovely, dear."

Like Ali's childhood therapist had pointed out, Gail didn't mean any harm by her words, she was looking for a way to connect. And since she'd lived so afraid that what she possessed inside wasn't enough, she'd placed all that value on external things. Like cars, and status, and appearance.

"Thanks, Mom. I was hoping you'd like it," Ali said, squeezing Gail's hand. Gail smiled ear-to-ear and squeezed back. "And I remember, Dad. Those were some fun times down on the boat."

Almost as fun as seeing him smile at how great the night had turned out. As promised, Bridget had included him in everything, even asking him to come to the appetizer tasting, and sleeping at his house last night.

Ali hadn't seen her dad that content since he'd had both girls under his roof for Christmas morning, two years ago. Not caring that they were grown women, he'd put reindeer paws around the fireplace, left cookie crumbs and a half-empty glass of milk, even dressed up like Santa to hand out the presents.

He was so happy he'd spent most of the evening shaking hands, talking to neighbors, introducing himself to Bridget's friends.

"Jamie is a sailor, too," Gail said proudly, and Ali could tell she was trying to bring the conversation back to a topic where she could participate. "He's taking Bridget sailing around the Gulf for their honeymoon."

"Bridget gets seasick," Ali pointed out.

Gail waved an elegant hand. "They have pills for that."

Ali might have laughed at her mother's comment, but Marty sent her an even gaze. "Jamie told me it's an eighty-five-footer. Complete with hot tub, four guest suites, and a putting green on the back. No sail. I think she'll be fine."

"Thank goodness," Gail said, placing a hand on Marty's arm and leaning in so her hands weren't the only thing brushing up against her ex-husband. "It's already booked. For right after the wedding."

"They've set a date?" Marty asked, his voice even, but Ali could tell that he was feeling left out.

"Three weeks from tomorrow." Gail fanned herself. "Talk about a whirlwind wedding, but I have a lead on a venue that's about twenty minutes north of here, right on the ocean." She turned to Loraine. "One person's failed wedding is another person's happily ever after."

"She's still looking to get married around here?" Marty said with a big smile, and Ali was as surprised, and pleased, as her dad. Bridget having her wedding nearby allowed Marty to be a part of every step, without the tax on his body from travel.

"She seems set on it."

"Well, that sounds like a reason to celebrate. How about I go get us all a slice of that cake over there. The chocolate one." Marty was practically foaming at the mouth.

"I'll get it, Dad, right after I get you some celebratory broccoli and ranch," Ali said, feeling like a parent with a challenging child. "Anyone else?"

"Well, be sure to grab some club soda, just in case." Gail's eyes darted around the room and a small crease appeared between her brows. A very small, *I've had a face-lift* crease. "And maybe find Hawk. I hope he didn't leave yet—the games are about to begin and I know how much he likes Trivial Pursuit."

Understatement, Hawk *loved* Trivial Pursuit. Even had a victory dance, which, irritatingly enough, he got to use more than Ali would like to admit.

"Hawk didn't leave. He's just getting something from

the storage room," Ali assured her, although Gail looked anything but. "And what games?" She looked at Marty, who was looking back equally confused. "Bridget didn't say anything about playing games or I would have planned something."

Not that she would have known *what* to plan. Her friends played games like Pin the Junk on the Hunk and Condom Toss. And if her mom was concerned about a little wine on her dress, then an exploding condom filled with whipped cream was probably out.

"Don't worry, dear, I thought ahead." Gail pulled a packet of papers out of her purse and handed them to Ali. "Bridget was concerned it might make you uncomfortable to play, but I assured her that this is her day and there was nothing to feel uncomfortable about."

Ali looked down at the papers and shrugged. "What could be so bad about Couples Trivial Pursuit?"

"Nothing as far as I can see. It is simple—people team up in pairs." She batted her lined lashes at Marty. "You can be mine," she whispered. "Then each team answers questions about the bride-to-be, the same questions I already asked Jamie to answer. Whoever gets the most correct wins."

Okay, pretty standard party game. It looked like a list of questions that would evoke lots of laughter. Not Ali's kind of party game, but fun all the same. "I still don't see how that would make me uncomfortable."

"That's what I said, but then Bridget read the questions I'd asked Jamie, and got all upset. Then she said you were planning the party, and I'd be stepping on your toes."

Overwhelmed with all the different needs her family

required to make it through the night without someone collectively losing their shit, Ali felt the impossible expectations close in on her. She could give a rat's ass what transpired at the party. In the end, what mattered most was Marty's happiness. Which meant pandering to keep Gail busy and pampering Bridget. God, she felt like she was a kid all over again. "I'm okay with it. How about you, Dad?"

Marty mumbled something about anything that makes his girl happy is fine with him when Ali read a little farther down the list—and stopped breathing. Beneath WHERE DID THE BRIDE AND GROOM MEET? and above GROOM'S FAVORITE COLOR? was a question sure to make someone uncomfortable. And it wouldn't be Ali.

HAS THE BRIDE EVER BEEN SKINNY-DIPPING?

The answer would be yes. With Hawk. It was the night Ali knew her sister was going to marry Hawk or get frostbite trying. Lucky for Bridget, and all of her elegant fingers and pedied toes, it didn't take until the next winter for Hawk to get down on one knee.

He'd fallen for her sister at, "Hello."

Then there was three down: WILDEST THING THE BRIDE HAS EVER DONE?

Join the mile-high club. Again, with Hawk.

BRIDE'S DREAM HONEYMOON?

Swimming with dolphins in Fiji. Check and check. It was where she'd spent three weeks with Hawk after their wedding. Planning their future, and convincing Hawk it was a forever kind of commitment.

Hell, she'd done such a good job, Ali had been convinced, too. For a time. But then her sister's wanderlust, the *I wonder what I'm missing* gene she inherited from

Gail, kicked in. Sadly, it was right around the time Hawk's career ended.

So, no. Bridget wasn't worried about Ali's feelings. She was covering her own ass. And the only reason Ali didn't say that to Gail was because the only person who would be more uncomfortable with these answers than her sister—would be her ex-husband. Especially when they reached the WHEN DID THE BRIDE KNOW HE WAS THE ONE question.

So when Gail complimented Ali on her shoes, and mentioned she had a clutch that matched, Ali made her way to the bar. She needed to talk to Bridget, but first she needed a drink.

Ali located Hawk's stash beneath the bar and was pouring herself a sip when Colleen Hanover approached the bar. She was two years older than Ali, two marriages in, and based on the slinky dress and naked finger, she was looking for husband number three.

"Something fancy that says eligible but not easy," Colleen said.

"I don't work here," Ali pointed out.

"And serve it in one of those." She pointed to a champagne flute. "It will make me stand out. Oh, and no sugar. Empty calories."

"A signature cocktail it is," Ali said, grabbing a goblet and extra sugar.

"Where is the man of the hour?" Colleen asked.

Ali looked around the bar, found Bridget talking to her bridesmaids. An hour in, and still no Jamie. He was late to his own engagement party. "He was flying in from somewhere, I'm sure he'll be here soon."

Colleen's face puckered in confusion, well, at least

that's what Ali thought was happening. Her eyes narrowed, and her brows twitched, but her forehead didn't move. "I was talking about Hawk."

Ali blinked. "Hawk?"

Colleen smiled, "Yes, there is a pool on Facebook—"

"Oh." Ali rolled her eyes. "Let me guess, you bet he'd use polishing his stick as his reason for not coming tonight. Sorry to disappoint, but he's here." With her. And he'd bought her shoes. "He just had to go grab something from the storage room."

"Oh, I'm not disappointed. The second I heard he was dating you, I bet that he was going to stay all night. Even close the place down."

"Really?" Ali asked, swapping out the goblet for a flute and skipping the sugared rim, surprised at how hopeful she sounded at the idea of *someone* in town believing she and Hawk were the real deal. "Most people think he's going to bail."

And leave Ali standing there alone.

A fresh wave of humiliation rolled over her and settled in her stomach, adding to the complicated knot of emotions already coiling from the first time she'd seen the poll. Two minutes after Hawk disappeared in the storage room.

Ali had begun to sweat then, over the reality that he could have skipped out. Hell, she wouldn't have blamed him if he had. But the only thing that kept her from bolting, too, was that he'd promised to come back.

For her.

And Hawk had never broken a promise. Not to her. He'd unintentionally broken her heart once upon a time. But never a promise.

"Don't worry, Hawk won't bail," Colleen said with so much confidence, Ali allowed herself to breathe. "He has something to prove."

Ali slid the full goblet across the bar top. "What does that mean?"

"That you need to be careful," Colleen said softly, as if she were looking out for Ali. "Hawk has had three semi-serious relationships since the divorce. Each one started when she came home, and ended when she left town."

"Are you saying Hawk purposefully leads women on to make his ex jealous?"

"God, no," Colleen said, taking a sip of her drink. "He'd never do that on purpose. Hawk is too nice of a man to hurt someone purposefully. But I am saying that he convinces himself he's ready to move on, that he's over the breakup, and then Bridget leaves and he loses interest in relationships, and another poor girl loses her heart."

Which wouldn't be a problem for Ali, because they weren't in a real relationship. They were friends doing each other a favor, so her heart might be fluttering, but it was firmly intact, thank you very much.

"That's not what's going on here."

"Good to know. Because once you've had Hawk, trust me, no other man compares."

Ali swallowed. If a man-eater such as Colleen couldn't handle a man like Hawk, what made Ali think she could?

He'd made her a promise, that was how. Hawk had promised her that their friendship wouldn't be affected. And if there was one person who had never let her down, it was Hawk.

"Thanks for the warning, but I've got this," she assured herself.

"Good to hear." With a smile that was more pity than convinced, Colleen took her drink and stood. "By the way, he's standing by the pool tables, in case you were still worried that he was going to bolt and leave."

"I know what I'm doing," Ali said, but Colleen was already gone, leaving Ali to question her own statement.

Did she know what she was doing?

Yes, she knew the truth and he'd made her a promise. But Hawk wasn't responsible for her heart, had no control over how she felt about him. He was charming by nature, and would never purposefully lead Ali on. But that didn't mean that she wouldn't read into things, like she'd done when they'd been younger and he'd chosen Bridget.

She still remembered the look on his face the first time he'd met Bridget. It was a look that Ali had seen a lot with regard to her sister. But seeing it on Hawk had been devastating. It obliterated any of the looks he'd ever given Ali.

It had also obliterated any hope she had of anything more with him. Because his look wasn't one of infatuation, like most men with Bridget. No. Hawk's had been love.

And men like Hawk had a singular focus when it came to love. Leaving Ali the odd person out—with both her sister and her best friend.

With a tired sigh, Ali picked up her glass and emptied it, letting the burn slowly slide down her throat and warm her stomach. Then poured herself another, because she was an adult and could do what she wanted. She was no longer the seventeen-year-old girl madly in love with her sister's boyfriend. She was a mature woman who knew what she wanted, and could handle one night of being pampered by a sexy man.

Her life right now was consumed with her sister's wedding, her mother's games, and making sure Marty lived to see a hundred. She could use a little pampering. And a little confidence that she did have this, that she wasn't being naïve, gal-pal Ali.

Ali grabbed the whiskey bottle, a plate full of chicken skewers—not wings but better than lamb-stuffed mushrooms—and headed toward the storage room. It was empty, but she wasn't surprised. When Hawk said he had something to take care of, she knew where he was really going.

Sneaking out the back door, she took off her shoes and headed up the fire escape on the back of the building. Bottle in her cleavage, plate in one hand, she made her way up the rungs, the cold metal refreshing on her feet.

She reached the roof and found Hawk sitting on the far ledge, his legs dangling over the edge, staring out at the glow from the lighthouse in the distance bouncing off the waves.

He'd removed his jacket, those broad shoulders pressing against the fabric of his shirt, and his hair was mussed from the breeze. Or maybe running his fingers through it. He looked big, beautiful, and a little lost.

She's seen him camp out up here a lot over the years. Had sat there with him a hundred times since they were kids. After a disappointing visit with her mom, or when his dad was being particularly cruel, or sometimes just to have someone to sit with and share a beer. This was where Hawk would come to think, and she was the only person he'd ever shared this spot with.

As a teenager, it made her feel special; as his "girlfriend," it made her feel uncertain. She didn't know why he was there, or if she'd be welcome. Or worse, if he'd come there to rehash his relationship with Bridget. All she knew was something about the night felt different.

"Please tell me you brought food that isn't covered in fish eggs or requires extensive linguistic skills to pronounce," he said, and she realized he'd been waiting for her.

"I brought chicken on a stick and Jack," Ali said, taking the seat next to him and dangling her feet over the edge. "No glasses."

"My kind of date." He turned and smiled, soft and warm, and *this*, Ali thought, her heart beating against her rib cage, *is the real deal.*

It might not be the kind of love she'd once dreamed of, but their connection and this relationship were real. Unique. And stronger than any one moment or situation.

She laid the plate of chicken between them and hoisted the bottle of Jack out of her cleavage. She took a sip and offered it to him.

His smile turned wicked, his eyes turned lower to the top of her dress, and her legs turned to mush. "When I said 'my kind of date,' I was referring to the body shot I thought you were offering."

"Are women that easy for you to charm?" she joked, but after her conversation with Colleen, she really wondered what his answer would be. "Never mind, I forget the kind of women you date."

"I'm only looking to charm one woman tonight," he said, taking the bottle, and *Sweet Baby Jesus*, the man was potent. And sweet, and knew how to make her laugh.

And she needed to laugh tonight. To have some fun and forget about what was going on downstairs. Remember how easy things could be with Hawk.

"Well, the night is almost over, playboy, so I'd say that A-game you were bragging about is coming up a little short."

He looked at her bare feet and grinned. "Really? Because how I see it, on a scale of one to ten, I'm already at about an eight."

"An eight?" she laughed. "You haven't even made it to first base."

"I've got you alone on a rooftop, and managed to get you out of your shoes." He grinned. "Nice toes, by the way." He gently tapped her feet with his shoe. "My team color, I'm flattered."

She looked down at her toes. "They're red. I like red."

"So do Blackhawk fans."

Oh, for God's sake. "It was the only color I had besides black."

"My team's other color," he mused. "Something you want to tell me, sunshine?"

"Only that it's hard to see the stars around your ego so scoot over." She shooed him, but the big lug didn't move an inch.

"That's not what your toes say." His voice was like sex as he looked down again, and it took everything she had not to wiggle them. "They say you want to hold my stick."

"Colleen Hanover is downstairs and she's wearing a red dress with black do-me pumps," Ali said. "I bet she'd hold your stick."

"No can do, I'm a one-woman man."

Ali gave him a dry look. "Since when?"

"Since I got myself a girlfriend." He took a sip. "Proper boyfriend code says I can only dream about my girlfriend, and that would be you"—he bumped her with his shoulder—"coveting my stick."

She grabbed the bottle. "You'd better put those dreams to memory, because come midnight, this girlfriend turns back into your neighbor, and your stick is free again."

"I already have a lifetime of dreams banked, sunshine." His smile went wicked. "A few starting as far back as high school and just about every night for the past year."

Ali choked, the hot whiskey burning her throat. His words stopping her heart. Then she reminded herself that this was Hawk being Hawk and she forced out a laugh, then offered him back the bottle. "Save the charm for the next girl. I've seen the full Hawk experience in action, and I'm not interested."

Her body argued. Part of her heart did, too. She wanted the full Hawk experience, just for a night, to see what it would feel like to be with him, to have him see her as a desirable woman.

"Charm only works if it's the truth, sunshine. And you know me better than to lie." He took a big pull then leaned back on both of his palms and looked back out over the skyline of their little downtown.

The weight of his words fell heavy on the night's air, and Ali's confidence. She went from feeling free and giddy to extremely self-conscious.

Hawk had been nothing but a gentleman with her tonight, and maybe that was the problem. Under all the flirting and pampering, Ali feared, lay a whole lot of obligation. Maybe Hawk was just being Hawk and doing what he always did when her family imploded—tried to be the glue that held them together, helped them smooth things out.

"And what the hell is the full Hawk experience?" he said lightly, but she could tell she'd pushed a button. "You'll have to explain it to me."

"I don't know," she said honestly. "Normally, when we hang out, I'm in my jeans and boots, never in a dress with fancy shoes eating finger foods that are inappropriate to eat with your fingers."

"Dress. Jeans. It doesn't matter. Lately all it takes is one look, and I can't stop staring."

She waited for him to laugh, but he didn't, instead that easygoing charm of his slipped, and he went serious. Dead serious. And if that wasn't enough to send heat racing through her body, his gaze locked on hers, steady and sure, and Ali also felt her body respond.

The longer he looked, the hotter she became, until it felt as if her body was on fire. Her heart was in her throat. And nothing seemed to exist except his words—and their connection.

"Shit," he mumbled and took another long pull of Jack. He hissed a breath through his teeth and looked back out at the water. "I shouldn't have done that."

"What, get a little hammered at your ex's party?" she said. "I think it is expected, I mean Garth Brooks even has a song about it. So I don't think anybody would judge you for letting loose. In fact, half the people down there would probably encourage you."

"I wasn't talking about the Jack," Hawk murmured.

Ali looked over and found his gaze traveling slowly

back up her bare legs, to her breasts, finally stopping on her lips. "Oh," she whispered.

"Yeah, oh," he said equally low, and she took some pride in the fact that his voice was rough and husky. "I came up here to think about how I wanted to end tonight. Then I thought about how every time I touched you tonight, you flinched, and I promised you nothing would change."

"I didn't flinch," she defended, and Hawk lifted a brow. "Okay, maybe I flinched slightly, but your touch was so gentle and I'm ticklish."

"On your hands?" He met her gaze. "When did you become so jumpy around me?"

When I asked you to be my pretend boyfriend and you agreed. "It's been a long night."

God, it was worse than she thought. He had only been trying to hold her hand and she jumped out of her skin. "And since when did holding your hand become part of the deal?"

He smiled. "When you put on that dress." His smile faded. "And I warned you, I was handsy. And the way you avoid my touch isn't convincing anyone of anything, other than you don't like to hold hands."

He reached over and gently set his hand on hers. Warm, sturdy, strong. Ali felt her breathing slow. "See," he said, "not so bad."

"Not bad." More like wonderful.

He linked their fingers and pulled her hand into his lap and her breath hitched. "Easy there, I'm taking it slow."

"What would you do if you were taking it fast?"

"Why don't we start with basics." He flipped her hand over and slowly began to rub it. Little soothing, body-melting circles into her palm. "When a man and a woman like each other, they hold hands."

"They also don't hide up on the roof."

He ignored this. "And when they're dating"—he brought her hand to his lips—"they do more than hold hands. And if we want anyone downstairs to believe we are dating, you have to work with me, sunshine."

Ali knew how to play her part; she'd been doing it her entire life. And for him to blame her, when he was the one who disappeared, fired her up. So before she lost her nerve, or good sense kicked in, Ali pulled at the collar of his shirt and tugged him close.

"Like this?" she challenged, and pressed her mouth to his.

She wasn't sure what she expected to come from it, other than teach him a lesson, but she never imagined he'd sit there and do nothing.

Talk about humiliating, for one long terrifying moment, he didn't move. She tried to comfort herself with the fact that he hadn't jumped off the ledge either. But when she opened her eyes and found him staring at her, his eyes wide with shock, she considered jumping off the ledge.

She pulled back to say, "*Kidding, ha-ha, you should have seen the look on your face*," when Hawk let loose a rough, incredibly manly groan, then took their kiss from a dare to hot-damn with one slip of the tongue.

And man, he wasn't kidding about his A-game. The guy knew how to kiss a girl silly. He wasn't a sprinter, more of a going-the-distance kind of kisser. The kind that could last all night long and be over too fast at the same time. He kissed as if he'd been thinking about kissing all night long, and there was nothing else he'd rather be doing.

He felt strong and reassuring, tasted like hot summer nights and long-forgotten dreams, and touched her as if she was precious. Special.

His choice.

"Ali," he said, and she realized that her name had never sounded so sexy. She thought about telling him, asking him to say it again. Maybe, while taking off her dress. But he was kissing her again and she didn't want to be rude and interrupt.

This was so much more than she'd hoped, yet it was exactly what she needed. If this was his way of being right, then she'd never worry about being wrong again.

"Ali," he said again, his tone one of reluctance. And even though she wanted to tell him that she wasn't flinching anymore, she pulled back.

"I don't think I flinched," she said, pleased that his breathing was as ragged as hers. "Did I?"

"I'm not sure." His lips came down on her hard and fast, pulling away with equal speed and leaving her spinning. "Nope, no flinching, and just in time."

"There you are," Bridget said from behind and Ali let go of Hawk's hand and sprang to her feet. "It's just like when you were kids, I could always count on you guys hiding out up here," she said as if she had just walked in on them playing a game of Quarters and not Seven Minutes in Heaven. "Let me guess, you're seeing who can make the most rocks on Mr. Beamon's shop roof."

"Bottle tops," Ali said, holding up the bottle. "What's up?"

"Jamie is here and Mom wanted me to get you since we're about to start Couples Trivial Pursuit," Bridget said, and Ali could only imagine her sister's horror at reading the questions.

"Don't worry about it, I'll tell Mom that we are playing something else," Ali said, dreading *that* conversation with her mom, but knowing that as the maid of honor, and Bridget's sister, it was her job to make sure things like this didn't happen.

Bridget's eyes darted between the two of them. Smile at full wattage, she said, "Why would I want to cancel the game? It sounds fun."

"Have you seen the questions sheet?" Ali asked, being purposefully vague for Hawk's sake.

"Of course," she laughed. "That's why I came up to grab you. I couldn't imagine that walk down memory lane without you guys."

Funny, Ali couldn't imagine playing that game with Hawk, knowing it would dredge up a lot of mixed emotions for him. For all of them.

He'd worked hard to move forward, and with one lie, Ali had pulled him right back into the past.

Chapter 8

As promised, Hawk was true to his word.

It had been two days since the party and absolutely nothing had changed.

Gail was back in Seattle. Bridget said not a word about Ali and Hawk, or what she'd witnessed on the roof. And Hawk? Other than telling Ali he was fine after discovering that Bridget, the woman who'd told him she never wanted kids, admitted to wanting four with Hubby 2.0, and was, in fact, a member of the mile-high club, qualifying with an old flame from her past, he'd made zero attempts to contact her. Not even when she'd used the diamond saw on a steel sheet at 4 a.m. With the shop door open.

He also hadn't changed his status from In a Relationship back to Single.

Ali kept her status It's Complicated, so there was no grand statement for her to make on their relationship—or lack thereof. But that didn't mean she hadn't checked his timeline every few hours for confirmation—only to see a post about three other missing kegs. Or obsess over why he hadn't spent a single night in his apartment above the bar. And if, indeed, he hadn't, then whose bed had his boots been under?

The good news was that party had been a success. Bridget was pleased with the turnout, which meant Marty was happy—and Ali could go back to her normal life. The bad news? Nothing about her world felt normal, and she was terrified that Colleen had been right all along. And Ali wasn't talking about the Facebook poll.

Bridget was gone, their history brought back to the surface, and Hawk had gone radio silent.

The old gal-pal Ali would have helped herself to whatever was in his fridge and told him to stop being butthurt. The new *I kissed him* Ali didn't want him to think she was the butthurt party, so she'd stolen three kegs and buried herself in her shop.

But it was a new day, and she was determined to enjoy it. So she decided to drop some groceries by her dad's house, then go for a run on the beach. Maybe even take the paddleboard out.

When Ali pulled up, Marty was already down on the dock tinkering with his boat, so she let herself in and headed straight for the kitchen to put the groceries away. And check all of his favorite hiding places for sweets.

Last month she'd found a half-eaten bag of mini peanut butter cups in the toolbox under the sink. Marty played ignorant, and shrugged it off as leftover Halloween candy.

Ali asked if the chocolate stain on his shirt was leftover as well. He grumbled something about being a grown-ass man and toddled down to the boat—where Ali was certain there was more leftover Halloween candy.

Because apparently, grown-ass men needed to have their hand held, so Ali had been doing daily sweeps ever since. He'd gotten better at picking hiding spots, but was still a terrible liar.

Checking inside the first aid kit on the bookshelf, Ali walked through the kitchen doorway and stopped in surprise.

The table had been moved away from the wall and into the middle of the room. The window seat, which had been used as a bookshelf, was cleaned off and now had a cozy cushion and a selection of nautical-inspired throw pillows.

Even more alarming, Loraine stood at the counter in her blue work pants, bright white sneakers, and Marty's IT'S GETTING HOT IN HERE apron, cooking up some eggs and bacon, and moving around the place as if she belonged.

"What are you doing here?" Ali asked, setting the grocery bags on the counter.

"Came to make a delivery and saw that Marty ordered some of that fancy farm-to-table bacon I read about in *Bon Appétit*," Loraine said. "They say you haven't tried bacon until you've tried Black Pig Company bacon. Now, I'm sixty-six years old. It would be a sin not to be able to say I've eaten bacon."

"So you're eating my dad's?"

Loraine lowered the spatula and sent Ali a look across

the counter. "You want me to tell Marty he has sixty dollars' worth of bacon up here?"

Ali thought about what *that* could do to a man's system. "Point taken. Eat away."

"Save me some," Bridget said, walking into the kitchen in pink flannel pajamas and sipping from a QUEEN B travel mug. She sat at the table and picked up a magazine.

"A bacon party and I didn't get an invite," Ali deadpanned. "I'm hurt." She set the groceries on the counter. "When did you get back?"

"I never left," Bridget said, licking her finger to flip the page.

"Well, that's obvious from the bra drying on the back of the chair and the fact that Dad is hiding on the boat," Ali pointed out. "Although I really like what you did to Dad's window seat. The kitchen looks bigger."

"It's an illusion. I raised the ceiling light and added some bright-colored pieces to lighten up the space." Bridget sipped her coffee. "And he's not hiding. He was washing down the deck when I woke up."

Marty's favorite pastime. "I thought you would have left with Jamie or gone to see that venue up north that Mom was talking about."

"Jamie had an early meeting in Seattle, then had to fly to Florida to see his parents," Bridget explained. "Rather than hang in an empty house, I figured I'd hang here for a few days. Not that Dad's been around much. He's either sleeping, on the boat, or running errands."

"Running errands is code for having a cold one with his buddies," Ali groaned. "You should take him up to see the venue, the drive would be good for him." And keep him out of trouble.

"No point." Bridget took a sip of her coffee. "After the other night, we decided to move the wedding to Florida."

"*After the other night?* What does that even mean?" Ali said, her head spinning from the whiplash of being blindsided. Her heart was suffocating under the weight of her guilt. Because she was pretty sure she knew exactly what it meant.

"It just wasn't our kind of scene," Bridget said, taking a serene sip from her mug and confirming Ali's fears. Her sister wasn't moving the wedding to Florida to please Jamie's parents, she was doing it to get back at Ali because of the kiss.

Only it wasn't Ali who would suffer, it would be Marty.

"Right, because when I think of your *dream* wedding, I think pink flamingos and muumuus." Ali took a deep breath, tried to calm the anger surging through her body. It didn't work. "Wow, in that humidity, your hair will frizz like a Q-tip."

"So I'll wear it up," Bridget said, smoothing out her cuticle. "It's closer to our honeymoon destination, and will be easier for Jamie's family."

"But it will be harder on Dad."

Bridget's hands stopped, and Ali saw her hesitate, but as quickly as she'd considered the option, she dismissed it.

"It's a six-hour flight," Bridget said, as if six hours were no big deal for a man who hadn't so much as driven to Seattle in a year. "He will be fine. Plus Jamie's parents already offered to let him use one of their guest rooms."

"And will they be so accommodating if he has to go to the hospital because he isn't sleeping well in the heat?"

"How do you know what is best for him?" Bridget challenged. "Maybe a chance to get away from all of the smothering that goes on here would do him some good. You're worse than Mom sometimes."

Ali's heart thumped so hard against her rib cage, it physically forced her to take a step back. Is that really how people saw her... as smothering and controlling?

Everything she'd done for her dad this past year, done for him since their mom had left, had been out of love. At times, she'd even put her life on hold to make sure their small family remained mighty.

"I guess I never thought that me loving Dad was holding him back from experiencing other kinds of love," Ali deadpanned.

"All I meant is that you don't have exclusive rights on Dad," Bridget said, regret softening her words, but it was too late. Softening the truth never softened the blow. "Other people love him, too. I'm not asking you to stop being you, just back off a little so he can share moments with the rest of us."

"Well, thank God you aren't asking me to give up being smothering and controlling, I don't know if people would recognize me," Ali said, wondering why she was always the one who had to share. She'd been receiving leftovers for years, and was starting to wonder if maybe, for some people, that was just how life went.

"I do love to see you two talking and being sisterly, but the chill in the air is making the eggs cold," Loraine said as if she were a daily domestic goddess and doling out quality family bonding time was her superpower. Then she looked Bridget up and down. "You can have a few slices of my bacon, but don't get greedy." Loraine looked at Ali. "It's the skinny ones you always have to look out for. Now sit. Both of you."

"No thanks." Ali grabbed a single slice and headed toward the fridge. "I think I've had enough sisterly bonding for today. I'm just here to bring Dad some groceries and check for chocolate contraband. Then I'll get out of the way so you can get your daddy-daughter time in, and I can get to my meeting."

Which was between her, the Pacific Ocean, and a paddleboard. A strict no family, no drama kind of event.

"You'll miss the celebration," Loraine said, placing a big plate of eggs on the table.

"We already did that. Two nights ago," Ali said, quickly putting the groceries away, relieved to find that Marty hadn't filled the fridge with off-limits foods. "Big party. The groom arrived in golf gear. The bride still said yes. I have pictures if you want to see."

"It was croquet knickers," Bridget defended, as if *that* made it manlier. "And he'd just come from a game with some business associates."

"Never trust a man in knickers," Loraine said. "Shelly Lynch, from over on Tenth Street, caught her husband in a pair of knickers. The next thing she knew, her lipstick was disappearing, and when she kicked him out, she was missing her favorite pumps."

"You can take your bacon to go, too," Bridget said, pointing to the door. "I'm sure people are waiting to get their mail."

"Mail! I nearly forgot. This came for you." Loraine reached into her purse and pulled out an envelope.

It was white, contract-size, had a green note attached to it with the United States Postal Service logo at the top, followed by Ali's name, and a line for a signature.

"Oh my God!" Ali snatched the envelope. "It's from *Architectural Digest*?"

"Signature required," Loraine beamed. "I brought it by your shop earlier, but you didn't answer." She had been taking out her frustrations on a piece of steel. "And since signing for you was illegal, I just stuck it in my purse."

"It could be nothing," Ali said, knowing that the only reason they'd send a package with a signature was if they needed permission from an artist.

Bridget gave an apologetic smile. "Or it could be something. Open it, Ali."

"Yeah," Ali said, deciding to take her sister's comment for what it was, an apology. "It could be something."

And she needed something right then to go her way. Something good that was hers, and hers alone. Something that didn't rely on anything other than her hard work and determination. No outside emotions, expectations, or qualifications.

Just Ali and her work.

"Open it, girl," Loraine said.

Desperate to do something other than argue, Ali lifted the flap, which was already expertly torn, and glanced at Loraine.

"Okay, so maybe I peeked," Loraine admitted. "But only because I knew how much this means to you. And if it was bad news, then I wanted to be able to soften the blow."

Ali looked at the big breakfast and her palms went damp. "Maybe I'll open this at home." Over a bottle of Jack.

"But then you won't have anyone to squeal with," Loraine said.

Ali rested her steel-toed boot on the chair. "Do I look like a squealer?"

"Doesn't matter, because I'm a great squealer."

"So am I," Bridget added, coming up behind Ali and resting a hand on her shoulder. "I'm sorry, don't let us ruin this moment."

Pushing down the frustration and hurt to deal with at a later date, when she was alone, Ali said, "No matter what's in here, no one say anything to anyone until I contact Nolan."

Bridget nodded.

Loraine grinned ear-to-ear. "I promise to keep my mouth shut until I get your okay." And when Ali skewered her with a *this is serious* look, she added, "I haven't said a word about you getting the cover, now have I?"

"The cover?" Ali choked. Loraine grinned. Bridget clasped her hands. And all of the stress from their argument vanished and a euphoric lightness filled her chest until she felt weightless. "I got the cover?"

"Well, Mr. Landon got the cover," Loraine said, pulling out the contract and flipping to the page that talked about the shoot. "But they're using his yard and the back of his house for the cover. And it says right here, 'The Marshal piece will be in the foreground,' she read, "and further down, look."

Ali read the next line and squealed. "They are requesting the artist be onsite for some evoking words on her piece." She clutched the papers to her chest. "They want me onsite while the shoot is happening!"

"That's huge," Bridget said.

And that was when Ali found herself squealing. Not a long, woo-girl squeal, but a little chirp of joy that refused to be held in. It felt so good, she did another one, until she felt her feet coming up off the ground. Loraine had lifted her up in a hug and was spinning her like a windmill in spring.

"Hawk is going to flip out," Bridget said, and beneath all of her sister's excitement, Ali sensed a small amount of longing. "He always said you'd do it. And you did. That's pretty cool."

"I couldn't have done it if he hadn't talked me up to Nolan in the first place," Ali admitted.

She also couldn't have done it if he hadn't been willing to help her get all of her supplies up to Nolan's place. And encourage her every step of the way.

Bridget gave a wistful smile. "That's Hawk, though. Fiercely loyal until the end. Always offering his support and belief in people and always there for his friends."

Ali wanted to argue that they were more than friends, but that would be ridiculous. Whether it was today or after Bridget finally decided to leave Destiny Bay, it was inevitable that Hawk would change his status.

And the sooner the better, because even though Ali was a master at pretending around those she loved, she was afraid that this game of pretend had turned too real for her.

Suddenly the victory didn't feel complete. It wouldn't until she was able to share it with her friend. She thought about calling him, then remembered he was avoiding her.

Maybe it wasn't such a bad idea for things to go back to being the same. Because she couldn't imagine them being different right then.

Not if different meant losing her best friend.

* * *

In Destiny Bay, it turned out, promising not to keep one's mouth shut did not limit the use of one's fingers.

Two seconds after Ali left the kitchen, Loraine started texting her friends. By the time Ali had cleared the house of all contraband—a Drumstick inside the icemaker and a bag of chicharrones hidden in the linen closet—there was already a Facebook event set up for a magazine release party. Because the only thing Destiny Bay loved more than one of their own making was free food.

Determined to get to her dad and tell him the good news, before someone sent smoke signals over Destiny Bay, Ali went down to the dock. Which was empty. She stepped on the boat and followed the whistling below deck and found the subject of her search stretched out on the bed.

His deck shoes lying on the floor.

In cargo shorts, a faded U of W shirt, and with one socked foot crossed over the other, Marty had his reading glasses on his face and his nose casually stuck in a book.

"Oh, hey, honey," Marty said, lowering the book and sounding surprised to see her there. Ali knew that, for her dad, surprise could easily be a front for guilt. "I didn't know you were coming over today."

"I come over every day." Ali sniffed the air, but caught

only the faint scent of air freshener over the salty brine of the Pacific. That's when she noticed the coffee mug on the nightstand, and the pair of dress slacks at the foot of the bed. "Bridget said you were washing down the deck, not that you relocated to the boat."

"I didn't relocate, just didn't want to wake Bridget when I got home, so I spent the night down here."

"Why were you out so late, Dad?" Ali crossed her arms.

"I was out with the fellas, I lost track of time," Marty grumbled. "I forget, is fun not on the doctor's prescribed therapy?"

"No. I'm glad you went out," Ali said, feeling awful. "You've just been tired lately, and I worry."

"No need to worry, I got home before nine, surprised to find Bridget asleep on the couch. So I snuck down here, then headed back to the house this morning to see if Bridget wanted to go for a sail. I took one look at the laundry hanging everywhere and decided I didn't want to share my coffee with Victoria and all of her secrets, so I came back down here to relax."

He set the book on his chest and rested his reading glasses on top, and that's when Ali noticed how tired her dad looked. He may have claimed to have slept like a baby, but she could see the subtle signs of exhaustion bracketing his features.

He shook his head. "Thank God you never did that."

"Sure I did, but since my bras could pass for headbands, you just never noticed." Ali sat on the bed next to him.

Up until she turned eighteen, Ali was small enough to pass for a twelve-year-old boy. Everywhere. A late bloomer, Loraine had called her. How accurate that term had become. Ali was pushing thirty and the most serious relationship she'd been in had lasted seven months with a logger from Spokane—who ended up being less of a lumberjack and more lumbersexual.

"I notice everything." He lifted a single brow. "Like how you're clenching your hands. What's on your mind?" Marty sat up and swung his long legs over the side of the bed. "Based on that smug smile, I'm guessing it's good news."

"My smile is not smug." Marty looked at her clenched hands and she forced them to relax. "Okay, fine, maybe a little." Ali handed her dad the envelope. "They picked my piece."

"Of course they picked you!" Marty's face went bright with pride and he smacked the papers across his knee. "Anyone in their right mind would take one look at your work and know it was something special. Unique. A one-of-a-kind treasure." Marty threw his arm around Ali and pulled her in for a hug. "Just like my girl."

Neither one of them was all that big on hugs, so it started out a bit awkward. But when Ali wrapped her arms around her dad's middle, she held tight. He might be beanpole tall, but he was sturdy and sure—and Ali let herself sink into his warmth. Sure, sometimes she felt as if she'd missed out not growing up with a strong female figure in the house, but with Marty, she'd never suffered from a shortage of love and support.

"It will be on the cover, too," she said, and Marty tightened his embrace. "And they want me to be there to talk about what inspired the piece."

"I couldn't be prouder," he whispered.

"Thanks, Dad." Ali breathed in the moment. The steady beat of her dad's heart, the sound of the waves gently lapping at the dock, the familiar scent of—BBQ potato chips?

Ali pulled back, suspicion high.

"I'm proud of you too, Dad," she said pointedly.

It was in Marty's nature to hold things close to his chest, but he'd never kept secrets from Ali. Until last year when he'd had a diabetes-induced heart attack.

It was only then, as she watched the doctors rush him into the OR, that Ali learned he'd been diagnosed with type 2 diabetes—two years before.

The reason for his secrecy, he'd said, was that she was a worrier and he hadn't wanted to worry her. But Ali knew the truth. Marty didn't want to be a burden. So she'd spent every day since proving to him—and maybe to herself—that love could never be a burden. Not when it was honest.

"I know this past year has been hard on you," she said softly. "Retiring, having to cancel your sail to Mexico, giving up chips."

Marty cleared his throat and went back to reading the letter from *Architectural Digest*.

"But it's important that you follow the doctor's guidelines." Ali pushed off the bed and walked over to the kitchen area. "You and I still need to make that fishing trip up to Alaska." Seeing nothing condemning on the counter, she knelt on the bench that circled around the small dining table and casually peeked in the overhead cupboards for something suspect.

Nothing.

"And chips won't get us there." She moseyed over to

the cubby above the radio. Maps, a can of mixed nuts, and a satellite phone.

"Are you looking for this?" he asked.

Ali turned around to find Marty holding a bag of beef jerky. He shook it for good measure. "This is one of the five approved snacks I am allowed to have." He popped a piece in his mouth. "Now, instead of snooping on your old man, why don't you go do something fun to celebrate."

"If you'd stop hiding things from me, then I wouldn't have to snoop." Or worry so much. "And I was going to go out on the paddleboard, but I'd much rather go for a sail with you. Not to Alaska, but maybe a little day trip out and back."

"If you'd stop the snooping, my hiding would be unnecessary," he challenged, but his eyes sparkled at the mention of a sail. "I meant something fun in town. With other people."

"Dad, this is Destiny Bay, and my kind of fun usually ends with me and the sheriff having a one-on-one. And while fleecing Dudley in poker is entertaining, doing it from a holding cell isn't exactly fun." She looked at her dad, the man who had made her childhood as full of love as it could be, then forced herself to let go—a little, "But why don't I ask Bridget to come along. We can make it a fun family day filled with the open sea, fishing, and maybe even grill up some fish."

"I haven't finished waxing the hull, and the ladder needs some work."

Ali looked around at the clutter and half-finished projects, and guilt settled hard. Marty was anal about his boat, tinkering and finessing until it shined.

Ali had been so focused on the article, on Bridget's wedding, and keeping up the pretense with Hawk, that she neglected to see that her dad's health was taking a toll on all aspects of his life—even his boat.

By this time last year, he'd finished all of his spring chores on the boat and was prepping for fishing season. Not that he could go far this summer, but she would make sure that whatever small trips he did get to take, his boat was in tip-top shape.

"Next weekend I'll help you finish up with all of that, but until then, I don't think Bridget will even notice."

"What about her seasickness?"

"Like Mom said, they have a pill for that," Ali said, and her dad chuckled. "Plus, it will help get her ready for her honeymoon at sea." Ali still couldn't believe Bridget had agreed to that. Not that Bridget didn't like to spend her downtime lying in the sun and sipping down umbrellaed drinks. She just preferred to do it poolside instead of seaside.

"I'd think after this morning that you and Bridget had reached your quota for quality family time."

Ali grimaced. That wasn't exhaustion she'd seen in her dad's eyes a moment ago. It was stress. "You heard that?"

"Didn't have to, I felt the frost all the way down here," Marty joked, but his smile didn't reach his eyes. He took Ali's hand in his and the overwhelming concern she'd carried with her for the past year doubled.

Growing up, her dad had been the biggest, strongest man in her life. His hands were powerful enough to lift engines out of machines, and soft enough to tend to a scraped knee. But as she held them now, all she felt was flesh and bones. And the new stress weighing heavy on his shoulders was partly her fault.

"I don't need you fighting my fights," he began. "Especially with your sister. My job as your dad is to protect the two of you, not come between my kids. If Bridget wants her wedding in Florida, then we celebrate her decision. That's what family does."

"But flying that far will be hard on you."

"Sweetheart, they transport dead people to Florida with less fanfare, and as far as I remember, I walked out of that hospital," Marty said with velvet steel. "This wedding is about Bridget and Jamie, not her extended family. And that's the way it should be. A wedding is always between two people."

Ali bit back the growing frustration, because weddings weren't about two people. If they were, everyone would go off and elope. As far as Ali was concerned, a wedding was about family, and sharing that special moment with the people in her life. But for Bridget, it was about what she wanted, and completely ignoring the needs of your family.

So yeah, Marty would go to the wedding and suffer through it with a smile. And Ali would be right there by his side, taking care of him, making sure he experienced everything he wanted to, while picking up the pieces along the way.

Then, when they got home, she'd deal with the fallout. Just like she had her entire life.

"You're right about one thing, Dad." Ali rested her head on Marty's shoulder. "Family supports each other. So why don't I go grab Bridget and ask her if she's up for that sail."

"Why don't you call Hawk, too," Marty said. "I bet he'd want to be here to celebrate."

Hawk would want to be there. Deserved to be there. This moment was a big deal, but it was ruined by the fact that she'd been doing the same thing she'd accused her dad of—lying. To everyone, including herself.

Even worse, because of her lies, the one person she wanted to celebrate with was MIA. And the last place he'd want to be was stuck at sea with the Marshal sisters.

"You're going to hear this sooner or later, and I want you to hear the truth from me," Ali said and sat next to her dad. She took a big breath—and her own advice. No more secrets. "Hawk and I were never really dating. We were just pretending to date to give Bridget a reason to leave."

"Huh," Marty said with a smile, and Ali wondered if he'd heard her correct. "And here I thought Bridget coming to town was a reason to finally figure out what's between you two."

"It's not like that," she laughed.

Only Marty never did. His expression was soft and serious, and full of understanding. "Why do you think he started spending so much time hanging around the house the past year?"

"Because you're fishing friends and he's a sucker for a free meal."

This time Marty did laugh. "The man uses a Ping-Pong ball as a lure, and trust me, the guy could share meals with better-looking cooks than me in this town. But he keeps coming here. Why do you think that is?"

"Because he loves and respects you like a father."

"Which is one of the reasons I keep inviting him back

every week, even when it's clear he's been sniffing around my daughter for years now." Ali opened her mouth to say that he was sniffing around his ex's house, but Marty silenced her with a finger. "Before you say something smart, I want to point out that Bridget isn't the daughter who lives here."

Ali closed her mouth, absorbed her dad's words, and felt her chest tighten. Not in a bad way, but it was painful because she longed for his words to be true. But she knew better than to blindly give in to a dream. "You need new glasses, then, because Bridget is blond and I'm brunette, and I'm pretty sure Hawk never dropped to a knee and promised to love me forever."

Because if he ever had, then both of them would never be alone again. Ali knew what a catch Hawk was, would never let someone like him go. Even when he married another woman, a part of Ali had clung to the hope that what-ifs created. What if it didn't work out, what if he realized he made a mistake and picked the wrong sister?

But all of those what-ifs led to nothing but a stagnant ache that, although it dulled over the years, never went away. And then the marriage didn't work out, and he was suddenly single again. But he never made a move to be anything other than the doting friend—until Bridget came home and Ali pulled him back into their world.

"Bridget's a determined woman. Once something catches her eye, she won't stop until it's hers, just like your mom." To Ali's surprise, Marty's tone was filled with admiration and deep love. "Hawk didn't know what hit him. And Bridget didn't know what she was getting herself into."

"I'm pretty sure when she said, 'Oh my God, yes, yes, I do,' she was on board with the whole thing."

Marty lowered his voice. "Hawk has spent his whole life looking for someone to love, and Bridget's spent her whole life running from it."

"She's a Marshal, it's what we do."

Marty slid Ali a look. "Good thing you're the black sheep of the family then."

* * *

The afternoon was fading by the time Ali pointed the boat in the direction of shore—and so was Ali.

Bridget forgot her affliction to moving water. Marty spent the way out detailing the finer points of sailing, Bridget spent the way back discussing the importance of proper wedding planning, and Ali spent the entire trip hard at work on the whole sharing concept.

Yesterday, she would have argued that Bridget was wrong, but after spending the day trying to be a part of the family, instead of the cog that held them together, Ali realized that when it came to navigating relationships, she was merely treading water.

And in her need to take care of everyone, she'd turned relationships that were supposed to be so simple and straightforward into something complicated.

Like now, watching her dad focus everything he had on Bridget while she detailed every bead and line of her dress. Things she knew Marty could care less about, but because it was important to Bridget, it was important to him. He wasn't giving his opinion, or explaining that Vera Wang was probably already booked, he was just listening.

Being a parent and sharing in his daughter's joy.

Ali had always been envious of their relationship in that way. Wanted to learn how to remove herself from the reality and participate in the whimsical side of relationships. To be impartial and avoid the conflict and hard decisions seemed freeing.

Completely foreign, but freeing nonetheless.

"Blue is a great choice," Marty said. "It matches your seaside wedding theme. And Ali loves blue." Marty turned toward the helm, the wind blowing his hair forward. "Don't you, honey?"

Ali blinked. "What?"

"Weren't you listening?" Marty asked, his voice barely carrying over the sound of the boat cutting through the water. "Since the wedding will be on the water, Bridget picked blue for her color."

"Sorry, I didn't hear, I was navigating," she admitted. "What happened to the fuchsia?"

"They couldn't get it in time for the wedding," Bridget said, and Ali gave a silent high-five to the universe. "But Mom found a boutique in Seattle that had the style I wanted and everyone's size in stock. They already shipped them out, and the dresses should arrive in Florida the Tuesday before the wedding. It's cutting it close, but there will be just enough time for a fitting and alterations."

"Blue works for me," Ali said, trying to adopt her dad's causal smile, his genuine interest. "When's the fitting?"

"Wednesday morning, first thing," Bridget said, and a strange nagging sensation pulsed at the base of Ali's neck. "I figured you and Dad could fly in on Monday so you can be there for all of the preparations and festivities."

"A whole week of festivities?" There was no amount of signature cocktails to make that week pass quickly.

"The fitting, the bachelorette party, rehearsal dinner, then the wedding."

Bridget wasn't kidding when she said that proper planning was important.

Ali did the math in her head, wondered how many slices of cake Marty would sneak, then that nagging feeling in her skull went nuclear.

"Wait," she said, blowing out a breath. "That is the same Wednesday as the shoot at Nolan Landon's house."

The day *Architectural Digest* wanted to talk about her work, her inspiration. Her big moment.

"I swear, Ali, I had no idea when I agreed to that date that it was the same timing," Bridget said, and to her credit, she did sound apologetic.

"Can you change it?"

One wouldn't think it was a huge request, considering the wedding had only been finalized last night. However, the look on her sister's face suggested that Ali wanted to walk down the aisle in nothing but her birthday suit while flipping the bird.

"That's was the only booking Raoul had."

"Is there another seamstress who could do it maybe Thursday?" Ali asked, knowing that there had to be more than one seamstress in the state of Florida. "I can catch a red-eye right after the shoot."

Even before Bridget shook her head, Ali knew it was a no-go. Marty couldn't take a red-eye. Not if they expected him to enjoy himself. And she wasn't all that thrilled about him flying alone.

As if reading her mind, Marty said, "I can fly out with Bridget and Jamie, and you can join us later."

"I can totally take Dad," Bridget offered. "But it still doesn't solve the problem of the fitting."

"Easy, I'm a size four."

"You're five-foot-one in heels, and depending on what bra you're wearing, you fluctuate between cleavage and small lady lumps," Bridget said. "Plus, there is my bachelorette party and the pre-wedding preparations, all of the things I'd want my sister to be at."

Arguing aside, Ali wanted to be there for her sister, too. And for her dad. But she also wanted, more than anything, to be at that shoot. Meet people from the magazine who could be important contacts to grow her career.

Experience what it's like to be first pick.

"What if I get fitted here and then get to Florida in time for the bachelorette party?"

"The dresses are already on their way, so unless you want to drive to Boise to get one, the fitting has to happen in Florida. Come on, Ali, this is a once-in-a-lifetime thing," Bridget said so seriously, Ali laughed—she couldn't help it.

"You know what?" Bridget's face went hard, but not before Ali saw a flash of hurt there. "Forget it. Come when you feel like it."

"Hey," Marty said, his face a puzzle of lines and creases. "We can figure this out. That's what family does."

Ali stood and walked over to Marty and sat next to him. "We'll figure it out." She looked at Bridget and willed her with her eyes to agree.

"Yeah, Dad. We'll figure it out," Bridget finally said

and then looked out at the water, making it clear that the family bonding time had reached its bitter end.

The rest of the trip home was in silence, Marty behind the wheel and Ali watching the steady current move across the top of the open waters. And thinking.

Thinking that this was exactly why she was still treading water, because anytime she started to make headway, it always ended up with her sacrificing for the greater good.

Chapter 9

Later that day, Hawk dropped off the last of the glasses that he'd rented for the party and started prepping for happy hour. He'd spent most of the past two days at the Bay View house, repainting the kitchen.

Located on the outskirts of Destiny Bay, and overlooking the Pacific, sat fifty acres of some of the most sought-after hard cider apples in the state, and the house that held more happy childhood memories for Hawk than his own. He'd been lucky enough to spend his summers here, with Luke's family. Those days and that land helped mold him into the man he'd become. So when Luke had the chance to buy the property last fall, Hawk jumped in and became an equal owner in the property with Luke and Luke's mom.

Only, Paula wasn't interested in moving that far out of town. Then Luke had to go and fall in love with Kennedy, get down on one knee and the whole works, leaving Hawk to take care of the place.

Not that he minded. He could spend the rest of his life on that property, yet every time he thought about packing up and moving in full time, he came up with another reason to hold off. He'd told himself it was because he'd needed to get the place fixed up first. Even though the previous owners had kept the property a working orchard, no one had lived in the house since Luke's dad passed away and they'd been forced to sell it ten years ago.

An inspection three months ago showed the structure was sound, but it needed new flooring, new paint, and a thorough cleaning. All things that he could have been working on over the winter months when the cider business was at its slowest. But Hawk had a feeling that his procrastination when it came to leaving his apartment above the bar had more to do with the brunette across the parking lot than remodeling.

He'd spent Monday ripping up the carpet in the front room, exposing some amazing hardwood floors. And yesterday, repainting the walls a bold but warm shade of gray. He'd been so busy he'd had zero time in his day to think about Ali.

Or how that kiss had been a game changer. In fact, he'd been too busy to even replay how she'd turned from hard-ass to playing grab ass in one touch.

At night, though, those images ran free. Including the one of the look on her face when Bridget interrupted them. And how her shy smile crumbled under the tension.

It shouldn't haunt him the way it had. But man, there was something about Ali and that sad fucking smile of hers that tore at his gut every time. Made him want to dig deep and find out where all of that sadness came from. But he had a feeling he already knew.

And it wasn't just her family who was to blame for the heartache in her life. Something he intended on changing. Ali's life had been filled with sacrifice and disappointments, and he refused to be another person to let her down.

Sure, their reason for being together ended when the party was over and Bridget left for Seattle, but that didn't mean Hawk was walking away. There had been a few rough moments the other night. Listening to Bridget talk about her hopes and her dreams and her new exciting chapter of family and forever. All of which didn't include him.

And it burned. He let it get to him and overshadow his time with Ali.

It wasn't until he got to Bay View that he realized he didn't want to be a part of that life. Not the one Bridget had described. Maybe when he'd been younger—desperate for a place to call home. Now he knew what he wanted and he was proud of his life, the one he'd created for himself right here in Destiny Bay. He liked his bar, and his friends, and he sure as hell liked the idea of more time with Ali.

First, though, he wanted to make sure she was okay. That *they* were okay. Dealing with her family was always hard on both of them, and the other night was no different. Except this time, he had some explaining to do.

So two hours later, when Ali stormed into the bar, her hips swinging and eyes flashing, Hawk leaned against the counter and smiled.

She wore a pair of show-stopping jean shorts, so short they barely peeked out from beneath an oversized T-shirt she was sporting. And that shirt was long-sleeved, hung off one shoulder, nicely showcasing a bathing suit strap that tied around her neck. Which was sky blue, matched her eyes and the confetti stuck to her delectable backside, and was designed to come apart in a single tug.

"What's all that?" he asked as if he didn't already know.

"You tell me?" Ali plopped onto the bar stool, bright-colored debris raining down around her.

Hawk reached out and plucked a piece of metallic confetti out of her hair. "Looks like some incredibly thoughtful and charming person put a lot of time into decorating your place."

"I turned on the ceiling fan and the room exploded in confetti and glitter," she said. "One whirl of the blades and it blew all over my apartment."

"Did it stick to the bouquet of chocolate cake pops?"

"I picked it off," she said, and even though she was acting all put out, Hawk knew the gesture had made her smile. Brought her back to a comfortable place with their relationship.

That's what he'd wanted. For her to know she was celebrated, without having to deal with the expectations that came with everyone watching. Or the uncertainty of where they stood.

Flowers would have led to more questions, but confetti and cake pops said she was understood.

"You ignore me for two days, then confetti-bomb my house." To make her point, she shook her head and more bits of bright paper fell like snowflakes.

"Don't forget the cake pops." He reached out and slid his finger along her lower lip, catching a leftover crumb. "Did you leave any for me?"

"Nope," she said, popping the *p*, but he couldn't help noticing the strain beneath that tough-girl vibe she was working so hard to give off.

"Good thing I bought backup." Hawk reached under the counter and pulled out a pink box filled with more cake pops and set it on the counter. She reached for them, but he pulled them out of reach. "They're celebratory cake pops, to be shared with someone special."

"Does that mean you're not avoiding me anymore?" she asked, her eyes on the box, her body dialed to vulnerable as hell.

Hawk felt like a jerk. Ali hadn't been mad about his disappearing act, she'd been hurt—and worried.

For him.

He'd figured her withdrawal at the party had something to do with their kiss, but looking at her now, the shy way she was avoiding his gaze, he realized it had everything to do with what happened *after* the kiss.

"I just needed some time to process," he said honestly. "In a space that didn't smell of signature cocktails and mixed signals."

Still looking at the box, she said, "You could have told me that."

"I could have, and next time I will," he promised earnestly. "But, sunshine, I don't remember my phone ringing either. Not even when you found out the good news."

Those expressive eyes of hers darted up, and then down to the box, as a faint blush tinted her cheeks.

Yeah, it takes two to successfully avoid someone in this town.

"How did you hear?" she finally asked.

"You mean besides Loraine running down Main Street, waving the envelope around, and screaming, 'She got it, she got it!'? Your dad called to tell me the good news, so I came into town to congratulate you. You weren't there."

"I was with my dad and Bridget," she said, watching for his reaction to the news.

It was the same reaction he'd had when Marty dropped that bomb on him earlier. Bitter resentment. Apparently she and Ali had gotten into some kind of heated argument. Marty didn't say what the topic was, but Hawk had a pretty good idea he was at the heart of it. And he was one unexpected appearance away from reminding Bridget of exactly what terms she'd agreed to in the divorce.

That Destiny Bay was his town.

"My dad took us sailing," Ali said.

Which explained the sunbathing, the sun-kissed skin, and look of utter exhaustion on her face. Balancing the line between letting Marty live his life and making sure Marty had a life to live was difficult. It was as unpredictable as running across the ice in church shoes. But every day Ali laced up and stepped onto the ice, knowing that she was going to wind up skating in circles or flat on her ass.

Yet he'd never once heard her complain. Not even when he knew she had to be at the end of her rope.

"So let me guess. You talked doctors' orders and fishing lures on your big day." Man, she deserved more. "I bet there wasn't even a burger on the premises."

She cracked a small smile. "Does low-sodium turkey jerky count?"

"Even worse than I thought." He leaned in, and placed his hand on hers. "Want to talk about it?"

"God no." She clunked her head down on the countertop. "I am so talked out, stressed out, argued out, familied out. Sometimes I just want..." She met his gaze, hers horrified and filled with regret. "Out. Does that make me sound like a horrible person?"

"No, sunshine. It makes you human." A side of her she rarely allowed people to see. She was too busy proving she had everything handled. "We all need a break every once in a while."

"Even you?"

God, the hero worship in her voice had him wanting to be the kind of man who was deserving. "Even me."

"It's been so long since I've had a break, I wouldn't even know where to go," she said and the wistfulness he heard in her voice drew him in.

Hawk had lots of breaks in his life. Good and bone shattering. But for every painful break that life had dealt him, there was a silver lining right around the corner. His dad hadn't given a shit about him, but Luke's parents had stepped in and offered him the kind of childhood and foundation most kids could only dream of. And sure, his marriage to Bridget hadn't worked out, but he'd experienced love, in all of its forms, and walked away from the divorce with more people to call family.

And for a guy who, up until age ten, could count his family members with a single finger, usually the middle one, that meant something.

But Ali? She had too many people placing their happiness on her shoulders for her to even see the silver lining. Something Hawk was more determined than ever to change.

"Good thing I know the perfect place."

She looked at him for so long, he thought she was going to shoot him down. But then she smiled. "Fine, but if you tell me it's in your pants, I'm out."

"Sunshine, you couldn't handle what's in my pants." With a wink, he pulled a to-go bag out from under the heating rack, and a bottle of cold hard cider out from under the counter.

"What's that?"

Hawk pulled out his phone and scrolled through his texts to find Luke's thread. His thumbs flew across the screen at lightning speed.

Can you handle the bar tonight? Great, thanks. BTW, your burger order got lost... in my belly.

"Dinner," he said, walking around the counter and taking the basket in one hand, the other resting low on her back. We'll pick up the rest on the way out of town,"

"What are you doing?" She swatted his hand away.

"Man, you really are bad at this." He handed her the cider. "In order to 'get out,' you actually have to leave. So this is us leaving."

She studied him quietly, her lost expression drawing him in and taking him under. "Why would you do that?"

"Take you out?" Jesus, she tore his heart apart. "Because it's what a good boyfriend does?"

"We're not dating anymore, party's over. Remember?"

Oh, he remembered all right. He remembered just how amazing that kiss was, and how good it felt to finally give in. He'd been circling around his feelings for Ali for so long, he was dizzy with want. And frustration.

He also remembered how thrown he'd felt when she'd distanced herself from him at the party. And what an idiot he'd been when he'd walked her home and given her that chaste kiss on the cheek, as if they were two friends returning from a fun night of playing pool and shooting the shit.

When their night had been anything but.

So yeah, he'd made her a promise that nothing would change between them, and he intended to honor that. Right up until Ali realized that she wanted more. Because not only was he done with letting his past control his future...

Hawk was done circling.

"Okay, well, then how about this is what kissing friends do," he said, slinging an arm around her shoulders.

"We are not kissing friends," she said quietly.

"Sure we are." He steered her off the chair and toward the door. "We are friends who kissed, meaning we're kissing friends. Now, watch your step," he said as he all but shoved her through the door of the bar. "We still have to drop by Burger Barn and pick up dinner, then make it to our destination before sunset."

"You said that was dinner." She paused, her eyes bright with humor. "Wait, are you admitting that Burger Barn serves a better burger?"

"Hell no." He placed their dinner in the leather saddle bag on his motorcycle, then grabbed his extra helmet. "But you seem to think they are better, and tonight is about you."

"Then what's in the to-go box?"

"Two of my world-famous Blue and Blackhawk burgers."

She straddled his bike, and *holy hell*, those shorts did amazing things for her ass. "What happened to tonight being about me?"

"Sunshine, tonight is about you. And as your kissing friend, it is my job to ensure the best night, even if your taste in burgers needs to be challenged." He slid the helmet over her head and climbed on the bike. "Now hold on, we've got a sunset to catch."

* * *

Hawk told himself to take it slow, there were a lot of twists and turns ahead, and if he wasn't careful, he'd careen right into dangerous territory.

Ali had been suspiciously quiet the entire ride. As they'd made the descent down the narrow path to a bluff, which sat right above the wave break and below Bay View, he could feel the frustration and ache roll off her and crash into him, like the tide slamming against the rocks. That didn't mean she hadn't snuggled so close against him that her body was shrink-wrapped to his, or that she objected when he took her hand the second they arrived.

In fact, she seemed to need the contact. And Hawk didn't mind providing it.

He watched her toes wiggle in the seafoam as they sat on the dock and stared at the tiny islands jetting out of the Pacific water. Her red-tipped feet, and the cute silver ring circling one of her toes, disappeared under the high tide as it swelled—and something raw and wild swelled within him.

She was thinking so hard, he could smell the gears burning. He'd given her an opening to talk about what happened, but every time he even circled close to serious, she changed the subject, or ate another cake pop. Not that he minded—watching her lick the icing off her lips was an activity he could watch for hours.

But if he had any chance to make tonight about more than just chemistry, then he'd need to have some kind of conscious thought process available to him. They needed to talk about Bridget, the kiss, and where they were going.

The faster Hawk got the first two out of way, the faster they'd get to the last, which was a topic he had strong opinions on.

Ali pulled her knees to her chest and wrapped her arms around her legs. Between the micro-mini-shorts, and her soft blue top, she appeared small and unexpectedly fragile.

"I can hear your smug smile all the way over here," she said, taking the last bite of her cake pop.

"This one?" He flashed her a grin. "I can barely hear it over all of that moaning you did when scarfing down my burger."

Ali shot him a glace, a penetrating flash of ocean blue. "I wasn't moaning."

"Sunshine, the fish poked their heads out to see what was going on." She nudged him with her shoulder and he nudged her back until she smiled, then he took her hand in his.

She looked down at their intertwined fingers. "Too bad no one is around to see this sweet moment."

"Huh, you're right. I hadn't noticed." He tightened his grip.

Her smile went shy and she looked out at the water, but she didn't let go. "So this is where you come to get away?"

Hawk looked behind him at the farmhouse in the near distance, the endless hills of apple trees speckled with white flowers, and a calming sense of rightness washed over him. "Yup, been coming here since I was twelve."

"Did you come here with Luke and his parents?"

"To this property, yeah. To this spot on the bluff, no. This was my secret place, and they knew when I came down here, it was to think."

She rested her cheek on her bent knee. "And what did twelve-year-old Hawk think about? Hockey, girls, Jenny Snider's boobs?"

Hawk laughed. "Every red-blooded male in high school thought nonstop about Jenny Snider's boobs; they didn't need a special place to do it." Knowing that in order to get her to open up, he had to share a part of himself first, he got serious. "My mom brought me here when I was a kid. During low tide we'd look at all of the little critters hiding in the rocks."

"My dad and I used to do that up in Sunrise Cove. We'd pack a lunch and spend an entire afternoon poking around the tide pools, spelunking, collecting shells and sea glass, then we'd come home and decorate stuff with the treasures we'd found."

Hawk tried to picture what a pig-tailed Ali would have looked like, tromping around in the tide pools, giving the crabs and guppies a scare. He chuckled, because he imagined it would look a lot like what she did for her art, only she was smaller.

"We collected shells, too. My mom would tell me that every day the tide would carry out things ready to spread their fins and explore, and bring in new critters, looking for a safe place to land."

"It must have been hard, losing her so young," Ali said, with soft understanding in her voice.

His mom never had the chance to explore, nor had she ever found her safe place to land. She'd been married young, had him young, and died young. She'd always said he was her biggest adventure.

"Yeah," he agreed. He had very few good memories from those early years, trying to deal with the grief, stay out of his dad's way. No matter how good he'd been on the ice, Bradley always demanded that he get better.

"After my mom died, I kept coming here," he said, remembering painfully just how bad those first few years without her were. "When I was feeling trapped, I'd climb down the cliff side and sit right here, looking out over the water. It was as if when I was here, nothing could cage me in. It was the proof I needed."

"Proof of what?"

"There was a world that was bigger than my dad's controlling hands."

Hawk took a deep breath to keep the familiar feelings of helplessness at bay, then looked at the ocean, past the outcropping of rocks and coastal trees, to the dark blue surface that sparkled in the fading sun, and expanded beyond what he could see. Cyprus trees rustled in the breeze and the water lapped gently against the rocky beach.

This view never failed to bring him peace. And today was no different.

They were completely isolated from problems that were awaiting them back in town, and Ali didn't seem to be in any hurry to leave. Most important, this was one of

Hawk's favorite spots, a place that had brought him comfort. And he wanted to share that comfort with her.

He could feel her gaze on him, steady and compassionate. "I never met your dad," she said.

Even though Bradley Hawk Sr. had lived in Destiny Bay for all of his fifty-nine years, very few people really knew him. Including his own son. After Hawk's mom passed away, Bradley spent his days up in the mountains logging trees, and his nights drinking himself stupid. And until Hawk had matched him in size, knocking his son stupid.

"You wouldn't have liked him," Hawk said truthfully. "He was a moody son of a bitch." Whom Hawk worked tirelessly not to become.

There wasn't a rule he hadn't broken, or a person he hadn't plowed down. Not if they stood in the way of his goal—securing his son a spot on a Stanley Cup team. In fact, Tom never wanted a son; he wanted a player to coach. Someone to control and mold in his likeness. Someone who could live out his lost dreams.

"You must take after your mom, then," Ali said. "She sounds like a sweet woman with a big heart."

A ball of emotion expanded in his throat at the mention of his mom. She had been the healing light in his life. Always ready with a big hug or warm words. When she died, their home became nothing but a cold, empty shell.

"Was that a compliment, sunshine?" he asked, trying to lighten the mood a little.

"Just an observation." Ali shrugged. "But I think it's sweet the way you talk about her."

"She was strong and loved being right, but she worked hard to make her family happy. She reminds me a lot of you in that way," Hawk said, smiling when he saw Ali blush. "It was like trying to break into a vault to get her to talk about herself, though."

Ali laughed. "Is that your way of telling me that it's my turn to share?"

"Only if you want to."

Her answer was to rest her cheek on the tops of her knees. "What's the point of going out, if all we talk about is what I am trying to escape?"

"Going out isn't about escape, it's about finding clarity and reminding yourself that you aren't locked into any one direction."

"Do you really believe that? That someone can change their direction by stepping out for a little while?" she asked, so much hope in those dark green pools, he found himself wanting to drown in it.

"I do." It was why he'd been so adamant about a fresh start with a fresh career in a fresh town. Destiny Bay wasn't a new place to him, but it didn't have the daily reminders to hold him back from a new adventure.

"And what happens when you want to step back in and everything's changed?"

"Change is what makes life exciting," Hawk said. "And you look like you could use a little excitement in your life, sunshine."

"*Architectural Digest* wants me to come to the photo shoot and get some shots with me and my piece. They also want to interview me, a little fluff article on an artist to watch."

Hawk pulled her in for a side hug. "Ali, that is great news. This is the game changer you've been working toward."

"I know," she said, and instead of excitement lighting that expressive face, all he saw was genuine regret. "But it is on the same day as my dress fitting for Bridget's wedding in Florida. I obviously can't be in two places at once, and Bridget can't change the appointment, and I don't know what to do."

Such an Ali move, to have an opportunity of a lifetime staring her in the face, but she was so focused on being everything to everyone, she was missing out on being herself. He knew how slippery that slope could be, had been there himself, and he didn't want to watch Ali miss out on her dreams because she was too busy making the dreams of others a reality.

"Easy, what do you want?"

"Well, Bridget really wants me there, and I'm nervous about my dad flying without me, and my mom would never forgive me if—"

Hawk gently cupped her face. "I don't want to hear about Bridget or dresses, I want to hear about you, Ali. I want to hear what *you* want." She looked at him with the saddest fucking eyes he'd ever seen—as if her wants had never played into the equation. "Right here, right now, this is the place to ask yourself what would make you happy. No outside expectations or responsibilities. Just a raw, instinctual want."

"I want to step out of the shadows and feel what it's like to have the light shining down on me." And if that didn't officially break his heart, then what she said next did. "Out of dozens of amazing artists, they chose me. And I want to experience everything that comes with that moment, but it will mean letting my family down."

"Remember, we aren't talking about your family."

Hawk ran a finger along her cheek, loving the way her body quivered under his touch. "But if we were, I'd tell you that, first, they'd want you to be happy, and second, and here is where I need you to really hear me." He dipped his head down, sure to look her in the eyes so she could see the conviction in his own. "What you've always seen as Gail walking away and letting you go, I've always seen as your dad loving you so much, and holding on to you so tight, she didn't stand a chance."

Sitting there, as the sun finished its descent into the horizon, casting a warm golden glow around Ali, Hawk began to crave that kind of connection.

"He loves Bridget, but he let her go," she whispered, her eyes soft with confusion.

"No, baby, after the divorce, Bridget cut herself off to his love. You gave yourself over to it."

A quality that both impressed the hell out of him and turned him on. Beneath that *I play hardball* exterior she wore like armor, lay a heart so big that, if he wasn't careful, it would swallow him whole.

"Is that what happened to you?" Ali asked, clearly misunderstanding which divorce he was referring to.

"Nah, I may have taken a longer time-out than planned, but I never left the game."

And he never would. His desire to find love was greater than his fear of being hurt. And when those soulful eyes of hers lit with hope—and a dump truck of vulnerability—creating an intimacy that was impossible to ignore, Hawk knew that he was ready to start looking again.

He'd been geared up on the sidelines for a while now, waiting to be called in, and watching the desire pulse at the base of Ali's neck, Hawk knew it was time to get back that laser focus of his, because it was game on.

"And when you're done playing games, then what?" Ali asked, resting her hands on his shoulders.

He took her hand and slid it over his chest to right above his heart. "Are you asking me what I want, sunshine?"

"Right here, right now. No outside expectations or responsibilities. Just a raw, instinctual want," she repeated his earlier statement.

He looked at her mouth, which was full and lush and, *damn*, perfect. Then he looked into her eyes, gently cupping her chin and tilting it so she faced him. His thumb traced a line from her jaw to her lips, while he waited for her to look at him.

"You," he groaned. "I want you. And I'm pretty sure you want me, too."

Chapter 10

Ali nodded because she needed him more than she needed her next breath.

The intensity of her feelings terrified her. They always had. Even at seventeen she knew what she felt went beyond the run-of-the-mill teenage crush. She'd been in love. Sure, it was a young, simple love, but it was love all the same.

Only he'd loved someone else.

So when he married her sister, she did her best to let him go. But no matter how painful it had been for her, and at times the ache was so acute it had been paralyzing, she was never able to set him completely free. Choosing the pain over the loss.

Now he was back, looking at her how she always looked at him, as if he'd never let go, and Ali gave in to the fantasy. Played out the what-ifs she carried with her for over a decade. He'd been hers for so long, she let herself believe that she was his, too.

He was asking for right here, right now—this she knew. Tomorrow, reality would creep in, and everything would go back to the way it was. But tonight, sitting on this beach, overlooking a world bigger than the two of them, Ali wanted to feel what it was like to be loved by the man who owned her heart.

"I want," she said.

"What do you want, Aliana?" he whispered, the sound of her name on his lips doing crazy things to her. Crazy girly things that made her feel delicate and desirable.

"I want you." She trailed her hands down his pecs to that flat stomach and lower, loving how his muscles rippled and curled under her touch. "I want you to pamper me so hard I won't remember how to walk come morning."

Hawk's eyes darkened, and his mouth was on hers. Hard and demanding, and just how she'd imagined. There was no warm-up, no testing the waters. He was kissing her as if he knew what he wanted.

And he wanted Aliana.

Their mouths were fused together, her hands gripping his shoulders for purchase, but his fingers were gentle, languidly exploring her face, her neck, the curve of her shoulder, slowly moving down her arm and bringing the wide neckline of her shirt with him.

He never stopped kissing her, but she felt his lashes flutter open, realized that she'd never closed her own. Then his deep brown eyes locked on hers, watching her as they kissed, and it was erotic and unexpected. As she watched him back, she felt his lips curl into a smile. Could feel the dimples on both cheeks come alive under her touch.

"You like to watch," Hawk growled, and she felt her cheeks flush.

Ali never considered herself a watcher. But Hawk was such a beautiful and commanding man, she'd never been able to look away. Not even now, when her body was begging for release. He was that good—a simple kiss and she was so turned on, she could feel her body shaking.

That smile turned cocky.

"It's not like I stand there peering through your bedroom window at night," she said, leaving out that night he was at the bar. His bedroom window during the morning, when he was walking around after a shower. She was more than guilty.

"I've peered through yours."

And to prove he wasn't the least bit ashamed, he lowered his head and placed an openmouthed kiss on her shoulder, those eyes of his never leaving hers. Not even when he moved lower toward her collarbone, his mouth working her with a softness that took her by surprise and a reverence that made her feel as if she was precious.

Ali wasn't sure what to do. Hard, challenging, complicated—that was what she was used to. But this was light, simple—too easy to be real. It confused her as much as it terrified her.

But then Hawk's finger tugged on the collar of her shirt, pulling it low enough to expose the top of her bathing suit, and he gave a wicked smile that was so Hawk, a small burst of hope welled up, making her believe that maybe it could be this easy. Maybe she didn't have to go into every situation looking for problems, or the escape hatch.

Turning off the little voice in her head reminding her that love was never easy, Ali gave herself over to the moment. She might regret it come tomorrow, but today she was living in the here and now. And right now she was going to savor every toned, muscled inch of Hawk.

The possibilities alone were enough to make her body quiver.

"Come here," Hawk said. "Let me warm you up."

Ali didn't bother pointing out she wasn't cold, not when his big, manly hands slid under her shirt and around to cup her ass. One minute she was sitting on the rocks, the next she was straddling his lap, her hands fisted in his shirt.

"Better?"

With a smile of her own, Ali tugged his shirt up over his head, exposing a chest and a set of abs that could be on the cover of a magazine. She rested her hands on his pecs and watched his abs jump. "Now I'm better. You?"

He returned the favor, lifting her shirt up and off, giving a groan of male appreciation when he saw her tiny bikini top. "Fucking great."

"I don't think we've gotten to that part yet," she teased.

He ran a finger under the halter strap of her top and followed it down to the triangle, his finger dipping beneath the fabric. "This isn't a bathing suit. This is a siren's call."

"You should see the bottoms." She rose up on her knees slightly, just enough to give a small inch of space between their bodies, and with a teasing glance down and back up.

"Although I do love watching, I'm more of a touch and feel kind of guy."

Hawk wrapped his hands around the backs of her naked thighs, and slowly slid his fingers up and under her shorts—not stopping until he found what he was looking for. Then her body found what it was looking for, a little pressure that was sexy enough to have her head falling back.

"You have a point, touching is so much better," she moaned.

"Wait until the touching leads to feeling, sunshine," he said, and to prove his point, his thumb gave another pass, around the edge of her bottoms, and then right up the center. Even through the fabric of her suit, she could feel the heat of his fingers at her core.

It had her feeling all kinds of things. Especially when he pulled the fabric aside, his fingers working their magic as his mouth covered her nipple. Nuzzling and sucking her through the fabric until her breath came in short, harsh bursts.

She looked down, watching him savor her body, and finding that his gaze was still on hers. Watching her watch him, his eyes getting darker with every level he took her to. She felt him smile a second before his finger sank all the way in.

"God, Bradley," she moaned and arched back.

"I like it when you call me that."

"Bradley?"

He grinned. "God."

She could have argued, but what was the point. Hawk was a sex god of the superior kind. He had her a few strokes away from what she knew was going to be the best orgasm of her life, and she was still completely clothed.

Scratch that. In one ninja move, Hawk lifted her up and her shorts off, without even breaking contact. Then with the smile that proved he was also a woman whisperer, he hooked a finger in the front of her suit and tugged her closer so he could take her mouth, while his other fingers took her right up to the edge—where she hung on as long as she could—then finally fell over.

And what a fall it was.

Mind, body, and soul, she plummeted into those warm brown eyes of his, certain that she could spend forever right there.

Her body ached with pleasure, and her heart struggled to stay in her chest, and just when she thought she couldn't take any more pampering, Hawk added the right amount of friction and—*Oh God!*—Ali came again with a loud cry.

Heat rushed through her body and the release she'd waited an eternity for exploded until all she could see was a bright light. And all she could feel was Hawk's strong body wrapped around hers. Her arms shook, her thighs tightened, and her lungs burned.

"Breathe," Hawk chuckled, slowly guiding her down to earth. And when she knew she couldn't cling any tighter, she let out a breath and opened her eyes. Their foreheads were pressed together, and Hawk was stroking her back. And smiling.

God, she loved his smile.

"I thought you were going to pass out," he said.

"I think I did." When her legs could support her, she

rested back and took a moment to admire the beautiful half-naked man in front of her. "I was thinking."

He laughed. "You mean to tell me during all that, you were thinking." Hawk rested back on his hands, their position causing his erection to press against her core, sending a nice little aftershock through her body. "I must have been doing something wrong."

She ran her palms down his chest again. Now that she'd allowed herself to touch him, she couldn't seem to stop. "I was thinking that you did it so right, you may have gotten me to change my mind."

He cocked one of his brows, making him look roguish and sexy as hell. "I'm listening."

Yes, he was. He always was. Listening, really hearing what people were saying, was another one of his superpowers.

"Watching is fun." Ali's fingers teased down his chest, back and forth, lower and lower they went until they found the waistband of his shorts. He was in athletic shorts, an easy *one tug and they'd be gone* style that she'd always wanted to play with.

So she tugged, and played, and tugged a little more, her tongue licking her lips when he let out a small groan.

"Watching is fun," he agreed, eyes riveted on her face.

"But I think the touching part is so much better," she said, and slid her hand beneath the waistband—and down the heated, long ridge that was begging for her attention.

He groaned, and so did she. Unable to stop herself, she did it again, wrapping her fingers around his length, and taking her time to explore every hard inch of him. Slowly, she stroked and memorized, watching his every move and reaction. Watching her hand work him until she felt her own body tremble with need.

It was erotic, watching him watch her as she slowly drove him out of his mind. *Sweet baby Jesus*, he was as impressive as she'd imagined. Even more so. And her fingers must have been pretty impressive as well, because Hawk's eyes rolled to the back of his head. His body arched in demand, while the muscles in his arms and neck corded tighter with every pass she made.

"Jesus," he said, his breath nothing but a rush of air. "Sunshine, all that touching is going to make the next part impossible."

"What's the next part?" she asked, her hands giving no sign that she was going to slow down.

"The feel part." He grabbed her wrists, stilling her. "And when I come this first time, I want to feel you tight around me."

It happened so fast, she barely saw it coming. One moment she was straddling him, the next Hawk was sitting up on his knees, her ankles locked behind him, and he was lowering her down on her back, with his shirt beneath her for padding.

"And while I'm doing all of that feeling," he said, pulling a condom from his back pocket and making short order of his pants, "I am going to be watching you, Aliana. Watching that body of yours come alive around me."

His voice was gruff, but confident, and Ali trembled with anticipation. She didn't like knowing people were watching her; she was always afraid they'd see all of her soft places, the vulnerable spots she kept hidden for fear of being hurt.

But she wanted to feel alive, wanted Hawk to find those spots, love away the hurt until she wasn't afraid to be soft. Wasn't afraid to show her true self.

But when Hawk slowly lowered himself into her, one careful hand beneath her head, the other around her back, protecting her from the ground beneath, Ali felt a helplessness rise up in her.

She didn't know how to explain it, but she felt lost and found at the same time. She felt the past melt away, the uncertainty of tomorrow grow, and her need for Hawk spiral until all she felt was—

Too damn much, she thought, horrified.

Too much to process, to watch, and too damn much to lose. So she tugged him to her until she could wrap her arms around him. And Hawk was also a great listener when it came to the unspoken, because he tightened his hold and whispered, "I know, I feel it, too."

And something about the slight tremor in his voice gave her the courage to feel it all.

Hawk felt the shift in her body and began to rock inside her. Slow withdraws and even slower thrusts, taking his time to build the rhythm, the trust—the connection.

A feeling she had been missing for some time now. And now that she'd found it again, she desperately wanted to cling to it with everything that she had.

"Stay with me," Hawk said, picking up the pace, and giving her a kiss to end all kisses.

And as the pressure built, and Hawk worked her body into a frenzy, and her heart into a knot, she knew that staying with him wasn't going to be the problem. Letting go was.

"God, you feel so..." *Right? Perfect? Like mine?*

Ali struggled to hear his words over her pounding heart, only he groaned before he could finish his sentence. Afraid she'd never find out, and not wanting to live with one more what-if, she cupped his face and said, "What, Hawk? What do I feel like?"

His smile was slow in coming, but soft around the edges. "You feel like sunshine."

"Sunshine?" She gave a small laugh.

"Yeah, sunshine." He kissed her again. "Sometimes it burns bright, sometimes it burns hot, but it has a healing warmth that I always wake up wanting to see."

Ali felt her eyes tear up, because that was the most romantic thing anyone had ever said about her. Most people saw the hot side of Ali, but Hawk took the time to really see her for all that she was. And that, more than anything, got to her.

Afraid she'd do something embarrassing, like cry or blurt out that she loved him, Ali locked her legs around his hips and rose up, relieved when his eyes slid shut in ecstasy.

"Jesus, Ali," he moaned, the need in his voice alone nearly sending her over the edge.

She lowered herself, and then tightened her legs again, the angles of their bodies pushing him deeper, farther. With a groan that said he was done playing, Hawk molded her to him as he crushed her between the ground and the even harder planes of his body.

His hands, however, stayed gentle, stealing Ali's heart even more, while his lips gently brushed hers, over and over as the friction grew, and Ali's body was once again screaming for release.

"Come on, sunshine," he whispered. "Let go."

I don't want to let go. I want to hold on.

"Then wrap your arms around my neck," he said, making her realize she'd spoken her deepest desire aloud. "And hold tight."

Ali did. She held on as Hawk took them both so high it was impossible to breathe, and then higher still.

"Now," he commanded softly.

Ali wasn't all that big on taking orders, but this time she was helpless. Hawk gave another thrust and sank his teeth into her lower lip and she came apart around him, just like he'd promised.

She squeezed her arms around his neck and held on with all she had. Her body was on fire from the orgasm surging through her. Hawk took her mouth with his, controlling the kiss, his body quaking with the need to erupt. Both hands beneath her now, he guided her into the rhythm he wanted, and then with a final thrust, he came hard.

He didn't crash down on her, instead he rode out the pleasure, his arms shaking from supporting them both, then slowly he rolled over, taking her place on the ground, and laying her across his body.

After a long moment, and when both of them had stopped gasping for air, Ali reached for her shirt. With nothing more than a grunt, he pressed her head back down on his chest and, taking the shirt from her, laid it over her back.

It didn't cover much more than her back; not that she was cold. She was lying on a big hunk of hot male, and Hawk's hands were affixed to her ass as if he had no intention of moving them anytime soon.

Too afraid to look up, for fear of what Hawk would see

looking back, Ali pressed her face into the curve of his neck, breathing in his scent, tasting the salt on his skin, putting to memory the perfect way his body felt beneath hers. Every touch, every kiss, every whispered word became a watermark on her heart.

Ali was no longer treading water, she was headed out to sea, only she didn't know if she had a life raft.

Chapter 11

Later that night, Ali was in bed, staring across the parking lot into Hawk's bedroom window. It was dark, of course, because he was tending bar downstairs. But that didn't stop her from peeking.

She considered walking into the bar and ordering a drink. Hawk, after all, had tried to convince her to go with him just an hour earlier. But the bar was where they normally hung out, and Ali wasn't ready to share him yet.

Maybe it sounded selfish, but she knew the second he walked into his bar, every person there would be drawn to him. That was part of Hawk's charm; he was such a funny and easygoing guy that people immediately felt better just being around him.

So Ali had given a regretful no, and Hawk had done his best to persuade her into changing her mind. Even giving her a kiss that felt as if it could have lasted until the sun rose. And wobbly legs or not, she'd stood her ground.

And now she was looking at spending her Friday down in her shop, working on her vintage-inspired produce stand piece.

Only first, she needed her angle grinder. Marty had borrowed it a few weeks ago, when he started spring cleaning on the boat, which meant refinishing all of the teak railings, and replacing the rusted rung on the boat's ladder. She'd seen it earlier that day in his toolbox.

Careful not to wake the house, Ali turned off her headlights before she pulled into his driveway and then tiptoed down to the dock. Once on board, she navigated herself below deck, and bumped into something soft—and breathing.

Ali grabbed the handle of a nearby fishing net, ready to swing when the boat lights flicked on.

She blinked. "Dad? What are you doing down here?"

"Getting ready for bed. What are you doing with my net?"

"I was going to pummel you with it." Ali lowered the net and sat on the bench, trying to make sense of what she was seeing. Marty, barefoot, in a pair of black slacks, a button-up, and a parrot-covered bow tie. "It's after eleven."

"My thoughts exactly. What are you doing here?" he asked, channeling that parent tone that had Ali expecting him to tag *young lady* to the end.

"I was coming to find my grinder," she said. "And you still didn't tell me what you're doing awake."

"Oh," he said with a small laugh. "I was out with the guys."

The dressiest "the guys" ever got was wearing a polo shirt when they went golfing. Ali looked at his Sunday suit and crossed her arms. "You're awfully snazzy for someone who's just been 'out with the guys.' Try again."

Marty loosened his tie and busied himself by pouring two glasses of milk. "Okay, fine, I was out. But not with the guys."

"Uh-huh," Ali said, taking a seat at the kitchen table. "Then who were you out with?"

Marty set a glass of milk in front of her, then stood while he sipped his. Ali watched the pink rise up his neck, the way he avoided eye contact, the way he was deflecting. He was sneaking around, but why?

Ali froze, then slapped her hand over her mouth. The fancy clothes, the new hair, sleeping on the boat, all the sneaking around. The question to ask wasn't why, but who.

"Were you out with a girl?" That pink went bright red and ran all the way up his face. "Oh my God." Ali stood. "You were out with a girl!" She paused, trying to think of anyone her dad had given a second look, and couldn't think of a single person. Except…

Ali gagged. "It isn't Mom, is it? Please tell me you're not dating Mom again."

Marty looked as horrified as Ali sounded. "I am not dating Gail."

"Okay, I know the kids are more causal these days, so let me rephrase. Are you having sex with my mom?"

"No." He did sound quite as horrified about *that* possibility as he had about reentering the dating world. *Gross.* "How could you think that?" Ali lifted a brow. "Okay, so I've made a few slips in the past."

"A few? You dated her five times and married her twice." Ali sat back. "They say the third time's the charm."

"I promise you, your mom and I are not having sex."

Thank God!

"Then tell me why you're out until all hours, sleeping on the boat, sneaking around."

Marty put his milk glass on the table and sat down across from her. "I've been racking my brain for years to find a way to reach your sister, show her how much she means to me. Then last week, she asked me to walk her down the aisle."

"She did?" Ali couldn't hold back the smile. "That's great, Dad. I know that means a lot to you and I am really happy that she asked."

She was relieved, really. The wedding was getting closer and Ali had been afraid that Bridget was going to ask someone else to do it. There had even been talk of Jamie's dad walking her down the aisle. And Marty's heart was struggling as it was. Being skipped over, again? Ali didn't think he could have handled that kind of rejection.

"Me, too, because it's the first time she's offered me a way in since high school, when she was crowned queen and asked me to escort her during the Homecoming Parade." His eyes glistened with hope. "I wanted her to know that I appreciate the chance to walk her down the aisle and I won't waste the opportunity to get to know her better."

Ali wanted to tell him that he wasn't the one who had turned his back or walked away. He'd had the door slammed in his face over and over by Bridget, and he'd never once given up. Never even considered walking away. Nope, Marty always showed up with his heart on his sleeve, and patience and understanding on his face.

"She's always talking about that *Dancing with the Stars* show," he went on. "So when I heard that Jamie's parents had hired an orchestra, one of those big eighteen-piece ensembles, I decided to surprise Bridget with a waltz."

"Oh, Dad, that is so sweet," Ali said, resting her head on Marty's shoulder. "She's going to love it."

Marty stepping out of his comfort zone and meeting Bridget in her world was exactly what her sister needed to move past the hurt and move on with growing their relationship. And even though Bridget's and Ali's relationship was strained at the moment, she really wanted that for them.

Wanted it for her dad.

"I hope so," Marty said, and even though he looked tired, he seemed to have a little extra twinkle in his smile and color in his cheeks. "But your dad here has two left feet, and there isn't that much time left to teach this old dog a few new tricks."

"Well, don't go overboard on the practice. She'll be surprised and touched even if you don't look exactly like Fred Astaire."

Marty chuckled, then went serious. "You know, she's opened a door for you, too, honey."

"I know," Ali moaned. Bridget had a dozen friends who she could have asked to be her maid of honor. All of them more suited for the role, and more suited for Bridget. But she'd chosen Ali. "Why does there always have to be some kind of dress code required for me to enter her world?"

"Because it's Bridget," Marty teased, but then went serious. A rare emotion for a man who lay around in

Hawaiian shirts and flip-flops. "This wedding is a chance for all of us, and even though your sister won't admit it, having you there is important to her. I'm sure if you try, you can find some kind of common ground to work from."

"Why does 'common ground' always sound like Bridget's way?"

"Love doesn't keep score, honey." Marty took Ali's hand, something else he rarely did. "And if this old dog can learn some new tricks, I'm sure you'll find a dress that you can stand for a few hours."

"You don't need tricks." He had an abundance of love working for him. Ever since Ali was little, she knew his dream had always been to bring Bridget back into the fold, for them to all be one big, happy family. "You're the real deal, Dad."

"It's easy to be real when I've got two amazing daughters in my life," Marty said, wrapping his arm around Ali's shoulders and pulling her in for a side hug. Ali rested her head against his shoulder and closed her eyes. "Even when one of them interrogates me about sneaking around when she's got seaweed stuck in her hair and smells like men's aftershave."

Ali jerked up and patted her hair. After a thorough search, she found no such seaweed.

Marty smiled. "I guess things with Hawk aren't so complicated after all."

Um no, things with Hawk were even more complicated than ever. She'd spent the evening with a sexy, gorgeous, amazing man who'd rocked her world and given her the best orgasm, make that *orgasms*, of her life. And instead of going for round three and waking up next to him, she was here. On her dad's boat. In the middle of the night. Drinking milk and looking for a grinder.

Ali sighed. "Nope, things are totally normal."

And whose fault was that?

* * *

Two days later, Hawk lay in bed, staring at the ceiling. The blankets were on the floor, a sheet was tangled around his calf, and all he had to keep him company was an epic case of morning wood, and the damn alarm he'd rigged in the alley.

It had been going off all morning, interrupting another hot dream of Ali in that blue scrap of fabric she called a swimsuit. Which, pathetically enough, was the closest he'd come to seeing Ali since their night on the bluff.

He wanted to see more of her. Not just the naked parts either, although they were high on his list. But he wanted to see her sweet parts, explore her secret parts, even her prickly ones. Hell, he wanted the chance to see all of her parts. And they'd been on their way to that the other night.

Then he'd had to get to work, and he hadn't managed to break away early enough to catch her before she went to sleep. When he'd awoken the next day, it was to a text that she'd made a trip to Boise. Something about finding the right dress.

Beep! Beep! Beep!

"Five more minutes," Hawk mumbled, putting his pillow over his face. But all it did was muffle the sounds.

With a sigh, Hawk scrubbed a hand over his face,

rolled out of bed, and headed toward the front door. Not wanting to wave his stick around again, he tugged on a pair of jeans and headed down the stairs.

He reached Main Street, just in time to see the Senior Steppers settling on two park benches with their morning coffee and a box of pastries from Sweetie Pies.

"You ladies taking a break?" he asked.

"We were finishing our walk when we saw the show, so we grabbed coffee and came back to make sure we got good seats," Fi said, taking a bite out of a muffin that was bigger than her fist.

Setting her coffee down, Ms. Collins held up her camera and snapped a picture of Hawk's chest. She put on her reading glasses to look at her work, and frowned. "Where's your stick?"

"Inside," he said.

Her eagle eyes narrowed in on him. "But my followers want to see your stick."

"Sorry, stick's off limits." He reached for her phone to delete the picture before she uploaded it to Instagram for man-candy Monday. But even his honed reflexes weren't a match for the woman's paparazzi-like skills. She shoved her phone between her cleavage and then gave him a challenging look.

Not going *there*, Hawk asked, "What show?"

Six bony fingers pointed toward the back of the alley. Where Ali, dressed in a pair of ass-hugging jeans, a tank top, and those silver heels, was dragging a keg half her size across the parking lot.

"Bitsy here put a cool twenty on her being mad," Fiona said, jabbing a thumb at the pastor's wife. "I say the girl's finally lost it."

"My guess was pure revenge," Ms. Collins said, giving him a pointed look. "So what did you do?"

Hawk turned back to the ladies, all of who were giving him a stern look. "What makes you think this has anything to do with me?"

Concern filled Bitsy's gaze. "The only reason a woman would be doing heavy lifting in shoes like that was if she'd been wronged."

Hawk turned back to watch Ali disappear back into her shop, only to return dragging another keg. "And you assume I'm the problem?"

The women shared a secret look, followed by a giggle that made Hawk's jaw clench. It was Fi who spoke. "Honey, you're a man, you're always the problem. Now make us proud, and go down there and apologize."

Completely confused, Hawk looked back toward the alley. Ali was halfway between their properties, her breathing labored, those little legs of hers really working as she tugged one keg after another across the asphalt. She looked a little ragged, a little sweaty, and completely sexy.

Hawk rested a hip against a tree and took a moment to enjoy the view. Every time she went to give the keg a pull, that heart-shaped ass of hers leaned way back, pressing so hard against her pants, he could make out every curve. It wasn't as inspiring as his dream had been, but it was a close second. Plus, it was proof that she was back in town and they could get on with that talk they had coming.

All that huffing and puffing had him wondering, though. Maybe the ladies were right, and he'd somehow messed this up. A thought that had his smile fading, until

Ali looked his way and stopped short at the sight of him standing there in jeans and bedhead.

But instead of laughing at waking him up, she gave a shy little *oops* followed by a wave.

Hawk threw his head back and laughed.

"You ladies go on with your theories, but I wouldn't put any money on them," Hawk said, strolling toward his keg thief. "She's isn't mad."

"Then what's she doing?" Fi called out.

"I think she's flirting," Hawk chuckled to himself as he walked down the alley.

He reached the stack of kegs and kept going until he was in her direct path. She was back to business and didn't notice him until he was right behind her, lifting the keg out of her hands.

"Hey, I was moving that," she said, looking up at him and—*damn*—the woman was adorable.

Her hair was in one of those cute ponytails she favored, her face was morning fresh and makeup free, and her expression was indignant.

"I can see," he said, lifting it up with one arm. "But I can get the job done faster."

"Oh," she said, seeing reason. And when those big mossy eyes met his from beneath her lashes, he felt everything inside him man up and take notice. "Carry on then."

Hawk moved the keg to the docking bay and stacked it next to the others. "Is that all?"

"Yup. Sorry if I woke you," Ali said. Only she didn't sound sorry at all. She sounded guilty.

"You didn't wake me, the alarm I set on my docking bay did," he said, reaching up to dismantle the blinking red light. "What are you doing?"

Ali's gaze, which was on his bare chest as he stretched to reach the alarm, jerked up to his face. And she sputtered.

"I meant with those." He pointed to the kegs with his chin.

"Oh." She straightened and smiled, big and proud. "I'm giving you your kegs back?"

He pulled the cable out of the electrical plug and stuffed it in his pocket. "And why would you do that?"

"Well." She took a big breath, as if she'd been contemplating the meaning of life, and giving him back his kegs was the answer. "I don't think it's right to keep your stolen kegs anymore."

He grinned. "You didn't seem to have a problem holding them hostage a few weeks ago."

"Right," she whispered to herself, then squared her shoulders. "Well, at that time, we were just friends, then we became kissing friends, and now we're sexy friends and it doesn't feel right to hold on to your things without your permission."

Hawk crossed his arms, sure to flex a little for her benefit. "Sunshine, most women would thank me for the best night of their life, then kiss me."

"I'm not most women," she said, not sounding insulted at all.

A truer statement had never been made.

"But if it would make you feel better." Ali set her hands on his chest, and slowly rose up on the tips of her toes, her hips brushing against his thighs, then higher until Hawk's stick was making a reappearance. When she still couldn't reach his lips, she crooked her finger for him to come closer.

Hawk didn't need a second invite. His pulse raced harder and faster as he dipped his head until his mouth was hovering, and then she made the final move. And what a move it was. Ali slanted her head, taking his lower lip between her two plump ones, and gave a long, slow tug, the impact nearly knocking him to his knees.

Only she wasn't done. Oh no, his girl let it go with a pop, only to repeat the same sweet torture on his upper lip—this time using her teeth. And Hawk lost all good sense.

Maybe he'd never had any around Ali. It would explain why it had taken so long for him to get to this point. With his hand on her waist and her tongue teasing his lips. Because had he known just how hard she would rock his world, he would have kissed her years ago.

A round of applause and a few flashes went off in the distance, and Ali pulled back with a sweet smile. "Thanks, Hawk."

She started to go back down on her feet, but he pulled her up against him. "Thanks for what, sunshine?"

"For being you," she said softly, and Hawk's heart rolled over and showed its soft underbelly. Because everything about this woman disarmed him. "And I really am sorry that I woke you."

He looked at that soft, sweet mouth and groaned. "I'm not."

Without warning, Hawk picked her up and tossed her over his shoulder, then headed toward Main Street.

"What are you doing?" she said, smacking his butt.

"Finally getting some sleep...ladies," he said as he walked past the Steppers and their flashing camera phones. Ali put up a fight the entire way up the stairs and into his apartment, but she was smiling while doing it.

"What's up with the shoes?" he asked as he walked down the hallway.

"I was breaking them in. I figure if I could lug kegs in them, walking down an aisle will be a snap."

With a chuckle, and a smack on that fabulous ass, he tossed her on the bed, and before she could scramble up, he stretched out next to her and pulled her snug against him.

With one arm he covered them with the blanket; the other was cupping her boob like he owned it. Then after nuzzling the back of her neck, he finally, *finally* closed his eyes.

Damn, she felt good in his bed.

Just as he was getting comfortable, his body settling into the idea of catching some much needed Z's, Ali rolled over in his arms, her face inches from his. "Are we really sleeping?"

He opened one eye. "Yes. And this time when I wake up, the first thing I want to see is sunshine."

Chapter 12

Ali looked at her reflection, at the billowing yards of tiffany blue silk, and smiled. No matter how many people looked at her funny, she couldn't seem to stop.

The smile had started Wednesday morning, when Hawk had dragged her to bed, and lasted straight through lunch, when he finally let her come up for air. It stuck with her through shoe shopping with Bridget, and the argument over the Hump-Day post on Instagram: Stanley Cup's Stick, MIA—although the town agreed on the *Missing in* part, there was heavy debate as to what the *A* stood for.

Now she stood on a chair in the middle of Sweetie Pies, during one of the most competitive games of coupon bingo in history, and she was smiling so hard, her cheeks hurt.

"I can't believe you drove all the way to Boise to get this dress," Bridget said, holding Ali's hair up.

"Of course she did, she's a good sister," Bitsy said, neck-deep in silk, her head stuck up under Ali's dress.

"I realized how important this was to you, and you're right, it is... a special day." She refused to say once in a lifetime. "So I called the magazine and told them that I had to be on the road to the airport by six p.m. They moved the interview to before the photo session, so I can make the red-eye, arriving in Florida just in time for the family brunch at Jamie's parents' house."

"And your dress should fit like a glove," Bitsy said.

"Thanks, Ms. Cunningham, for doing this on such short notice," Ali said to the small woman moving beneath the dress.

Bitsy poked her head out from under the skirt and smiled around the needle in her teeth. "I'm no Raoul, but I've won the town's quilting bee six years running. And if my hands are good enough to stitch a life-size wall hanging of the mayor," the older woman whispered, "then I think I can hem a dress by next week."

"I-27," a voice said over the loudspeaker, which was really a microphone hooked up to an old boom box. "I-27."

Bitsy paused, glanced at her card and screamed, "Bingo! I got bingo."

"Last time you called bingo, you had just put markers on the numbers that looked good," Fiona accused.

"I can't help it if I pick winners," Bitsy said, and with a promise to be back in a flash, the older woman marched her winning card up to the judges' table. Leaving Ali and Bridget alone for the first time since their argument.

"She's right, you know, you are a good sister," Bridget

said, taking a seat on the chair and spooning off a piece of apple pie. "You made it all work."

Ali shrugged. She'd been making things work her whole life, so figuring out how to merge two schedules wasn't as difficult as it sounded. Leaving her dad to his own devices for two days, that had been the challenge. But Bridget had assured her she'd keep an eye on Marty, and since Ali was working really hard on letting go of things that didn't matter, so she could grab on to what did, she'd gone. Plus, it was a chance for Bridget to see just how far Marty had come in his recovery—and more important, how far he had yet to go.

"How was he?"

Bridget leaned back in the chair and laughed. "A handful. I had no idea how much help he still needed. If I didn't remind him to take his medication, he'd just pretend he didn't have to. And who tapes a Snickers bar under the coffee table?"

Ali laughed, enjoying the connection that came from talking with her sister about Marty, rather than arguing. "I once found a candy bar taped to the back of the toilet tank. I told him if he was that desperate, he could have it. But now that I'm back, you can focus on the wedding."

"I didn't mind being with him." Bridget picked up an extra spoon and offered it to Ali.

Ali took a bite, let the gooey goodness melt on her tongue. A little bite of heaven right there in Destiny Bay.

"Dad said you took care of his flight and travel," Ali said. "I know he doesn't say much about his finances, but a flight to Florida would have been hard for him to afford."

The money he'd already spent on the party, the tux, the dance lessons had made a dent in his monthly allowance. Ali had paid her dad good money for his shop, and if Marty was careful, he could live off that and his retirement for a good long while.

Bridget shrugged. "It was no biggie. Jamie and I decided that since we moved the wedding to Florida, we'd cover his costs. We'll cover him, too. I mean, look out for him while he's there. So I'll fly out Monday and Jamie will bring Dad with him Tuesday."

Ali nodded, unsure how to bring up a topic that had been bothering her for a while now. How did she tell her sister that she needed help, without letting Bridget think that Ali couldn't handle Marty's growing needs?

Ali would never want Bridget to feel obligated to pitch in; Marty deserved more than that. Just like she'd never want him to think that his illness was a burden on Ali.

"Dad's loved having you here," Ali began, testing the waters.

Disappointment darkened her sister's eyes. "He's spent half the time down on the boat."

And there it was again, her family's incredible communication skills hard at work. Sometimes Ali wondered how they managed to stay together as long as they had. "Well, then join him on the boat."

Bridget rolled her eyes. "So you and he can bond over knots and wind speeds? No thanks."

"I won't come over."

Bridget paused, spoon in her mouth. "Are you serious?"

"Sure, I'll come by to check on the groceries and his meds, but I'll leave the rest of the day to you two. You can help him wash down the deck, or polish the handrails, whatever sounds fun," Ali said, wondering why sharing always ended up with her left out. "I know he's really enjoyed these last few weeks. And he's looking forward to spending time with you at the wedding."

"Thanks," Bridget said with a smile. "It means a lot. And you don't have to worry about the groceries and meds, I can handle that." Ali went to argue and Bridget held up a hand. "I'm already there, it's silly for you to come out. Plus, don't you have the project you're working on for the Galleon Orchard?"

Yes, she did, and it was due for delivery next week. With hours still left to go on it, Ali could use some quality focused time with the piece. But she wasn't willing to risk everything they'd done in Marty's rehab for a few extra hours. "He can be a handful, and it's important that he sticks to the doctor's plans."

"I did it for two days, I can finish out the week." Bridget went quiet, and looked down at her pie. "Plus, it would be good practice for when he comes and visits us."

Appetite lost, and regretting the few bites of pie that were turning in her stomach, Ali set her spoon down. "He wants to come visit? When?"

"Jamie and I have been talking to Dad about him coming to our place maybe one week a month," Bridget said, and Ali felt sweat bead on her forehead. "It might be nice for him to get a change of scenery."

"Have you talked to Dad about this?" Ali asked, a strange panicky sensation working its way up her throat. "I mean, does he like the idea?"

"Of course he likes it. He said the sail would do him good, especially to get him ready for when grandkids come along."

Ali was going to be sick. Sure, this was exactly the kind of help she'd been hoping for. The kind of relationship Marty had dreamed of. But instead of one big happy family, Bridget was asking him to come into her shiny new world. Alone.

Not only wouldn't she be a part of it, she wouldn't be there to make sure her dad was taking care of himself.

"Are you okay?" Bridget asked.

No, she was one Kodak moment away from a complete meltdown. Surely, everyone could hear her heart thrashing against her chest, because really? Bridget thought that Marty was in any condition to *sail* to Seattle? Alone?

"The doctor said it might be a while before he's ready to go far on the boat alone."

"I know, Ali. I'm not a complete idiot," Bridget said, crestfallen.

Ali felt like a jerk. "I don't think you're an idiot, it's just been a while since you've spent a lot of time with him. Two days is nothing, a whole week? He's..." Ali searched for the right words to explain the situation, and settled on, "He's different now."

"Which is why I want to spend more time with him," she admitted. "Plus, Jamie will be gone a lot for work, and it gets lonely in that big house. Dad can have his own room. On the bottom floor so he doesn't have to do the stair thing."

Marty would like that, and his doctor would like the idea of Marty relaxing. And Bridget had every right to want some time with her dad. Even if it did make Ali nervous. "I could drive him one way, at least until he's cleared to drive the distance by himself."

"We'll work it out," Bridget assured her, repeating

what their dad had said the other week, and Ali found herself smiling. Believing that maybe Marty was right, and this wedding was exactly what the family needed to come together.

To finally work together.

"We always do," Ali said.

They both settled into comfortable silence, nibbling on the pie, when Bridget's phone rang. She pulled it out of her pocket and smiled. "It's Jamie." She answered and put the phone to her ear. "Hey, baby."

Ali heard Jamie's muffled voice, and Bridget looked up at Ali. "Hanging with my sis, and eating pie...No, she found the dress here and will bring it with her, but tell your mom she'll make it to the brunch...The family brunch." Bridget's face fell. "No, it's on Thursday morning...But it's at *your* parents' house."

Bridget held up a finger, then turned her back for privacy and whispered, "I understand, but you promised that you wouldn't leave me alone with your mom *and* my mom." She hovered further into the phone. "I know it's important, but I worked really hard on this party, and your mom is so excited."

Ali could tell by her sister's tone that she was excited as well.

"No, I get it. I know, it's what you do...yeah. I love you, too."

Bridget hung up and turned back to Ali, her eyes big and her smile bigger. "Jamie got a call from Nolan today. I guess he's willing to meet and wants to do it after the shoot, thank you for the introduction."

Ali paused. "So while I'm flying out to Florida, the groom will be flying back to Washington?"

"Ironic, huh?"

Ali would have gone with *sad.* If it had been that important to Bridget that Ali be at every pre-wedding event, then she could only imagine how important it was to have her fiancé by her side. "Nolan is a pretty laid-back guy. I'm sure he wouldn't mind meeting Jamie some other time."

"There is no other time. Jamie needs to get started on this project the second we get back from our honeymoon. So unless I want to spend a day or two alone on a boat in the middle of the Gulf, it's better he gets it over with," Bridget said, and there was a resignation in her tone that Ali knew all too well. It was the same thing Ali had seen as a child, every time she'd looked in the mirror.

"Is that what you want," she asked softly. "To get this over with?"

Bridget's hand crept across her throat. "No," she said, but her eyes went misty. "Oh God, is that what it seems like to everyone?"

"Screw everyone else. What matters is what it feels like to you."

Bridget gave a self-deprecating laugh. "Easy for you to say. You don't care what anyone thinks. And why should you? You have the perfect life."

Ali snorted. "Right, because living with your dad until you're twenty-seven is really cool. It also makes dating so much fun."

"You get to make your art, answer to no one but yourself, eat pie every day."

"I never knew you were into metal art."

Bridget rolled her eyes, then dabbed them with a napkin. "You know what I mean. You have a career. Something to point to and say, 'Hey I did that.' "

"You have a huge house, you're getting married, and get to use phrases like 'Let's brunch' in daily life and not sound like a poser."

"The house belonged to my ex, the lifestyle is courtesy of my fiancé, and I hate brunching," Bridget admitted.

"Okay, what's yours?" Ali asked, and when Bridget looked ready to cry again, she took her hand. It was awkward, but Kennedy did it whenever someone was upset, so Ali gave it a try. "What did you set out to do?"

"Have a fabulous life." Bridget sniffed. "God, it sounds so lame, even to me."

Yeah, it sounded lame, but then again who was Ali to judge someone else's dream? Hers had been to find a career where she could use a blowtorch all day, because she liked how it felt in her hand. The bending metal into cool shapes came later.

"Define *fabulous*."

"I don't know," Bridget said, sounding as lost as she did embarrassed. "I like to make things pretty and find a place for everything."

Now they were getting somewhere. "Like what you did with Dad's house?"

"Yeah," Bridget said. "When Mom was in one of her dating phases, I used to spend a lot of time rearranging my bedroom. Every weekend I would move stuff around, try to find the perfect spacing. Or I'd set the dining room table for just myself, using all of the pretty plates." She laughed. "Did you know Mom has a china pattern for every marriage? Two from Dad's."

"I'm not surprised." When Gail tossed out the old,

she made sure that when it came to bringing in the new...everything was new. Furniture, houses, personalities, political views.

The only consistent thing in her life was Bridget. Who was now doing the same thing.

"After the honeymoon, why don't you look into event planning," Ali suggested, even though she wanted to tell her to put the wedding on hold until she figured out if marrying Jamie was the best thing for her. But Ali was practicing the art of remaining neutral, listening rather than telling Bridget what her problem was. "I bet there are some openings to start as an assistant to help make contacts."

"I met a woman at one of Hawk's parties and she asked me to help her with a big event for the NHL, and if things worked out, maybe it could become a steady thing."

"That's great!"

Bridget looked up, her face unreadable. "Hawk was drafted by the Blackhawks the next week, and he had to be there for training. So I had to pass."

"Why didn't you do the party and then go meet Hawk?" Ali asked, trying to get the topic away from the biggest obstacle left between them.

Bridget took a sip of wine. "Hawk said that, too, but his career was taking off and I needed to focus on helping him get to the next level."

"Maybe it's your turn to get to the next level," Ali said.

Bridget gave a nostalgic smile. "That's what Hawk said after his accident. That it was my turn."

"Then why did you leave?" Ali asked, because, if they were going to talk about Hawk, they might as well *talk* about him.

"I don't know." Bridget licked her spoon and set it down. "I was so good at being a hockey wife. Used to the long seasons, him being on the road, the parties, the press. Once that was gone, and he was home all the time, I got scared."

"Scared to spend that much time with him?" Ali said, thinking that waking up with Hawk every day, ending the evenings in his arms, would be something to treasure. Not something to run from.

"Scared that spending that much time together would only cause the excitement and love to fizzle out," Bridget said with so much conviction, Ali didn't know whether to hug her or sock her. "And I was right, he moved on."

"Only because you left him, even though he loved you," Ali pointed out, not understanding how her sister could walk away from a man who had so much love to give. Then again, wasn't that what she'd done with Marty all these years?

Tested him to see just how far she could go before he came running after her.

"I guess I'm more like Mom than I thought," Bridget whispered softly, and for the first time in her life, Ali was thankful to be the odd Marshal woman out.

Chapter 13

Exhausted and covered from head to toe in little bits of metal and sawdust, Ali dropped the sander down on the workbench and flipped up her mask. The sun was barely setting on Saturday, and Ali was ready for bed. With Bridget taking care of Marty, Ali had been able to work on the commissioned piece around the clock for the past few days—a luxury she hadn't had since his heart attack.

And it showed in her work. The structure was exactly what she'd pictured in her mind. Clean steel wrapped around driftwood and old cider barrels, secured with vintage bronze railroad nails. It was strong and powerful, but had an element of femininity, a sensual shape to the lines that she'd never used in her work before.

Rubbing her tired eyes, Ali promised her bed that as soon as she cleaned up, they could hyphenate together for a few weeks. It was a lie, of course. She only had until tomorrow morning, when she was scheduled to deliver the piece to her client.

Too tired to take off her coveralls, Ali closed up the shop and headed upstairs for a cold drink. She had a nice aged Scotch that she pulled out for these kinds of occasions.

Needing a celebration and a nightcap all in one, she poured two fingers over ice and set the glass on the counter. She unzipped the top of her coveralls and, letting them hang off her hips, took a seat at the counter as she took the first sip.

The smooth liquid burned all the way down her throat, loosening the tension behind her shoulders. She took another, and when the fiery heat reached her belly, she did a quick one-two and removed her bra.

Ali let out a relieved moan and rolled her shoulders. She loved her work, but all of the heavy materials and equipment tended to take a toll on her body.

Afraid she'd fall asleep if she didn't move, Ali stood and stretched, walking to the windows to watch the sun take its final dip into the bay. The gas lamps on Main Street gave a warm glow, showcasing the hive of activity below. Weekend tourists sifted through the quaint mom-and-pop shops, families were enjoying a weekend stroll, and across the parking lot, a good portion of Destiny Bay was getting its Happy Hour on.

Ali considered going next door, ordering a drink, and celebrating the moment with friends. But that would require a shower, a fresh change of clothes, and seeing her sister—who was taking Marty to the grill for dinner.

But it would also mean seeing Hawk. Ali's body

hummed to life at the thought, and those flutters, which had been bothering her all week, kicked it up to wild flock levels in her stomach.

It was pathetic really, she thought with a smile. It had been only three days since their kiss that spurred the great stick debate, and she already missed him. Her gaze traveled to his bedroom window and paused when she saw a shadow move from inside.

Pretty sure he was already at the bar, and wondering if maybe he'd come back up to grab something, Ali walked closer to the window. When she still couldn't get the view she wanted, she pressed her face closer, until she was leaving little hot breath marks on the pane.

Her eyes trained in on a single focus point, she held still and watched, sipping her Scotch. After a long moment, she decided she was just tired and went to head to the bathroom when the light across the parking lot clicked on and—*Sweet baby Jesus!*

Ali spun to her left, plastering her back against the wall. The quick movement sent her Scotch over the side of the glass, and her heart plummeting to her toes.

Because right there, on the other side of the window, walking from the bathroom to his closet, was Hawk. Wearing nothing but shower water, a towel, and a sexy hawk tattoo over his right shoulder.

Ali waited a good minute, to be sure if he had seen a suspicious movement, say by a peeper, that he'd moved on. No matter how many times she told herself to knock it off, to go take a cold shower and stop being a creeper, she couldn't resist one last stare.

One look out the window and her mouth went dry—the exact opposite of what was going on below the equator. Because instead of finding him looking through his closet—he was looking at her.

Arms resting on the windowsill above his head, the bottom sill cutting him off right where the towel started, he focused his gaze directly on her, that double-barreled smile out for good measure.

Then he added a little lift of the brow, which turned the smile into a grin and implied a certain level of male smugness. A little male smugness was okay, she decided, since it had been male supremeness that had her staring in the first place.

She lifted her glass in toast, and when he winked, she took a sip. Then her phone rang. She looked at the number and back to the window.

One hand was still supporting his weight on the sill, making his arm go into Hulkian mode. The other hand was holding his phone to his ear. He waved his pinkie her way.

With a smile, she swiped Answer.

"You aren't very good at the whole window-watching thing," Hawk said. "The point is not to get caught."

The sips of Scotch must have already started working, or maybe it was fried brain cells from seeing Hawk nearly naked. "I actually like it when you watch me watching you."

She heard his breath go gruff through the phone. "Sunshine, if I didn't have to go run the bar, I could watch you all night."

"I won't keep you then," she said, letting her coveralls fall to the floor, leaving her in a tank top and boy-cut panties.

"Luke can cover the bar for a few more minutes." Even

though the light was behind him, shadowing him in a silhouette, she could still feel those intense dark brown eyes zeroed in on her. “All those times I’d sit with you in your shop and throw back a beer while you were in your coveralls, you were wearing—”

“Nothing but panties,” she finished and plopped down on the couch, then flicked on the light behind her so he had a clear view.

Watching him through the window was hot. Him watching her? So erotic she felt her body dampen. “And all of those times you were watching hockey from your bed, you could have been watching this.”

“What makes you think I was watching hockey?” he said, and Ali felt her heart stop. He let that go for a moment, giving her sternum time to do one final thump against her chest, then added, “What do the hearts on your panties say?”

Stunned that he could see that much detail, she looked down at the red and pink hearts and grinned. “ ‘Eat me.’ ”

He chuckled, soft and low and so sexy, her body shuddered.

“What are you drinking?”

“Scotch.” She held up the glass for him to inspect it.

“Nearly empty. You know, friends don’t let friends drink alone. I should come over.”

“We’re not friends, we’re sexy friends, remember? There’s a difference. And you can’t come over, you have a bar to run.”

“I have a few minutes.”

“You never take a few minutes.” She took a stealth sniff of her shirt and grimaced. “Plus, I need to shower first.”

A groan of pure agony and disappointment came muffled through the phone. Then Hawk paused, both eyebrows lifting in a move so sexy, Ali licked her lips. "I can wash your back." She tapped her watch. "Right." Deep exhale, followed by, "Wait? Is that the Scotch you hide above the fridge? Holy shit, you finished your piece."

"Just a few minutes ago."

His voice softened. "How did it turn out?"

"Inspired," she said and knew it was the truth. Once she got focused, the piece almost built itself. The process had been intense and consuming, and even though her limbs were mush, she wanted to keep going.

Kind of like sex with Hawk, she thought deliciously.

"You're an inspiring woman," he said, with pride so thick, Ali felt her eyes burn. "I can't wait to see it."

She wanted him to see it. Wanted to show him this new side of her art, the side of her that she'd kept hidden until now.

Until Hawk.

"I deliver it tomorrow morning," she told him, knowing he'd be dead asleep when the delivery truck arrived.

"Well, then I guess that means a sleepover at your place," he said. "You provide the bed and I'll bring the pj's. I have an old jersey that would look great with your legs."

She pulled her knees to her chest and hugged them. "Are you sure?"

"Like I said, the watching is fun, but I am more of a touchy-feely kind of guy," he said lowly. "Leave a key under the mat and I'll head over after I close up the bar."

She heard him disconnect, and then with a wink, Hawk

walked back to the bathroom—the towel nowhere in sight.

* * *

Ali had just fallen asleep when her cell buzzed. Her first thought was Hawk calling to say he'd closed up early and was on his way over. Her body throbbed at the thought, but as she looked at her cell, she knew it wasn't him.

"Hey," she said into the phone, trying to clear the sleep from her throat.

"Hi, honey, it's Loraine," the older woman said.

"Oh, did the snorkel gear I ordered for Bridget come in?" It wasn't the most romantic wedding gift, but she knew her sister would have fun—once she got over getting her hair wet.

"I'm afraid I'm not at the post office. I'm at the hospital with your dad."

Ali bolted up, wide awake, her feet already diving into the nearest pair of shoes. "Is it another heart attack?"

"They won't tell me. But I know he overdid it a little at dance class and his sugar levels were low, so I called an ambulance."

Ali told her pulse to slow down, told herself that he was okay, that it wasn't another heart attack. But all she could remember was finding him on his boat. Facedown on the deck, head bleeding, and unresponsive. She'd thought he was dead, that she'd lost him.

And she made herself a promise that day that she'd never let him get to that point again. Even if it meant putting her life on hold for a while, until he got back on his feet. But he wasn't there yet, and now she was getting a call.

Terror clogged her throat. "What hospital?"

"Destiny Bay Memorial. They're moving him to Urgent Care."

Ali scribbled it on a notepad next to the bed, then grabbed her sweatshirt and keys. "Thank you so much for taking care of him and for calling me. I will be there in ten minutes."

Chapter 14

Ali made it in six.

Her heart was racing as fast as her speedometer as she saw the red lights of the emergency room. The drive had been a blur; all she remembered was getting the call and then seeing the turnoff sign for the hospital.

The parking lot was packed, ambulances and cars everywhere, her mind spinning too fast to search for an empty spot. Pulling up to the curb, Ali cut the engine and tore out of her car. Ignoring someone telling her she couldn't park there, she tossed them the keys and pushed through the emergency room door, heading straight toward the nurses' desk.

"Hi, hello?" she said, and a woman on the phone held up a finger to wait. Ali had a finger of her own, but knew it would not help her get to Marty any faster. "I see that it's busy here, but I need to see my dad. His name is Martin Marshal." Ali reached out and grabbed the phone from the nurse's hand. "Martin Marshal, he was brought in—"

"Honey, over here."

Ali turned and saw Loraine, dressed in a layered red and black gown with black lace gloves, waving her closer.

"Sorry," she told the nurse and rushed over. "Is he okay?"

"It was a mild attack," Loraine explained, and Ali pressed her hand to her own heart—certain that it had stopped. "But the doctor says he'll be just fine. He's a little dehydrated, so they're giving him fluids now and the doctors want to keep him overnight for observation."

It was as if a wrecking ball had slammed into her chest at full force. Wind knocked out of her, Ali held on to one of the chairs for support. "What happened?"

"He looked a little wilted when he came to dance class tonight. It's the late class so it's not uncommon for some of the folks to look a little sleepy." Loraine pulled helplessly at the skirt of her gown. "But he looked really sleepy. We've been partners for a few weeks now, so I've gotten good at reading him. Like I can tell he's been practicing at home because he's been getting really light on his feet. But when he looked lighter than normal, I asked him if he was okay. He said he was just flush from being out on the water all day."

Ali pressed the heel of her hand against her eyes. "He said he was on the water all day?"

"I hate to say this." Loraine looked around, then lowered her voice. "I think he's been out on the water every day. Something about trying to teach Bridget how to deep-sea fish for her honeymoon."

Ali took in a big breath. It did nothing to stop the rage

from building. Bridget had promised her she'd take care of him, that everything would be okay.

This situation. *Their* family. As far from okay as they could be.

"Does he know you called me?"

Loraine shook her head, the red flower in her hair coming loose. "He looked so sorry for ruining dance class, I didn't have the heart to tell him I'd have to wake you up."

"Thanks for waiting, you can go home. It's late."

"You sure? I can stay," Loraine offered and Ali shrugged. This was becoming old hat for her. She'd spent more nights sleeping in a hospital chair than she cared to admit.

"I got this."

With a final thanks, and a hug that nearly did her in, Ali walked into her dad's room and felt her heart catch painfully. The biggest man in her life seemed small enough to be swallowed whole by the hospital bed. And something about seeing her father, her hero, hooked up to an IV, oxygen, the works, made her want to cry. Just give in and have a long, hard cry.

Damn it, they'd worked so hard *not* to get back to this place.

Five days.

Not even a full week was all it took for everything to come crashing down, and for her dad to end up back in the hospital.

Mild didn't lessen the worry. He'd had a heart attack.

At least this time he hadn't been alone.

Marty opened his eyes, and even though she knew he was tired, he flashed her a big, loving smile. "Hey, honey. You're dressed for a sleepover."

He patted the side of the bed, as if they were back home and Ali was naive enough to believe that parents could make bad things disappear. Ali was playing out the worst-case scenario even as she padded over and crawled in.

"You're dressed for the waltz," she said, resting her head against his chest.

"Tonight was tango," he said, his voice altered by the oxygen mask on his nose. "And you should have seen my toe flicks."

Ali tilted her head up to look at her dad. "I bet all the ladies were wanting to dance with you."

"I couldn't fend them off, even if I tried." He waggled a brow. "But that Loraine kept them at bay."

"I bet she did," Ali said, wondering when Marty was going to realize that Loraine wanted his toe flicks all to herself. "I bet she would have told you to take it easy, had you explained up front that you'd been out on the water all day."

Marty gave a guilty smile. "I wasn't on the water all day, and I didn't leave the shoreline."

He also must have left the extra water bottles and high protein lunch at home. "How about yesterday or any other day this week?"

Marty studied the television, which was playing a *Keeping Up with the Kardashians* marathon. "I went out far enough to fish, but I had a sitter with me."

"And did you explain to your sitter, who doesn't know jack shit about sailing, what to do if you had another diabetic attack?" Ali asked.

"I was teaching her how to deep-sea fish, so she could impress Jamie on their honeymoon," Marty said, as if *that* made everything okay.

"She shouldn't have to impress him, they're getting married," Ali said, her voice thin and shaking. "And you shouldn't have to impress her either. Love doesn't work that way. Just like you said love doesn't keep score, love can't be earned. It just is." She sat up so she could face him. "Either he loves her or he doesn't. Knowing how to deep-sea fish or do a toe flick doesn't change that. And it never will."

When Ali had finished, she realized that she was standing and she was so close to tears, her voice was hoarse. Her hands were shaking and her chest was a tangle of knots, which kept pulling tighter and tighter, making her wonder if that was what her dad had felt before he hit the boat's dock.

Before Loraine had called 911.

"Maybe not. But at least I know that it has nothing to do with me," Marty finally said. "People don't all bloom at the same time. Some people are late bloomers in life, and others in love. Some struggle with both. I might struggle with the life part of the equation, but I know how to love."

"I know," Ali whispered, not even wanting to imagine what her life would be like if she lost that. "It's a gift I have felt every day from you. Which is why I hate seeing people take advantage of that."

"People can't take advantage of what I offer freely." Marty patted the bed, and when Ali sat, he took her hand in his. It felt frail and cold, but steady. "You came into the world knowing who you were, your sister is still figuring it out. But I'm going to love her until she learns how to love herself. That's my job and my privilege as her father. Just like it will be my great privilege to love you, even though you sit me on the sidelines because you have everything already figured out."

"I'm single, spend my weekends with my dad, and still play with my old tools," she choked out. "Trust me, Dad, the struggle is real."

"Your dad seems like a righteous guy, and last I heard, you were canoodling with the town's hottest catch."

"Who says *canoodling*?" she whispered, resting back against the headboard.

With a watery grin, Marty put his arms around her and pulled her into his side. "The only thing you struggle with, honey, is waiting for the rest of the world to catch up to your plan. But they will catch up, I promise."

Ali hoped that this was one promise that would come true, because she was pretty sure she'd been Hawked—and there was no coming back for her this time.

* * *

It was three in the morning by the time Hawk made it to Ali's apartment. He'd snatched his old jersey, as promised, and that thirty-year-old bottle of Scotch he'd been saving. It was warm inside her place, and Hawk smiled, hoping Ali had kicked off the covers in her sleep and was in nothing but those panties.

Quietly he made his way down the hallway to find the sheets tossed back, just how he'd imagined. But the bed was alarmingly short on EAT ME panties, and his sleepover buddy. That's when Hawk saw the scribbled note on the nightstand, and he knew exactly where Ali was.

That he wasn't there with her, and that she had to go

there alone, brought back a sense of helplessness that he hadn't felt since his career ended.

He grabbed a small tote and filled it with things he thought might bring comfort, then headed to the hospital. The drive was a nightmare. The town had only three stop-lights. He'd hit every one. Giving him more than enough time to wonder why she hadn't called him.

He would have closed the fucking bar the second she had. He'd done it before, when Marty had his heart attack. But she hadn't called.

The only reason he could come up with was, they were sexy friends. He could have clarified that the other day in his apartment, or even tonight on the phone, but somehow he'd stalled on giving them a title.

Sure, the town thought they were dating, and in reality they were. But he wanted a real conversation with her, about starting a real relationship, when he didn't have to deal with his ex walking through his life and stirring up shit that didn't need to be stirred. So, like an idiot, he'd decided to wait until *after* the wedding, when Bridget was gone and he had his town—and Ali—all to himself.

Only Ali was at the hospital and she hadn't felt comfortable enough to call.

Jesus, he thought as he found out Marty's room number and walked down the hallway, he hoped to God it wasn't another heart attack.

But when he opened the door to the private room, all of his thoughts focused in on the person he'd been the most concerned about.

Ali.

She was huddled in a chair, a blanket wrapped around her feet, her eyes red and puffy as if she'd cried herself to sleep there. And she had, his gut told him. She'd taken care of Marty, and waited until the nurses were gone and he fell asleep. Then she silently dealt with her grief and fear—alone.

Well, she wasn't alone anymore.

Hawk crouched down to look at her perfect face, amazed at how beautiful she'd become. She was cute when they'd been younger, but as a woman, she was stunning. Strong and sweet, and so damn amazing, his heart ached.

He tugged the blanket up over her shoulders and was about to sit down in the other chair when she opened her eyes. "He's going to be okay."

"I know." Ali would make sure of it. He'd never met a fiercer person than Ali when it came to her loved ones. But looking at the worry etched into her face, the big bags under her eyes, he wondered if *she* was going to be okay. "How are you holding up?"

"Fine." And to prove she could handle everything life threw at her, she straightened and gave a big stretch.

Not buying it, Hawk carefully lifted her off the chair and took her seat, cradling her on his lap. Her arms went around his neck and she snuggled into him, pulling her legs in and holding on tight. Hawk pulled the blanket around them, noticing that she was in nothing but pajama shorts, a tank top—and slippers.

"How long are they going to keep him?" Hawk asked, stroking her back.

"I'm not sure. His hydration is back to normal and they've been monitoring his levels. They want to run a few more tests after he eats a good breakfast, then they might let him go home."

Her arms tightened, but he didn't mind. Having her in his arms allowed him to breathe for the first time since seeing that note on her nightstand. "Has he been waking up?"

She shook her head, her hair brushing his chin and getting tangled in his scruff. "After I got here, we had a talk, then he fell asleep and hasn't woken up since. Either he hurts more than he's letting on or trying to avoid another conversation."

Hawk tipped Ali's face up, and those sad, green pools swallowed him whole. He couldn't make tonight disappear, but he could make everything from here on out better. "Let me take you home—"

"No." She stood up. "I want to be here in case he wakes up or if they have any more questions. They might even release him early and I don't want him wondering where I am."

Like Ali wondered where her mom, and her sister, had gone. She'd had to watch while, one by one, the people she loved disappeared out of her life. And she was afraid to close her eyes, in case her dad vanished, too.

Hawk got her situated back in the chair and he went to talk to the nurse. A few minutes later he came back and squatted in front of her.

"They won't be releasing him until after a final EKG, which is scheduled for two p.m., and will determine if he needs to stay another night." At his words, her eyes closed with anguish. "The doctor has some nice drugs in that IV to ensure he won't wake up until morning."

"I know but—"

"Ali," Hawk said, with gentle force. He took her hand. It was shaking—the adrenaline crash was hitting her hard, and in about thirty minutes, she would be down for the count. He wanted to get her home before then. "If he wakes up, the nurse assured me she will call my cell."

"I don't want to leave him."

"You're not leaving him, you're getting a reboot so you can come back even stronger tomorrow." He took the blanket off her lap and pulled her to a stand. "Plus, the nurse has a few more questions that you can answer on the way out."

* * *

Ali was half asleep when they pulled into the parking lot. Guessing she'd feel more comfortable at her place, he took her hand and led her inside. He was about to ask if she was hungry, but she bypassed the kitchen and went straight to the bathroom.

And closed the door.

Hawk busied himself with pulling the sheet back up, trying to give her space. This was probably the time she'd allow herself to break down, only he was here and he could tell she didn't know what to do. So she put a door between them.

It had been an emotional night, so he'd give her a door for the moment. He had a call to make. Bridget answered on the second ring, and started crying when he told her about Marty. She said she was heading down to the hospital and promised to say there until he brought Ali back in the morning.

Ali had been handling this all on her own for too long. And she'd hit her breaking point. It was time her sister stepped up and became that woman he always knew she was capable of being. Then he gave Luke a call and asked him to drop by in the morning to deal with the scheduled pickup.

With Marty covered, Hawk went back to the person who needed the most care.

Ali.

His sweet, loving Ali.

The bathroom door was closed, but that didn't stop him. He gave a quick tap, and when she didn't answer, he let himself in. Ali sat on the edge of the tub, her feet tucked up under her, and she was crying.

Big silent tears that broke his fucking heart.

"I got you," he said as he scooped her up, careful of the new bruises on her legs from working all week, and carried her to the bed. He set her down and moved in beside her.

She scrambled up his chest and wrapped her slim arms around his neck and he realized that he had it backward. She had him. From the moment they met, she had his back, his trust, and now his heart. Right there in her hands.

There wasn't a piece left of Hawk that Ali hadn't laid claim to. He'd been in love before, but he'd never been *here* before. He wasn't just dreaming of a future with Ali, he could feel it, taste it, see it.

He'd had enough experience with dream girls to know that Ali was the real deal. What he felt for her wasn't a frenzied, immature lust. It was sure and steady, built on a foundation of friendship and respect, and had the depth to go the distance.

He just wasn't sure, with their past and her family, what kind of path to expect. At her core, Ali was a pleaser, taking on the role of peacemaker for her family. A quality that he respected as much as he feared. Because Ali would do anything to hold her family together—even if it meant sacrificing her own happiness in the process.

"Will you hold me?" she whispered, her voice a soft cry that vibrated through his chest.

He ran a hand down her back and pulled her close, cradling her against him. "For as long as you want, sunshine."

"Just until I fall asleep."

"Then how about I hold you for as long as I want?" he asked, and she nodded, her tears falling on his shoulder.

He'd never heard someone pour out that kind of emotion without making a sound. Her body shook, her breath came in anguished puffs, but he couldn't hear the grief. He could feel it; it was rolling off her in waves, silent waves. It was as if she was afraid that giving it a voice would make it real. Or alert someone to her vulnerability.

After a long moment, she tilted her face up, her eyes so sad, his soul ached to erase the pain.

"Hawk?" Her voice was hoarse and raw.

He traced her tears with his thumb. "Yeah, sunshine."

"Will you be here when I wake up?"

God, she knew how to break his heart with a simple question. She'd had so many people walk out on her, she didn't know what to do if someone actually stayed. "If I'm lucky, I'll get to wake up next to you every morning from here on out."

"I'd like that," she whispered.

Hawk tilted his head down and gently kissed her forehead, then whispered, "Now sleep."

She closed her eyes and Hawk rubbed her back, steady

and melodic, until he felt her breathing even out and her body relax into his. It was strange, how someone so different could fit perfectly into his arms.

Into his life.

* * *

Normally when Hawk was invited to a woman's house for a sleepover, sleeping was not the main objective. Yet there he was, sporting the hard-on of a lifetime, with Ali cradled into the crook of his arm, content to just watch her sleep.

Not that he could move even if he'd wanted to—which he most certainly did not—since his arm had gone numb about three hours ago. But having her this close, all warm and soft, pressing into his body, was driving him batshit crazy. She needed sleep, and he needed—well...

He needed her to move her hand a breath south, bringing a whole lot of good into his morning.

Hawk had convinced himself that this insane attraction stemmed from forbidden fruit—a bad case of the one who got away. It had been the basis of their ruse.

A fun fauxmance was all this would be, she'd said. And he'd bought into it. But it was impossible to pretend for long when dealing with the realest woman on the planet. Ali was selfless, nurturing, and a woman who deserved the best kind of forever. She put up a good front, distracted him with her tough-girl 'tude, but the longer their relationship went on, the more he realized what a big heart she had, and just how easy she was to fall for.

Ali had been a steady force in his world since high school. He couldn't remember a time when she wasn't around or in his thoughts. Good times. The bad ones. Around her, he'd never felt alone.

Even during the divorce, Hawk remembered the deep ache that came with the knowledge that he just might lose Ali in the process. In fact, he'd been more concerned with coming back to Destiny Bay and building his relationship with her, than staying in the town where he'd built connections and a career.

And watching her now, sleeping in his arms, he knew why. She was special, as much a part of him as his career had been—as his mom. Ali felt like family. She got to him unlike anyone else, and she got to him in ways he'd never expected.

Sexy, naked ways.

He must have made a sound, because he heard her give a contented and breathy moan, felt her breathing change, and knew she was awake.

And that he was in trouble.

"You're awake," she said, those big mossy eyes lifting to his. She gave a little stretch, rolling on her side and sliding her leg over his. And her hand, yeah, it was sliding down his stomach, far enough for her to know firsthand just how awake he was.

"I never took you for a cuddler, sunshine, but I got to say, it looks good on you." He cocked a brow at her hand and Ali jerked it back. "How did you sleep?"

"I slept great." She came up on her elbow, her hair a mess of sexy waves. She gave a shy smile. "Thank you for being here last night."

"Anytime." He tucked her hair behind her ear, then ran his thumb over her cheekbone. "We have an hour before we have to leave. Want me to make up some breakfast?"

"I never took you for a nurturer, boo, but I gotta say, it looks good on you." Her gaze roamed his body, followed by her fingers. "Almost as good as my sheets."

God, she was sexy.

"So, maybe coffee and leftover pie?"

"Maybe," she said, moving up his body to deliver the gentlest of morning kisses.

Always a giver, Hawk kissed her back, a sweet and gentle brush of the lips that was meant to soothe, ease her into the morning. After last night she needed some serious pampering. But when it came to Ali, one kiss was never enough.

He'd come here to be a support in her time of need, but Ali's needs had clearly gone from comfort to carnal, because suddenly her hand was engaged in an interesting game of what's behind door number one.

Nothing good, that's for sure.

This was one of those moments when someone had to put on the brakes, point out that she'd had a rough night, and suggest that maybe they talk it out. Over breakfast. Only she didn't seem to be in a talking mood. As for breakfast, her mind was set on something a little hotter than pie. And what kind of jerk told a lady what she could and couldn't have for breakfast?

Not this guy. Nope, Hawk was all about the lady's needs and wants, and Ali wanted him. Something that became obvious when she slid her hands beneath the waistband of his jeans, giving him the best good morning of his life.

So instead he kept his mouth shut, reminded himself that it was always ladies first, and pulled Ali on top of him. If his change of plans fazed her, Ali didn't show it. In fact, she came to him soft and pliant, and so damn sweet.

"Hawk," she moaned. No, it was more of a groan—and before he knew it, his thumbs were sliding beneath the hem of her pajama bottoms. She took that as a green light to go back to work on his jeans, unbuttoning them with her fingers, while her mouth slowly, languidly worked his.

Which he had no problem with because it caused her shirt to gape open, and with a little one-two action of his nimble fingers, they were up and under and, *his life was complete*, she had gone for a bra-free kind of night.

Just like she'd gone home with him because she'd needed a friend. And there he lay, friend of the year, with his hands up her top while she was looking ready to go down on him.

Even though he wanted her to go down, and of course he'd return the favor, but he'd promised himself not to be one more person who took advantage of her, and she'd been pretty messed up a few hours ago.

"Ali," he said, cupping her face. "You've had a rough night, and you're going to have a long day. We don't have to do this. I'm okay with just talking."

She sat back on her knees, her eyes locked on his, then she smiled. "Last night was just the start of a really long process. There'll be months of talking and worrying. Right now I don't want to think of anything but this." She ran a hand down his abs—and lower—cupping him over his jeans. "I don't want to think of anything but us."

And to prove it, Ali reached for the bottom of her shirt and pulled it up and over, and Hawk sucked in a breath.

She was stunning. Petite, athletic, and with just the

right amount of curves to have his body saying, *Oh yeah.* Then she was kissing him, and man, the woman kissed like she lived—bold and unapologetic.

"As long as you're sure?" he chuckled against her lips.

She mumbled something about *Shut the fuck up and kiss me*, but it was hard to decipher with her tongue down his throat. And in case *that* wasn't crystal fucking clear enough, she made short order of his pants, then draped her naked body over his.

But instead of going for the gold, she took a minute to study him, as if looking for something. And Hawk prayed to God that he had what she needed, because this was as real as it was going to get for him.

Thank Christ, she must have found whatever she was searching for, because she met his gaze and whispered, "I'm always sure with you, Hawk."

At her words, calm stillness took over, starting in his chest and radiating out until everything inside him caught wind and all he felt was peace.

Direction.

Clarity.

Her smile, her confidence, the way she made him feel. It was addicting as hell. He could hold her all night and still itch to touch her. Kiss her until the sun went down and she'd still taste like his.

And damn, he wanted her to be his. Even more, he wanted to be hers. Her friend, her lover, her family.

"Come here," he said, and when she wrapped her arms around his neck, he cupped those heart-shaped cheeks and pressed her against him, showing her how sure he was.

Her mouth was on him in seconds, hungry and demanding. And her hips, *holy shit her hips*, were doing this swivel action that was mind blowing. She slid up the length of him, then slowly back down, her hand on one side, her body on the other. Never taking him in, just teasing the skin, increasing the friction, the pressure, until breathing was impossible.

He was one stroke from going off like a rocket, but he gritted his teeth, because Ali was back on her knees, her head flung back and those glorious breasts jutting out for his viewing pleasure. And talk about pleasure, Ali was taking hers, rubbing herself into a frenzy.

So when her moans turned to groans, and finally quick releases of air that said she was almost there, Hawk decided he'd be the guy to take her anywhere she fucking desired.

Sitting up, he grabbed her hips and rocked to his own knees, setting her on his lap and setting a fast and hard rhythm that had sweat beading on his brow.

He'd give anything to slip right inside her, feel her with nothing between them. But this was about Ali, so he focused on her until her nipples hardened enough to graze his chest, and her slick heat moved with ease over him, and when her head rolled back and she cried out his name, Hawk slid on the condom and brought her on home.

"Oh God, Hawk," she cried as he entered her in the height of her orgasm, causing a second wave of pleasure to roll through her—and through him.

Not giving her a chance to recover, Hawk laid her back, and with her ankles still locked around his hips, he drove all the way in and pulled nearly all the way out, only to slide slowly back in.

"Don't," she cried, fading off, and Hawk stilled.

"Don't what?" he asked.

Those bedroom eyes opened and she grinned. "Don't you dare stop."

When it came to Ali, Hawk was quickly realizing he didn't know how to stop.

He'd do whatever it took to go the distance. To stay. Right there in her bed.

In her life.

So when she wrapped those arms around his neck and held him until there was nothing between them but emotions, he was pretty sure his heart lodged itself in his chest. And when she pushed up and he was coming down, he felt as if he was going to explode out of his body.

"Anything you want," he promised.

"Anything," he said again as he withdrew all the way. "You." He slid all the way back in, to the hilt, and she cried out his name. And when he felt her first tremor of release, he gave her everything he had and she took it—all of it. Giving him even more in return.

"Want," he groaned as she shattered around him, her body coiling until he felt his body tighten to the point of passing out. His vision went hazy, his lungs gave out, and then he exploded so hard, his arms buckled.

He never let go, even as he collapsed and rolled them to the side. Holding her close so he could breathe her in.

Ali didn't seem to mind, her limp arms doing their best to hold on. And Hawk knew right then that she was his. That all this time he'd had been looking for that one great love, and it was waiting for him right next door.

Chapter 15

For a guy who had a million and one things to do before opening, Hawk had no business spending the afternoon on *Chasing Destiny*, refinishing the railings and polishing steel. But that's what happened when you fall asleep with a beautiful woman in your arms, and wake up to her moaning your name.

You do ridiculous things—like offer to clean your ex-father-in-law's boat for his homecoming.

Marty was doing better, but the doctor wanted to keep an eye on his levels for a few more days before they released him. So Ali had gone down to have dinner with him. Hawk had considered going with her, but knew she wouldn't rest until the boat was ready for Marty.

And Hawk wanted to help her in any way that he could. Her plate was overflowing, so while she was busy being Ali, and taking care of everyone around her, he was going to take care of her. His goal was to finish up here in time to surprise Ali with dessert, and a set of strong arms.

Perfect for a little pampering and, hopefully, some more of that naked pampering they were so good at.

So when he saw the dock swaying, he flexed those biceps and got them ready, in case she wanted to get started on the party early. Only when he looked up, he found Bridget walking down the dock with a glass of wine and an ice-cold beer.

She'd been there when he'd dropped Ali off at the hospital earlier that morning. Outside of thanking her for staying the night and discussing the details of Marty's release, the sisters had barely spoken. Bridget's big blue doe eyes were willing him to smooth things over; Ali's were begging him to leave.

The tension between the sisters was palpable, and his presence was just adding gasoline to the flames. He got it, but it still rubbed him the wrong way.

But watching Bridget now, that brittle smile and the cold beer in hand, he saw Ali's point. They'd all been playing the same roles for so long, it was hard to redefine the boundaries. Even more concerning, Bridget didn't understand that the boundaries applied to her, because it was clear that she was in need of a hero.

Too bad, Hawk had no desire to put on that cape.

The tide was changing direction and he'd promised Ali he'd deal with any contraband and stock the fridge with healthy choices. Something Marty better start making if he wanted his outcome to change.

A sentiment Hawk took to heart.

Bridget climbed on the boat, the breeze blowing her hair back. Her eyes were red, and her face was puffy.

She'd been crying. Hawk's heart dropped. "Is Marty okay?"

"He's fine," she said, leaning against the railing. "Or he's going to be. They're releasing him tomorrow morning."

"That's great." Hawk picked up his discarded shirt off the railing and slid it on. The temperature was only in the low seventies, but the sun reflecting off the deck had been brutal. "Ali's still at the hospital."

"I know. I came to pack my stuff and saw you down here." She swallowed. "You looked like you could use a cold one."

She handed him the beer, and he took a long pull. "Thanks."

"Don't thank me." She shook her head, her eyes going misty. "I should be thanking you, for being here to help out with my dad, and doing all of this when you didn't have to." She met his gaze and gave a watery smile. "You really are a great guy."

Torn between wanting to shoulder her tears and not ever wanting to go *there* again, Hawk changed the subject. "Are you headed to the airport?"

"First thing tomorrow morning," she said and faced the water, her hair spilling down her back, turning a shiny gold in the setting sun. She wore it loose and unstyled, the way he used to like it. "I have to go cancel the venue and take care of a few things, then I'll come back."

"I'm sorry, I know how excited you were, but Marty will be happy to know you're close. Will you reschedule the wedding for when Marty can travel or will you move it back to the West Coast?" he asked, knowing Marty would rather risk another heart attack than miss his daughter's wedding.

"No, I'm canceling the wedding. Calling it all off," Bridget said, her back to him.

Hawk froze. "You are?"

"I was sitting in the hospital room as person after person came to check on my dad, on my family. It was six in the morning," she said softly, "and they were already lining up with this huge outpouring of support. And I realized my support couldn't make it here until tomorrow, because of a board meeting he just couldn't manage to hand off to his VP."

After the short time he'd spent with Jamie, Hawk wasn't surprised. But he felt bad for Bridget all the same. She'd placed a lot of her dreams on that marriage working, and he knew how hard it was to watch a dream like that die. "Have you told your family?"

"Jamie doesn't even know." He watched as she covered her mouth with her hand, trying to control the emotions from spilling out. "He doesn't even know I'm unhappy." She closed her eyes, and a tear escaped. "How stupid is that?"

Hawk thought back to the last year of their marriage, and how he'd had no idea Bridget was unhappy. It wasn't as if there weren't any signs; she'd even told him she was struggling. But he'd been so busy with the season, he'd chalked it up to growing pains. To the sacrifice that came with being married to a guy who was married to hockey.

"I'm sorry, Bridget." Hawk placed a hand on her shoulder.

She turned around and her eyes went wide with surprise. "Oh my God, you really are. Most people would tell me I was getting what I deserve after what I did to you. But here you are, genuinely sorry for me."

"You weren't the only one who made mistakes, I did, too," he admitted. "I never fully blamed you, and I'll never stop wanting what's best for you."

"I want to come home," she whispered, sounding ready to break. "I want to be closer to my dad so I can help take care of him. Seeing him in that hospital bed made me realize that I might not get another chance to make things right. And I want to get serious about a career in event planning."

"That's great." He took a seat on the bench and waited for her to do the same. "You are organized and creative and great with people, so that would be a natural fit for you. People loved how you transformed my bar, and even though it wasn't my preference, I have to admit it was stunning. If you focused, I'd bet you could even open your own event company someday."

"I hope so, because I reached out to Susan at Myers's Orchards," she said, and an uneasiness settled over him.

"Susan Myers? The mayor's wife?"

Bridget nodded. "She plans all of the weddings and events at the orchard, and she's looking for someone to help her with wedding season. Plus, I've already had people tell me the same thing about the engagement party, Ali's friend even said she'd hire me in a heartbeat to plan some events for Sweetie Pies." Kennedy may have said that, but she'd never hire someone if it meant making Ali's life harder. And having Bridget in town would cause a never-ending cycle of trouble.

"I bet I could get a few clients of my own by the end of the year." She sounded so excited, as if she was talking about moving to Paris or New York, two places Hawk would be supportive of her moving to. In fact, there was only one place she couldn't move. And that was Destiny Bay.

Hawk held up his hands, palms out, in a clear sign to slow down. But he could tell by her smile that she was just getting started. She was approaching this move like she had the wedding. Full steam with blinders on.

"Why Destiny Bay?" he reminded her, because he knew his ex and she was caught up in the dream of it all, not stopping to consider what it would really mean to live in the same town as her family. She would want the perks of being close by, but until she got a better handle on who she was, she'd avoid all of the responsibility.

"My dad is here, Ali's here." She met his gaze. "You're here. Why not?"

Oh, hell, no.

"Because that was the only thing I asked for in the divorce," Hawk said, panic reaching out and grabbing him by the throat. "You got everything. The house, the cars, the mutual friends. All I wanted was to come home and start my life over."

"I know," she whispered. "I wanted that, too. But I was thinking, what if we started over... together."

That noose tightened until his lungs burned. "I don't even see how that could work. I want kids, a family, a simple life. You want... none of that."

"What if I wanted that now? The house with the picket fence, the 2.4 kids, the small town life full of picnics on Sunday and dinner at my dad's," she said, and Hawk struggled to make sense of what she was offering over the blood rushing through his head. "What if I wanted all of that with you?"

She took a step closer, her big fathomless eyes calling out to him to make everything better. A part of Hawk, the lovesick twenty-two-year-old who'd waited a lifetime to hear those words, wanted to grab hold of her and never let go. But the older Hawk, the one who wanted something real, who wanted to sink into love and make it last a lifetime, reminded him that *that* ship had sailed.

"You don't really want that," he said softly. "And you sure don't want it with me. Everything in your life is uncertain and you're reaching for something familiar. Using the past as a safety vest, but trust me, it won't work," he said with certainty, because he'd done the same thing. And all it had helped him do was keep his head above water.

She wrapped her arms around her middle. "It might work this time."

"It won't." And it never would have, he realized with a clarity he'd been missing. "Because we never worked. It's easy to remember the high points, and we had a lot," he said, thinking back on their marriage. "But we also had a lot of low times. And man, Bridget, when they were low, they were low."

And hard on both of them. They'd cycle from the highs to the lows, but they had no idea how to be with each other in the middle, where things were comfortable, loving, safe. It was as if they lived for the chaos. A place he'd spent his childhood trying to escape, and his twenties recreating.

"It might be different this time." She rested her palm on his chest, and he waited for the familiar zing of awareness that came anytime Bridget put her hands on him. All he felt was a peaceful release of the past leaving his body.

The pain and the heartache making room for hope and a new love.

"It will be different," he said. "Because we will both find it with someone else."

"Oh my God." Bridget's face fell, and she pulled her hand back as if burned. "You're in love with Ali."

Hawk froze, waited for that word to bounce right off him, but it didn't. It stuck in his chest and grew until that was all he could feel. The panic disappeared; the itch to deny it and move on was nowhere to be found.

"I think I am," he said. "When I think of kids and family and someone that makes me happy, makes me better, it's Ali."

He looked at the woman whom he'd once vowed to make happy, and knew that it wasn't his job anymore. He's been devastated when she took that from him, trapped by the loss, but now he realized that she'd actually set them both free—to find their own happiness. And he intended to find his and never let go.

"I can't be that with you here, Bridget." He and Ali needed time to cement what they'd found. Focus on what lay ahead, instead of their past walking up behind them anytime Bridget felt lonely. "Which is why I have to ask you to live up to your end of the deal and leave town."

"So just pack up and leave?"

"It's what you're good at," he said, stating what was true.

Bridget's expression turned guarded, tense. "Maybe I don't want to be that person anymore. Maybe I want to stick this one out, make it work. Figure out what I want and start a new life."

"Fine, just don't do it here."

Anywhere but here would work. He and Ali needed the space to focus on their relationship without the past hiding around every corner. And hopefully, when the time was right, Ali would realize she loved him back.

"Me leaving won't change anything," Bridget pointed out. "My dad will still be sick, Ali will still put family first, and I will always be your ex-wife."

"I didn't fall for her because she's your sister, I fell for her because she's Ali."

"I know," she said, her voice low. "But I also know that you live to make people happy, and the only way my family is going to be happy is if we finally have the time to heal."

The earlier panic tightened until his head throbbed and his lungs burned, because the easiest way to shatter Ali's world was if she learned her family was once again torn apart—because of him. Ali was loyal to a fault, and she would always protect her family.

Problem was, he'd come to think of her as his family.

"I'm not asking for a second chance, Hawk. I can see that isn't a possibility now," Bridget said. "But I am asking you to forgive me. And that means letting me come home."

Chapter 16

Dinner had been cleared away and Marty was resting. Ali was ready to head home, but was hoping to hear the results of her dad's latest round of tests before she left for the night. The nurse had said she'd check on them—that had been two hours ago.

She rested her head back against the chair and found herself smiling. She was pretty happy for a girl who'd spent the day in a hospital. Because her dad had turned a huge corner today, and she knew in her heart that he wasn't going anywhere anytime soon.

And neither was Hawk.

If I'm lucky, you might let me hold you forever.

For the first time since she was a kid, Ali had felt completely cherished last night. He'd not only taken care of her dad, but also taken care of her in a moment when she didn't know how to take care of herself.

Hawk had not only gotten her to the hospital before

Marty woke up, as promised, but also arranged for her piece to make it to her client so she didn't have to worry about it. Even more touching, he'd held her all night. Those big arms of his wrapped tightly, lovingly around her. Giving her the time she needed to let go, and the reassurance she needed to hold on.

Then he'd made love to her.

He hadn't said the word, but Ali had felt it. Strong enough to break through her walls and seep into her soul. It was thrilling and humbling and comforting all at the same time.

A healing force that gave her the courage to believe in dreams. Believe that maybe she was enough. That together, all of their flaws and differences somehow made for a perfect pairing.

She reached for the phone to call him and let him know she was running a little late, but it went straight to voice mail. She thought about texting him when Bridget showed up with an overnight bag and a little pink pastry box.

"How's he doing?" she asked, taking a seat next to Ali.

"He ate almost all of his dinner, even the broccoli, and then the nurses took some more blood. I was just waiting on the results." She looked at the box. "What's that?"

"A little cupcake from Sweetie Pies. Kennedy was afraid you weren't getting enough chocolate in your diet."

Bridget opened the box and Ali counted three mini death-by-chocolate pies. After a steady diet of vending machine sandwiches and green Jell-O cups—Marty refused to eat anything green that wasn't mandatory—the pie looked amazing.

She thought about Hawk waiting for her, but figured he wouldn't blame her for eating dessert twice in one night. Plus, she was still waiting on the results, so might as well enjoy the wait.

Ali picked up the pie, took a big bite, and moaned—quietly, so as not to wake Marty. Once alert, he could sniff out a single M&M from fifty feet away.

Ali took another bite as Bridget tossed her bag on the floor. The flap opened, showing that there was enough stuff in there for a sleepover. "Are you staying the night?"

Bridget picked up a pie and nodded. "You've been here all day, I thought I'd give you a break."

"Thanks," Ali said, relieved that Marty wouldn't be alone if he woke up. "But don't you have to leave early for the airport tomorrow morning?"

"I canceled my flight." Bridget took a bite of her pie, and sat back with a groan. "These are amazing."

"You mean rescheduled," Ali said.

"Nope." Bridget popped the last bit in her mouth and smiled around the whipped topping. "Canceled it. I called Jamie on the way here and told him that if he couldn't make it to be by my side when I needed his support, then I can't marry him."

Ali choked on a piece of crust. "Are you serious?"

Bridget smiled, and this smile looked different. Lighter and freer. "Serious about a lot of things, including getting my life together. I'm taking your advice and going after my dream of being a party planner."

"I can't believe you are actually doing it."

"Well, believe it. I already talked to someone about

being an assistant until I get my footing, and then I'm going to open my own company. Once-in-a-Lifetime Moments," she said as if she could already see her business cards. "Think about it, I will get to plan a bazillion weddings without ending up like Mom, a six-time divorcée."

They both laughed, then Ali reached for the last pie and broke it in half to give part to Bridget. "Don't worry about Dad, though, I am going to make him a priority. You won't be stuck handling everything anymore."

Ali opened her mouth to remind her that they'd tried that before, and it had landed them here.

"Wait, before you say it's a lot of work, and that I'm in over my head, you're right. About all of it," Bridget said quietly. "I'm tired of letting people down, so I'm going to change that. Starting with a class about caring for aging loved ones so that I know what Dad needs. And know that if something goes wrong, I have the skills to make the right calls."

Ali's heart gave a little tug. "He'd love that and I could use the help."

Bridget smiled. "And I could use a sister again. Which is why I'm asking Dad if I can move in for a little while. Just until he gets back on his feet."

"You're moving home. Like Dad's home?"

"Why does everyone sound so surprised when I say this? Yes, I want to be here while Dad heals, is that so bad?"

"What about the job you were talking about?"

"That's the best part, it's here in town," Bridget said, and Ali tried to tell herself that this was a good thing. It provided the post-release care her dad would need, and eliminated having to hire a live-in caretaker. Also, Bridget had the right to be near Marty. He was her father, too.

But working in Destiny Bay, starting her career here, making the networks she'd need to start her own business. Everything hit Ali like a bucket of dried concrete.

"Once-in-a-Lifetime Moments," Ali said, uncertainty and desperation colliding. "You're going to open that here? In town?"

"Destiny Bay doesn't have an event planner, and after talking to Hawk about coming back home, I realized that I could really make a go at this. That this is where I want to be."

"Hawk knows about this?" Disbelief rattled around her chest, making it hard to hear. Because if he'd known Bridget was considering moving back, he would have called her. Or at least texted her to give her a heads-up.

She checked her phone. No missed calls or texts. In fact, nothing from Hawk all day.

"You were right, he is an amazing man," Bridget said, her eyes filling. "Even after everything I put him through, he's willing to forgive the past and let me come home. Start fresh."

Ali opened her mouth, but too many questions and emotions formed all at once, choking her. Sending that earlier confidence back ten years. Hawk said he wanted to hold her forever, but that had been when Bridget wasn't a viable choice. But now Bridget was coming home—and Hawk had put their past behind them.

Which led her to the most important question, the one that had been bubbling up in her for so long but she'd never taken the time to ask. What about her future? *Their* future?

Ali's hands began to tremble because she had started to allow herself to picture it. To give in to the hope that it was possible. Wanted more than anything to believe that it could happen.

"It's not nice to tempt a changed man." Marty's voice was groggy with sleep and from the medication.

"We didn't mean to wake you," Bridget said, moving to the side of the bed to take his hand.

"I was having dreams of swimming in a vat of chocolate pie." He squeezed Bridget's hand, then looked at Ali and gave a tired smile. "Still not as good as time with my girls, though. That's all I want, is more time with my girls."

"Well, then today's your lucky day, because we aren't going anywhere," Bridget said, then looked out the door. "Except maybe to ask the nurse what's taking so long with those results."

"I'll go find out," Ali said, needing to get out of there. To see Hawk. To see what had happened since he'd dropped her off.

To see if he still meant what he'd said. Or if he'd said it in a vulnerable moment.

"I can do that," Bridget offered. "You've been here all day, let me handle things so you can go home and get some rest."

Right, this went back to the whole sharing people she loved when all she wanted to do was keep them to herself.

"Yes, honey, go rest. We can visit tomorrow," Marty said, and Ali nodded, choking on all the what-ifs and past fears making her head spin.

And her heart ache.

She kissed her dad on the cheek and told Bridget, "Text me with the results when you hear."

* * *

Ali pulled into Bay View, her heart taking another hard hit when she saw Hawk's motorcycle parked in the driveway.

When she'd arrived at her apartment and found it empty, she'd held out hope that Hawk was still at Marty's finishing up, or perhaps the grocery store. So she'd texted him, asking where he was. He'd responded with sweet and simple, Working something out. PS. pie's in the fridge.

I'll wait, she'd replied.

Ali knew what it felt like to wait. She'd been waiting for love her whole life, it seemed, but she thought her time had finally come. Hawk loved her; she had no doubt about his feelings. Just like she had no doubt that he still loved Bridget. He always would; he'd told her as much.

But Ali decided that this was one love she wasn't willing to share.

So she waited, in her pajamas, on the front porch steps, for him to come back. For him to explain away the confusion and uncertainty that grew with every minute that passed. She waited as the day started its final descent over the Pacific, until that voice in her head telling her she wasn't enough came back, and when enough time passed for Hawk to work out world hunger, Ali decided she was tired of waiting.

She knew what she wanted, had for a long time, and now she needed to see if Hawk wanted the same thing.

See if he wanted it with her. Because she would rather know now than wait until that hope got any further out of control.

Cutting the engine, Ali picked her way through the orchard and down the steep pathway to the beach, with only light from the moon and her growing frustration to find her way. The closer she got to the beach, the more slippery her descent, the loose sand and gravel cutting into her sandaled feet, the possible reason for what he had to work out making each of her steps more and more difficult.

She'd meant what she'd said to her dad. Love just is. It doesn't need to be worked out, or weighed. And it doesn't change when another opportunity arises.

Ali's foot slipped and her pulse pounded wildly in her throat. That legendary calm she relied on to keep her grounded had leaked out somewhere between town and here, leaving her feeling raw and exposed.

By the time she hit the bottom of the trail and stepped out onto the bluff, her hands were trembling, and by the time she found Hawk, the soft spot in her chest, where he'd taken up residence, began to ache.

He was sitting on his rock, ankles crossed and legs pulled to his chest, the moon lighting his profile as he stared out at the black waters. All it took was one glance in her direction for Ali to know exactly what he'd been working out.

How to move on.

Twelve hours ago, he'd been in her bed, looking at her with love and wonder, as if she was the one. And now they were at his thinking spot, the place he came to when he felt trapped and needed a reminder of just how big the world was, and that wonder in his eyes was replaced with dread.

"I didn't mean to intrude," she said when he looked up at her.

"Yes you did," he said, standing and coming over to her to take her hands. "I hope you brought pie."

The sensation of his touch was both comforting and terrifying.

"This didn't feel like a pie kind of conversation," she said, and her voice had a little more bite to it than she'd expected. "In fact, I'm so tired of waiting for this conversation to happen, I'm actually pissed at myself for putting it off so long."

Because then she wouldn't be in this situation again, with her heart on the line and wondering if one more person who she loved was going to choose to love her back.

Nausea burned the sides of her stomach until she was certain she was going to be sick. Standing here, in front of him, knowing that he could drop a bomb of truth on her that would forever shatter her world was petrifying.

But she'd shattered before, twice, and both times she'd managed to pull herself back together. And she could do it again. What she couldn't do was continue on for one more breath not knowing if he still dreamed of being with another woman.

Ali looked at those deep brown eyes that she loved and had come to trust. "Are you still in love with Bridget?"

There was a heavy beat of silence, where she held Hawk's steely gaze. He was working hard to find the right words, or maybe he was waiting for her to speak. Either way, the silence grew until it became a physical force separating them.

A muscle in Hawk's jaw ticked. "I don't know, Ali. Do you think I could still be in love with someone else?"

"I don't know," she said, feeling more lost than ever. He didn't look guilty or concerned; he looked hurt. The kind of hurt that changed everything. "That's why I'm asking."

"You don't know?" He dropped his hands and stepped away from her. "Is it that you don't know or you don't believe me? Because I made it pretty fucking clear last night how I felt about you."

"Last night was pretty intense and I was a mess, and you were comforting me," Ali said. "Sometimes people say things in the heat of the moment and then things change and they want to take them back. I didn't know if you wanted to take them back."

"And what if I did?" he asked, just staring at her. His face cool and distant. "What if I did want to take them back and give it a try with Bridget? What would you do?"

Dread moved through her, robbing her words and stealing her breath. She'd wanted to know the truth before it was too late to come back, but the sharp ache lacing through her body told her it already was. "Do you? Want to take them back?"

"You first. I asked you a question and I want the answer."

"I don't know what I'd do," she said honestly, wondering how this got turned around on her.

"Then that's a fucking problem I can't fix," he said, and if a rogue wave had dropped her into the side of the cliff, the impact would have been laughable compared to the anger flashing in his eyes. "Because when I told you I wanted to hold you forever, I meant forever. I meant, even if it came down to winning another Stanley Cup or being in your arms, running the bar or being in your arms, going back and replaying that game so my career never ended or being in your arms, I'd pick being in your fucking arms every time. But you have one conversation with your sister and *you don't know?*"

"Hawk, I—"

He held up a silencing hand. "I don't know what Bridget said to you, but I could never have slept with you if I was still in love with Bridget."

"You've slept with other women," she said quietly, remembering foolishly how she wanted to know what it felt like to be them, just for a night.

He whipped around. "I slept with other women, but I was always clear where I stood. Just like I was honest with you, sunshine." Now her nickname sounded like a curse. "Hell, I was more honest with you than I've ever been with anyone. I showed you who I was; there should have been no doubt in that."

"I guess I just got scared," she explained. "We started out as a joke to mess with Bridget, then it became so real so fast that I started to question where the fake ended and the real began. Then Bridget tells me you're the reason she's coming home and I let her get in my head."

"We started out as friends first. *Friends.* Who knew each other's secrets and fears. I let you inside places I never like to visit. So no, Ali, as far as I was concerned, nothing between us was ever fake." He sounded raw, betrayed.

"I am so sorry I doubted that. That I doubted you," she

said, putting as much apology and regret in her words, even though she knew deep down that it wouldn't erase the hurt.

Hawk was honest and loyal and one of the best people she'd ever met. If she'd given him the respect and trust he deserved, the trust he'd earned with her over the years, they wouldn't be here. And he wouldn't feel so completely devastated—and betrayed.

"You shouldn't have doubted *us*." He punctuated the word with a hand to his chest. "The old us or the new us. So what if I talked to Bridget? You should have seen that coming the second she realized she was unhappy. But I didn't support her coming back because she asked me, I did it because having your family together is important to you. It makes you happy. And Jesus, Ali..." His lip quivered and he ran a hand down his face. "All I wanted was to make you happy. From day one. So I came down here to figure out how to do that, how to give you the family you deserve, and still keep you."

Giving a defeated shrug, Hawk turned to face the ocean. She could see his chest expand as he took in one jerky breath after another.

His anguish cut Ali to her core. She'd been so busy trying not to get hurt, she'd hurt the most important person in her life. Placing one hand on her aching heart, she came up behind him and rested the other on his shoulder. "How could you ever think you'd lose me?"

"I don't know, Ali," he said, his voice getting lost over the crash of the waves. "You didn't want me coming to family dinners until your sister left, didn't want me at the hospital because it might upset Bridget, who'd upset Marty. You've spent the past few years keeping me at a distance because of how it would affect everyone else.

"Well, guess what? The big elephant you never want to talk about is moving home and she will be at every family event, every birthday and special moment, until she moves on to the next thing. But by then, this thing between us will be over, because it won't work with you trying to live two lives."

"I'm not trying to live two lives," she said, willing him to turn around. "I'm just trying to live this one right."

"I know, sunshine. It's who you are," he said, resting his hand over hers, as if he needed the contact to continue. "You know what I told Bridget?" He looked at her over his shoulder, his eyes empty and sad. So damn sad, she tightened her grip. "I told her that I love you, for that same reason. I guess I just hoped that I could be the guy that made your world whole, not the one who tore it apart."

"But you don't," she said fiercely. "You make my world light and fun, and you make me feel alive. I was just so scared that deep down I couldn't ever be what you really wanted."

Hawk made a sound as if his body had released everything it had to give, and she felt his shoulders sag, and disappointment roll off him in waves.

"Ali, for someone who knows what it feels like to have her love and her worth discounted, you sure know how to take a guy out at the knees."

It was in that moment that Ali knew she'd lost him forever, because instead of holding on, he gave her hand a final squeeze and let go.

Ali stood there as he walked up the trail, refusing to

blink even when he disappeared into the darkness. But when she heard his motorcycle start, she knew she was truly alone.

She told herself to hold it together until she got back to her apartment, but her legs gave way on her first step and she crumbled to the ground. The rocks biting into her knees, the sand rubbing her hands raw. She dropped her head to her chest and let the tears fall.

Hawk had put his heart in her hands and instead of holding tight—she'd crushed it. Right along with any hope of forever.

Chapter 17

Ali sat on the stern of the boat, her legs dangling over the side as she watched the morning tide slowly eat away at the sand.

She rested her head against the railing and breathed in the brine of the sea air, hoping it would make breathing easier. It just burned her lungs.

The sun had yet to peek through the morning fog, and a light mist covered the deck and seeped through her jeans. She didn't care. She was too drained, too empty to move.

She was supposed to swing by her dad's house and pick up fresh clothes for his release, but Ali needed a moment to compose herself before she faced her family. So she'd come to the place she felt the most at peace.

Chasing Destiny.

That had been two hours ago. And instead of peaceful, all she felt was hollow. She ran a hand over the refinished teak railings and a sob welled up.

"Thank you, Hawk," she whispered, welcoming the fresh batch of tears that had bubbled up.

It hurt to cry, but at this point she welcomed the pain. It felt better than the vast emptiness that had started in her chest when she'd watched her future walk out, and slowly eaten away at her until it had finally swallowed her whole.

But as the tears burned her throat and poured down her face, she realized that no matter how long she sat there, staring out at the ocean, she was never going to be free from the emptiness.

The tears would eventually dry up, and the crushing weight would eventually ease, but she was never going to experience love. Not the kind that had been possible with Hawk.

Allowing herself one last tear, she wiped her cheeks on her sleeve, then stood. When the world didn't feel as if it was going to spin her right off, Ali made her way toward the house to pack a bag for Marty.

Her dad was excited about coming home, and she didn't want him to be dressed in a hospital gown. But when she let herself in the back door, she found her mother at the kitchen table—holding a pair of her dad's skivvies.

"What are you doing?"

Gail looked up, her hand pressed flat over the fly of a pair of dancing parrot boxers. "I'm folding Marty's clean laundry. Sitting here waiting to hear about how he's doing was driving me crazy."

"So you decided to do laundry?" she asked, and Gail shrugged. "You don't even do your own laundry."

Gail glanced at the stacks of folded clothes. "Neither

does your dad apparently. I went to find the sweatpants you texted Bridget about and the man didn't have a clean pair in his drawers."

Ali counted at least five loads of clothes. "How long have you been here?"

"I left last night when Bridget called me from the hospital. I figured you girls might need some help around here."

"Thanks, Mom. I've been so busy and..." Ali swallowed down the growing lump. "Just thanks."

"Well, it's nice to know I'm needed," Gail said, folding another pair of boxers. This one had honey badgers on it.

"You're needed," Ali said, and she didn't know why that made her throat go tight. She blamed it on the last few emotional days, but suddenly the grief was too much to contain. "I need you, Mom."

Gail looked up and dropped the boxers. "Oh, sugar, what's wrong?"

At the sound of her childhood nickname, Ali dropped to her knees on the kitchen floor and an ache so raw that it had a sound, pushed its way to the surface. It also had a taste and a feel. And a name.

Despair.

Before she could absorb the pain, another one rolled through her chest, and by the time the third one racked her body, her mom was there. Holding her on the floor and rocking her back and forth.

"I've got you, sugar," Gail said, pressing her mouth to Ali's head and placing little kisses on her forehead. "I've got you."

She knew her mother wouldn't have her forever; that wasn't in Gail's nature. But right now, Gail was there, so Ali poured herself into her mom, and let it all burst free.

Seconds, minutes, an hour? Ali had no idea how long they sat there, but when she opened her eyes, the sun was out and her head was in her mom's lap. Gail was gently stroking her hair.

Ali had forgotten that about her mom. How when Ali had a nightmare, Gail would sit on her bed and stroke Ali's hair until she fell asleep. Sometimes she'd even be there in the morning, her arms around Ali, holding her tight.

"Better?" Gail asked, her eyes full of concern.

"I think so." Ali went to sit up, then changed her mind. "Maybe another minute."

"Take as long as you need, that was some release there," Gail said. "You had me worried."

"I had myself worried," Ali admitted, finally feeling as if she could sit up and not fall over. But she didn't go far, leaning against the wall next to her mom.

"Why did you leave Dad?"

Gail let out a deep breath. "There were a lot of reasons, but I guess the biggest one was that we stopped talking. There's a seven-year gap between us, so I was married young, had you girls young, and we were so busy trying to keep our heads above water, we stopped working at it."

"Did you start doubting he loved you?" Ali asked.

Gail laughed. "Sugar, with a man like Marty, one never has to guess at his feelings, the guy loves like every day is his last." No wonder why Hawk and her dad were such good friends. "But the longer we were together, the more I realized just how different we were. We had different ideas on just about everything, and when it came to some things, neither of us would back down."

"Things like me and Bridget?" Ali asked. She'd been more than aware as a child that having kids had been the biggest strain on their marriage. Marty had wanted more, and Gail was struggling to keep up with two. Looking back, Ali realized her mother hadn't been old enough to drink, but she'd had two babies in diapers.

"Yeah, he was such a natural father that it felt at times as if he didn't have room for a partner, or maybe he wanted another kind of partner."

Gail was never going to win Mother of the Year, but before the divorce, she'd been loving and attentive, and then it had suddenly stopped. "Then why didn't you just ask him?"

"I was afraid of what he'd say," Gail said. "And fear is a powerful motivator."

It had ruled Ali's life. Look at the mess she'd caused because she was too scared to believe that Hawk could really love her. If Ali was being honest, and that's what this moment seemed to demand, besides her father, she'd allowed fear to taint every relationship in her life.

It had kept her from making bonds, taking chances, and finding happiness. It had kept her from her family. From finding love.

And that needed to stop.

"Why did you take Bridget and leave me?"

Gail turned her head to look at Ali. "Oh, sugar, is that what you think?"

Ali shrugged. "You divorced and then you just stopped coming around."

"It was hard seeing your dad, watching you grow up

between rotating weekends and holidays. The older you got, the more roots you planted here, and the less frequent the visits. You'd always seem so sad when you came, and I never knew what to say to make it right. Until it was easier not to say anything."

All this time, Ali thought her mother hadn't been interested in building their relationship. Didn't have room in her life for a daughter who was so different. The truth was, Ali hadn't made an effort either. She could have found a common ground if she'd really wanted to. Looking back at all the wasted time, she wished she had.

"I was a handful on those trips."

Gail looked crestfallen. "No, that's on me, not you. Your dad and I fought and fought over custody, and I knew he wasn't going to let you go. Rather than lose both of my girls, I gave in. But as you grew up and I saw the strong woman you were becoming, I knew that he'd been right. Marty's love is freeing; mine can be controlling. The way he was with you was something beautiful to watch. You needed him. So much...I couldn't take that from you."

Wasn't that exactly what Hawk had said? That she was so fixated on the love she'd lost, she was discounting the love that was right there in front of her. Marty had loved Ali for exactly who she was in every moment. Encouraged her to be bold, be herself. So tangible and pure, Ali never had to question its authenticity.

Her heart sank, because that was exactly what she'd done to Hawk. Questioned his love. By focusing on the small stuff, she missed what was really important. Hawk may have never said the word, but his love was always right there, whenever she needed it. Given freely, without expectations or obligations.

Gail tucked a piece of hair behind Ali's ear; it was a motherly gesture that soothed her core. Ali rested her head on her mom's shoulder and watched the sun dance off the kitchen floor. "I'm glad you're here, Mom."

"I was going to wait until you called to say you needed me," Gail said. "Then feared you'd never call. So I decided to come over just in case you did."

"I know I'm not the best at asking for help, but I needed you here."

"I love to be needed, especially by my daughters." Gail pressed a kiss to the top of Ali's head. "With Bridget, I never have to guess. That girl calls me to help her pick out her shoes. But with you, I never know. You're so independent and sure all the time..." Gail took a deep breath. "I want to know what the right move is with you, but I hardly ever get it right."

Ali wasn't trying to hold people at a distance; she just didn't want them to feel obligated to come to her side. If they were there, she wanted it to be because they wanted to be. But maybe her mother needed the same assurances.

Ali tilted her head up and met her mom's uncertain gaze. "How about you just ask me?"

"As long as you promise to do the same." Gail smiled. "Now, you want to talk about what all of that was a minute ago?"

"I think we already did."

Gail chuckled. "You always knew your own mind. It's that unshakable oomph of yours that drives."

"You hate my oomph."

"I love your oomph," Gail rested her cheek on Ali's head. "You get that from your mom."

Ali wrapped an arm around her mother's middle and closed her eyes. She let the feeling of being held sink into her soul and warm her, from the inside out. Calm her fears.

Ever so slowly, that peace she'd been searching for came closer until it was right there. Within reach. All she had to do was grab on.

Call it clarity, oomph, or just knowing what she wanted, but this time Ali wasn't letting go. She could only hope that Hawk still felt the same.

* * *

"No. The last time I let you talk me into hosting a private event, I ended up in a monkey suit at my ex-wife's engagement party," Hawk said.

"From what I heard about the smooching on the roof, you should be thanking me," Luke said, then grimaced.

"Fuck you," Hawk said.

"I'm kind of seeing someone," Luke said, resting his elbows on the bar top, taking way too much joy in Hawk's current situation. "Plus, pussies who run home to cuddle their stick don't really do it for me."

"I didn't run." He'd ridden his bike, like a grown-ass man.

That had been three days ago, and he hadn't seen Ali since. He glanced out the bar window and looked up. Her place was still empty.

He'd heard that Marty had been released, and assumed Ali was spending her days taking care of him, but Hawk had thought she'd at least come back to grab some clothes. Or the chocolate pie in the fridge. She'd never let that go to waste.

Maybe she had, and she'd purposely waited until she knew he'd be sleeping or gone. He wouldn't blame her. She'd come to him like she had a thousand times before, a friend with a concern.

Only he'd reacted like some insecure ass.

"Lucky for us, this group specifically requested you bring your stick," Luke said, sliding over the schedule for the day. "They want to tour the orchard at Bay View as a possible location for a retreat. If it looks like a fit, they'd spend the day at the orchard, picking apples or some shit, then have a cider tasting back here at the Penalty Box. So bring the charm; this could be great for us."

Hawk slid the papers back across the table. He was all tapped out in the charm department. Actually he was tapped out in the giving-a-shit department as well. And spending his day talking hockey and war stories with a bunch of suits sounded as exciting as shattering his other shoulder. "If this is so great, you do it."

"Sorry, bro, no can do. Covering your ass the last few nights at the bar means I have been neglecting my duties at home. So while you handle this little meet and greet, I'll be handling my fiancée."

"I know and I appreciate it."

More than he could ever explain. After that night on the bluff, Hawk needed time to work through what had happened. When a bottle of whiskey and pounding sand hadn't helped, he'd ended up at the Bay View house, expressing his feeling demolition style.

With everything spinning out of control, he needed

something to focus on. Something that wouldn't break when he touched it. Something he could fix.

"Unless you have other plans." The look Luke gave him was one of pure challenge.

Hawk put the empty keg to the side. "There were a few things I wanted to finish up at Bay View, but they can wait."

"I was talking about Ali."

A topic Hawk was trying to avoid, with no luck. Another reason Bay View held such appeal. Talking about Ali led to thinking about Ali—and that shattered fucking look on her face.

He'd done that. He'd hurt her. Big-time. She'd finally opened herself up to the possibility of love, and instead of embracing her courage, he'd told her it wasn't enough.

She wasn't enough. Sure, she'd delivered a similar blow. But over the years he'd given her enough reason to allow for doubt.

"You going to call her? Tell her your stick isn't as much fun to cuddle with, you miss her, and you're sorry?" Luke asked.

He did miss her and he was sorry as hell. But he didn't know how to make it work. Her family needed her right now. And she'd been clear that he wasn't a member anymore.

Hawk leaned against the bar and rubbed his hand over his chest, trying to ease the raw ache that had been gnawing at him. It didn't help. Nothing he seemed to do helped. It just got worse, deeper, hollower. "I don't think she needs one more complication in her life right now."

"Easy," Luke said. "Then don't be a complication. Be

a friend, or pain in her ass, or whatever the hell it is that you two consider flirting. Just don't be one more person who she loves that walks away."

Hawk froze. "How do you know she loves me?"

Luke laughed. "Because unlike you, I haven't had my head shoved so far up your ex's ass over the years, so I'm able to see the way Ali looks at you, man."

His friend hadn't seen the way she looked at him the other night. His gut twisted just thinking about it. "I'm over Bridget."

"I know that, but I don't think you realized that until a few weeks ago," Luke said. "Or you would have known that Ali has loved you since college. And I think you loved her back."

"Yeah, like a kid sister," Hawk said, then realized that wasn't true. He'd had feelings for Ali, but she'd been a junior in high school, and he'd been ready to head off to college that next fall. Then he met Bridget, and well...

Here they were.

"Shit." He didn't want to be here. Not with Ali. He wanted to be the guy who made her smile. "I crushed her."

"Maybe," Luke said quietly. "But this is Ali we're talking about. She never stays down for long. And you're a fighter, Hawk. That's what you do, so why are you ready to call it so early in the game?"

"Because I don't want to fuck this up any more than I have," he admitted.

"Or are you afraid of getting fucked over?" Luke asked, and intuitive bastard that he was, he'd nailed it.

This was as much about Ali as it was about him. He'd promised himself after his divorce that he'd never be played like that again. But the only way to take home the trophy was to commit fully to the process.

He'd committed himself to finding love with Ali, but he'd been too gun-shy to commit to making that love work. And at the first body check of the game, he'd called foul and benched himself.

"Fuck." He sat down on a stool, or maybe it was his legs that gave out. He wasn't sure, but suddenly the weight of what he'd done was too staggering to remain upright.

"That right there, my friend. That is the look of true love." Luke clapped him on the back. "Now I suggest a nice bouquet of flowers, maybe some wine, and lots of groveling."

He was going to do more than grovel; he was going to lay it all out there and commit to whatever she needed to meet him at center ice. From there he'd take her hands and slowly guide her to the goal. Or maybe, they'd wind up on her side.

He didn't care. As long as they were together.

"Kennedy's going to kill me," Hawk said. "But can you handle the meet with the clients today?"

Luke sighed, like a man who wasn't going to get his. Not that Hawk minded; Luke had been getting his regularly for the better part of the year.

It was Hawk's turn.

"I'll do the wine and dine part here," Luke said. "Because Kennedy would kill me if I didn't. But you have to meet them"—he looked at his watch—"in twenty minutes at Bay View. Give them the highlights, that cover of *Sports Illustrated* grin, and then send them my way and I'll close the deal."

"I owe you," Hawk said, grabbing a bottle from beneath the bar and heading toward town. He'd meet the clients, then he'd hunt down Ali.

But he wasn't going to grovel. Ali deserved pampering. Cake pops, whiskey, honest words...and lots of pampering.

* * *

Twenty minutes later, Hawk pulled into Bay View and was driving around the orchard toward the back of the property when he saw his clients. From the distance he could see four of them, sitting around the picnic table on the back porch.

As he drew closer, it appeared to be a family—eating a picnic on his porch. He was used to people coming up from the beach and wandering around the property, as if this were some kind of tourist attraction. But what the hell? No one had ever ventured near the house, and this family even had a wicker basket and checkered tablecloth.

"Not going to happen," he mumbled as he parked his bike. "This is private property. You'll need to take your picnic back down to the beach."

"Oh, I'm sorry," the older man sitting closest to him said. "This is my son-in-law's house. I didn't think he'd mind."

"Marty?" Hawk said, getting closer and coming to a hard stop. His heart pounding against his rib cage for him to keep moving forward. "What are you doing here?"

"You've missed the last few family dinners," a soft, sexy, and nervous voice said from the back of the table.

"So we thought we'd bring the family and burgers to you."

Hawk watched as Ali moved out from beneath the shadow of the porch and slowly down the steps, looking like a warm burst of sunlight on a frozen winter's day. She was in a cute denim skirt, with a summery top that matched her eyes, and a sad smile that matched his heart.

She didn't stop until she'd closed the distance between them, leaving only a step of separation. "That is, if you're still interested."

* * *

Ali's heart beat so loudly, she couldn't tell if he'd answered. It didn't help that her father was asking if Hawk had brought dessert, because, in his opinion, there was a serious lack of dessert on the table.

But when the silence became too much to bear, she added, "If not, then..."

"Then what?" he asked, his expression unreadable.

"Then I guess I'll just have to invite you back next week." She tilted up her chin, to show him that she meant business. "And the week after."

"And then what?" he asked, taking the smallest step forward.

Ali bit her lip to keep it steady. She wasn't sure what to make of all his questions, but she was going to be sure to leave nothing unsaid. "Then we'll bring dinner to you, at the bar. I know how much you love Burger Barn."

"That won't be necessary," he said.

"It won't?" she asked, looking up at his handsome face, looking for a sign as to how to make this right.

"No."

Ali fought to keep it together. "I know my family is crazy, but beneath all of the drama, we have a lot of love to give." She looked up at him. "I have a lot of love to give, Hawk."

"I know." He closed the final step and took her hands and smiled. "That's why it won't be necessary, because there is no way I could ever say no to making a new memory with you, sunshine. Whatever you are offering, I am interested."

She thought about their last conversation, and how she never told him that he was everything she wanted and more. "Hawk—"

"Let me finish," he said, bringing her hands to his mouth. "Whatever you want to give, I promise to protect and treasure. If you need time with your family, I can be patient. If you need someone to take Marty to an appointment, I've got an extra helmet," he said, and she chuckled. "And when you need someone to hold you when it gets rough, I'm your guy. I love you, Ali, exactly for who you are and for how fiercely you love the people in your world." He bent down, getting eye level so that she could see his truth. "All I ask is to earn the right to be a part of that world."

"He's one smooth talker," Marty said, but Ali ignored him and focused on the man in front of her. On her future. Her heart pounding so rapidly, she was afraid it would explode with happiness.

"You already are a part," she said, sliding her arms around his middle. "You're the funny parts, the loud parts, and quiet moments. You're the part that makes me laugh when I want to cry, and makes me feel safe when I do cry. You're the part of my life I thought was missing, but you've always been right there."

He held her close. "I always will be, no matter what."

"I'm going to hold you to that, because you are the best part, Hawk," Ali whispered, emotion making it hard to speak. "You once asked me what I wanted, what would make me happy. No outside expectations or responsibilities. Just a raw, instinctual want."

"You said to step out of the shadows and feel what it's like to have the light shining down on you," he said, and Ali didn't know if she was more touched that he'd remembered, or that when he said it, he sounded as if he was making her a promise.

"I was wrong. I want to walk in the light, with you by my side," she said.

"Sunshine, you are my light, and I want to wake up every morning holding you in my arms and feeling your warmth next to me."

"Only if I get to hold you back."

"How long are we talking?"

She looked up into those soft brown eyes, loving eyes. "I was thinking that forever sounded right. That's how it works with family."

Hawk gave a shuddered breath. "Forever works for me."

"I love you." Ali went up on her toes and showed him just how much. And when they were both smiling through the kiss, she asked, "Bradley Hawk, would you like to come with me to family dinner night?"

"Say yes," Bridget said. "Ali already packed you a burger."

"It's not a burger, son. It's made out of turkey and wrapped in what they claim is a lettuce bun. I've never heard of a bun being made of lettuce, but as long as you brought pie, we're good," Marty said.

Ali laughed at her family, then cupped his cheek. "Say yes, Hawk."

"God, yes." Hawk pulled her in so tight, she couldn't breathe, but Ali didn't care, because the second his mouth came down on her, she could feel. All of his support and admiration—and his love. She could feel it surrounding her. And she'd never felt happier.

"I love you Aliana Marshal," he whispered against her lips. "I always have and I always will."

"I'll never doubt it again, and I'll never let you go," she vowed.

"Even if I told you there's a bouquet of cake pops for you on my motorcycle?" he asked with a grin.

"What fun are cake pops when you have no one to share them with?"

Look for the first book in the Destiny Bay series, *Last Kiss of Summer*.

An excerpt follows.

Chapter 1

Kennedy Sinclair had taken only two steps toward her new life and already her toes were beginning to pinch.

"I don't think I have what it takes," she admitted, plopping down on the changing room bench to loosen the buckles on her new *Comme Il Faut* ballroom dance shoes, sighing as the blood rushed back to her feet. The red satin straps were trouble enough—looping tightly around the ankle and pulling across the tops of her toes, pinching off all circulation—but the heels were the real problem. Staggering toothpicks that added enough height to cause lightheadedness and excessive teetering. A result, no doubt, from attempting to perform aerobic activity in depleted oxygen zones.

Or her body's preference for practical.

Too bad for her feet, she was done with practical. At least for the summer, she thought, taking in her matching cardigan set, glasses, and hair secured with a pencil at the back of her neck. Sure, right then, she supposed she resembled the bookkeeper that she was. But in a week's time, the summer semester at the culinary school she did bookkeeping for would end and she would be in Argentina—spending the next few months in the most exciting way possible.

Getting engaged.

"Engaged," she whispered to herself. A warm bubble of giddiness bounced around her stomach and tickled her heart.

Her boyfriend of four years, Philip, had been selected for an educational exchange program, teaching elevated Southern cuisine for the fall semester at one of the top culinary schools in South America. Not that anyone was surprised by the honor. Philip was handsome, charismatic, and the youngest master chef at Le Cordon Bleu School in Atlanta. In addition to being the perfect boyfriend—he scored a solid 9.9 on the compatibility test she gave him on their first date—he was so dedicated to his career that he'd elevated the school to worldwide acclaim.

Sometimes he was almost too dedicated. Not that there was anything wrong with that. Dedicated people tended to be reliable and stable. They had the ability to see things through—something her perpetually unemployed mother could benefit from. But lately Philip had spent so much time heating up his teaching kitchen, he couldn't even manage a simple tangled-sheets stir-fry when he got home.

So when he asked Kennedy to go with him to Argentina, days after she'd found a sizing slip to her favorite vintage jewelry shop, she'd nearly exploded into tears.

And had been walking around in a bliss-induced haze ever since.

She'd once read that traveling together ignites romance and intimacy between couples, opens the lines of communication, and builds healthy relationships. So it was the perfect time for them to reconnect, to take their relationship to that next level in an exotic land—to make that commitment into forever.

For her to have a long-overdue orgasm.

What better way to embrace what was to come, than with a new pair of shoes that made her feel sexy, spontaneous, and exotic. Daring even. There hadn't been a lot of opportunity for that in her life. She'd been too busy trying to find a safe harbor in an unpredictable childhood, which left her a little uptight. Okay, she was obsessed with organization and order, but now that she had a secure future ahead of her, and a stable man by her side, it was time to push the comfort of their relationship a little and experiment with new things.

Standing again, precariously balanced on her heels, she looked at her toes in the changing room mirror, then to the sensible cream flats she'd been dancing in for the past few months they'd been taking lessons. The flats matched her outfit—and her future if she didn't do something now to spice it up.

A loud thump sounded from the changing room beside her, followed by a low moan. Thinking someone had teetered right out of their heels, Kennedy pressed her ear to the wall.

"Is everything okay in there?" she asked, dropping to her knees when the only response was another thump, this one vibrating the wall between them.

A similar pair of mile-high red heels stood on the other side of the divider, fastened around a set of gorgeous tanned legs, which had a little gold anklet with an orchid charm dangling.

Oh my God! It was their tango teacher, Gloria. The woman who had inspired Kennedy to come to class early and try on the red shoes in the first place. The twenty-two-year-old Latin ballroom champion had legs to her neck, enough hip action to tempt the pope, and wore raw sex appeal like most women wore perfume.

And speaking of hip action!

Kennedy covered her eyes, then peeked through cracks of her fingers to watch as a pair of black and white, very classy, very masculine, wing-tipped shoes stepped toe to toe with the red heels, one of which lifted off the ground to lightly trace up the outside edge of her partner's leg and wrap around in a perfect *caricia.*

The wing tips stepped even closer, another thump ensued, then Kennedy heard the telltale sound of a zipper lowering.

Frozen, Kennedy watched as the wing tips started rocking in a perfect T-A-N-G-O rhythm, working toward, what Kennedy *knew*, would be a standing O. Back and forth, they swayed as the soft moans turned louder and the panting drifted under the dressing room door.

Kennedy found her hands were a little sweaty because for the first time in her life, she didn't have the right answer. Should she sneak out of the room and run for it?

A good choice, except she'd never been all that graceful and didn't have a sneaky bone in her body. Even worse, the hinges on the changing room door squeaked when she had come in, and getting caught would make for an awkward class. And she really loved their class.

It was the one hour a week when she had Philip all to herself, his undivided attention as he'd swept her across the floor, making her feel elegant and feminine. For a woman born with the coordination of a gazelle in snowshoes, it was something of a feat—something she wasn't willing to lose.

Which left hiding until they finished. An option that rather intrigued her. In fact, Kennedy felt embarrassed, intrigued, and a little bit naughty all at the same time. She also felt a tinge of disappointment, which started in her chest and moved up into her throat, because leaving the lights on was as kinky as Philip got. In fact, this might be as close as Kennedy would ever be to a standing-O-Tango.

With that sobering realization, she took a seat, pulled her knees to her chest, and stared at the wall. Which was all kinds of ridiculous.

It wasn't as if she could see anything through the wood divider, but sitting there in her red shoes gave her the courage to imagine. Only she didn't have to imagine much since the thumping got louder—and so did the dancing duo next door.

"*Ai, papi,*" Gloria said, her accent making every vowel sound like a promise. "You are such a good *lo-bar*."

"Uh," was all Mr. *Lo-bar* said. A single release of air that was neither sexy nor expected from an experienced Latin Lover. It was more of an admission that he'd had all he could handle. Not that Kennedy was judging—she had crested her comfort level about two moans back.

"Yes! Yes, *papi*," Gloria mewed and Kennedy closed her eyes. She had to. She was a private person by nature and tried her best to respect others' privacy, so the guilt began to build low in her belly. But before it could settle, Gloria cried out. "Just like *zat*, *Phil-ep*."

Kennedy's eyes flew open and the guilt quickly faded to confusion and finally shock. She climbed on the bench to get a look at this Latin lover *Phil-ep* who uttered a simple "Uh" in the throes of passion.

Breath left her body as her heart tried to adjust, to make room for the familiar ache of disappointment pressing in. Because there on the other side of the divider, with his pants around his ankles and another woman around his waist, was the man she lived with, the man she'd planned to spend the rest of her life with, executing moves with Gloria that told Kennedy this wasn't their first tango.

No, it appeared that *Phil-ep* was just exotic people's talk for a cheating, rat bastard of a boyfriend, and suddenly the past few months made sense. His shift in schedule, his sudden interest in "extra" dance classes, the way he pretended to be asleep when Kennedy would snuggle up behind him at night.

She didn't remember making a sound, or maybe the blood rushing through her ears made it hard to hear, but suddenly Philip looked up—and froze. At least she thought it was Philip. Right height, right build, right piercing blue eyes behind wire-rimmed glasses, but he looked different somehow.

"What are you doing here," was all he said. No "I'm sorry," or "Whoops, I tripped and accidentally ended up having sex with another woman," or "Please forgive me."

Just "What are you doing here," as though this were somehow her fault.

Maybe it was. What kind of woman didn't know when her boyfriend was sleeping with someone else?

The kind who puts all her eggs in the wrong basket. A trait that had been passed down from Sinclair mother to Sinclair daughter for five generations. A trait that Kennedy had spent a lifetime trying to overcome, without much luck.

Until today.

"You know what, *Phil-ep?* I have no idea what I'm doing here," she said then stepped off the bench.

Grabbing her purse, she walked out of the changing room, proud that she wasn't toppling over in the heels.

"Wait," Philip said and she heard a lot of rustling of fabric from his stall, but she didn't stop, refused to wait. She'd waited four years for him to pop the question, four years for him to take her on a vacation, to show her the world like he'd promised, and now she was tired of waiting.

Only Philip had always been an efficient dresser and incredibly quick, as Gloria must already know, so he was out of his stall and in front of her before she could make her escape.

"Let's talk about this."

"I am a visual learner, Philip, I think I understand. Tab A, slot B, no further explanation needed." Plus, there was nothing he could say that could make this any less painful—or more humiliating.

"I didn't mean for it to end this way."

Except that, she thought, her heart beating so fast she was afraid it would pop right out of her chest. He'd just broken up with her, in a public dressing room, with his fly down and his mistress listening to every word.

Part of her wanted to ask *why?* Why did everyone else always seem to move on before she got the memo that it was over? And why, damn it, didn't anyone ever think to get her that memo?

"Well, it didn't end 'this way,'" she said. "Because I reject your pathetic breakup since I broke up with you the second you became *Mr. Lo-bar.*"

He stuffed his hands in his pockets, only to remove them when he realized his fly parted. "I never meant to hurt you, Kennedy. It's just that we're so"—he looked at her starched pants and shirt and sighed—"solid."

"Most people would think that solid was a good thing." It was one of her biggest strengths, right along with reliable, steady, accountable.

The look he gave her said that he wasn't most people; that he was no longer looking for solid. Maybe he never had been. Maybe she'd been nothing more than someone to fill the gap between life's high points. A position Kennedy knew well.

"It is, but we've become so predictable"—he shrugged—"boring."

"Excuse me?" she said, the words getting caught on the humiliation that was clogging her throat.

"There is a color-coded, itemized itinerary for our Argentina trip on the fridge." He said it like that was a bad thing. "With Gloria, everything is fun and unexpected and new. Exciting."

Kennedy wanted to argue that she could be fun and exciting, too, try new things. *She* was the one who submitted his application for Argentina—not that *she* was going anymore. *She* had signed them up for dance classes. But then she thought of Gloria and her Latin moves and impulsive tendencies, and figured Philip wasn't willing to settle for classes anymore when he could have the real thing.

"With her, *I'm* exciting," he added.

"Exciting?" she asked, heavy on the sarcasm. The man thought golfing without a caddy was living on the edge. "You need a humidifier to sleep at night."

At one time Kennedy had thought he'd needed her, too. Just last semester he told her how he slept better, breathed easier, had less stress in his day knowing that she had his back at work and she'd be there when he got home.

Every cell of Kennedy froze in sheer horror because—*oh my God*—she was his humidifier. Kennedy Sinclair, winner of Berkeley's esteemed THE WORLD'S YOUR ABACUS award, was a certified life humidifier. Ironic because in that moment, with her whole *solid* world crashing down around her, she found it hard to breathe.

* * *

Whoever said one could never really go home obviously wasn't a Sinclair, because later that night, with all of her worldly possessions in the trunk, a bag of mostly eaten cookies in her lap, and a light dusting of powdered sugar everywhere in between, Kennedy pulled into her grandmother's drive. She'd made this journey a thousand times as a kid, the inevitable walk of shame to Grandma's house whenever her mother's world fell apart.

Only now that she was an adult, making the same pilgrimage felt so much worse. Maybe because it was *her* world falling apart or maybe because instead of packing for her first big adventure—which didn't come from a book or movie—she was once again packing up her entire life, forced to start over.

It was as if Sinclair women were destined to wind up alone and displaced. A disturbing thought, since Kennedy had done everything right, everything in her power to avoid ending up like her mother. The right school, right profession, right man. Yet there she was, single, homeless, and as of tomorrow, unemployed.

From a job she really loved. Balancing books at a culinary institute was the only way to blend her profession and her hobby—baking sweets.

Shoving another cookie in her mouth, Kennedy bent down to pop the trunk, crumbs falling out of God knew where and littering the floorboard. Wiping her mouth on the sleeve of her hoodie, she stepped out of the car, grabbed her suitcase, and walked up the brick pathway to the modest-sized Queen Anne–style house.

Even before her feet hit the landing, she knew Grandma Edna had stayed up and was waiting for her arrival. The "dreaming swing," which hung in the corner of the porch, was moving idly. Perched happily inside with Amos and Andy, her two cats, was Edna Sinclair.

All soft curves and frosted tips, she wore a teal house robe, matching crocheted slippers, and a warm smile. She also had a single sheet of toilet paper wrapped around her curlers and secured with bobby pins.

"I'm home," Kennedy said, dropping her suitcase on

the welcome mat, which read, WENT BIG AND CAME HOME.

"Figured it was either that or I was about to be robbed." Edna glanced at Kennedy's black hoodie pulled over her head and yoga pants. "Glad it's you, seeing as I made cookies and the boys don't like to share none."

The "boys" sent her their best *disrupt our pet time and we will pee on your bed* glare.

"I made cookies, too." She held up the bag, which was surprisingly light, and joined her grandmother on the swing. They both had to scoot down to accommodate Andy's swishing tail. "Snacked on them on the way over."

"I can see that," Edna said, brushing at Kennedy's shoulder and unleashing an avalanche of crumbs onto Amos's back. He growled, his little whiskers doing double time.

"Chocolate butterball cookies." Kennedy rubbed at a large cluster of crumbs that had collected in her cleavage, but it made only a white smear, so she shrugged and gave up. "They're Philip's favorite. I made a batch while I was packing."

"Did you leave him any?"

Kennedy shook her head. "Just a dirty kitchen. And my resignation."

"That was nice of you." Edna patted her knee and Kennedy's eyes started to burn. "Most women would have assumed letting the air out of his tires was word enough."

Most Sinclair women would have shot first, asked questions second, and then let him pull up his pants after they felt they'd been properly heard. But Kennedy had always been the more reserved one in her family.

"I wrote it in Sharpie across all of his dry cleaning that I had just picked up," she admitted.

"There's that creative, passionate girl I know," Edna said and an unexpected flicker of excitement ignited at her grandmother's words. No one had called her creative and passionate since she was a girl. Instead of being embarrassed by her impulsive behavior, she gave in to it, surprised at how liberating it felt.

Almost as powerful an emotion as the choking fear of not knowing what was next. Of how she was expected to pick up and move on—again.

Torn between laughing and crying, Kennedy settled on staring out at the Georgia sky and letting the gentle evening breeze be her guide. Like Kennedy, Edna lived in the greater Atlanta area, which meant that the city lights snuffed out most of the stars, leaving an inky blanket over the city. But tonight, there were a few bold ones whose twinkle was bright enough to break through the night and be seen. And for some reason that made Kennedy smile.

"I miss that girl," Edna said, wrapping a pudgy arm around Kennedy's shoulder and pulling her close.

"I do, too." Without hesitation, Kennedy snuggled in deeper, wrapping her arms around Edna's middle and breathing in the familiar scent of cinnamon and vanilla and everything that was safe. One sniff and Kennedy felt her smile crumble and the tears well up.

"They were doing it during the light of day against the wall of a dressing room," she whispered. "With their shoes on. He's never asked me to keep my shoes on."

"Of course he didn't," Edna cooed. "You're a respectable woman who knows the value of a good pair of shoes."

Oh God. Even her grandmother thought she was respectable, and everyone knew that *respectable* was just another word for boring. And boring people wound up living in their childhood bedroom at thirty with the neighborhood crazy cat lady as their roommate. "What if I wanted to keep my shoes on?"

"With what he's been stepping in lately, you should count yourself lucky," her grandma cooed.

"Gloria's the lucky one. He's taking her to Argentina next week." And there went the tears.

She tried to hold them back, but sitting there in her grandmother's arms, once again being the one snuffed out by something—or someone—bigger and brighter, brought back every time her mom had taken off with some guy on some other adventure, leaving Kennedy at home.

"He's the one who cheated, the one who lied, and he still gets to go teach in Argentina, and cross something off his bucket list. And I am stuck in another life time-out." A realization that not only sucked, but also challenged every belief she'd ever held dear. Including the belief in herself.

"That just means you get to check something off your *own* list now."

"That was my list. Argentina was *my* dream." Then it became their dream, and somehow Philip would get to be the one to live it.

"Ah, child, then find a new dream, something fun that doesn't include listening to all that wheezing the jackass does when he gets excited," Edna said, stroking Kennedy's hair.

Kennedy chuckled. "One time he snored so loud, our neighbors thought we were doing it all night."

"Probably thought he'd taken one of those blue pills," Edna said in the same tone she'd read a bedtime story. "Philip doesn't strike me as the most resilient man."

He wasn't, but Kennedy hadn't been interested in sprinters; she was looking for someone who was slow and steady. Only her best chance at going the distance had handed his baton to another woman.

"How can I have fun when I know he's out there living his life, having shoes on while making whoopee, and tangoing all over my future?"

A future Kennedy had worked so hard to make safe. With a man she thought she could trust.

Edna tsked. "Even as a little bit of a thing, you were so busy making checks and balances, you let the fun pass you by. Maybe this was God's way of saying you need to let go of the future you planned, and take some time to taste the icing."

The size of a large child, Kennedy still was a little bit of a thing who didn't know the first thing about life's icing. Hadn't had the luxury. Between her unstable childhood then working toward gaining fiscal stability, she hadn't had a lot of time for dreaming, let alone something that whimsical. Sadly, the closest she'd ever come to eating the icing was a fun four years working the morning shifts at a little bakery near campus to put herself through business school.

"I wouldn't even know where to start," she admitted, her voice thick with emotion.

"How about with one of these?" Edna pulled an old journal out from beside her and set it on Kennedy's lap. It was pink, pocket sized, had a well-worn spine and a picture of a cupcake with sprinkles on the cover.

The hurt and disappointment had settled so deep inside, it had turned into aching numbness by the time she'd walked out of her downtown loft for the last time, so she assumed any more pain would be impossible. Yet as she clicked open the gold-plated latch, which was rusty from years of neglect, and saw the swirly handwriting at the top, her chest tightened further.

This disappointment felt different, as though it originated from someplace old and forgotten, and it packed the kind of punch that made speaking impossible.

Kennedy wasn't sure how she managed to let herself stray so far from her life's goal. She hadn't felt the kind of hope and excitement that was apparent in the words she'd written since she discovered that while most people were looking for a copilot to happiness, not everyone had what it took to be more than just a brief stopover. Sadly for Kennedy, she'd figured out early on which category she fell into.

"'Life's short so eat the icing first,'" she read as her finger traced lightly over the words on the first page. Edna had given it to her the summer she'd turned thirteen, when Candice Sinclair had taken off with a truck driver from Ashland, leaving a brokenhearted Kennedy behind with her grandmother.

Kennedy was still naive enough to believe that one day her mother would take her along. That one day the two of them would see the country together like Candice promised. By July, Kennedy had realized that if she were going to live an exciting life, then she'd have to make it happen herself. And she took the *icing first* rule to heart and entered an apple and rhubarb pie in the State Fair. She'd found the recipe in an old cookbook, and Edna had spent hours with her in the kitchen helping her perfect it. Her entry won third place in the junior category, earning her two tickets to the theater in Atlanta. Something she'd always wanted to do, but her grandmother could never afford.

"Look at you, set to take on the world," Edna said, pointing to a photo of Kennedy as a teen. She stood in front of a table filled with winning cakes, lanky and still finding her feet, but the smile she wore was so bright, it burned Kennedy's heart.

She was wearing her favorite blue summer dress that her grandmother had bought especially for the fair, and pinned to the front was a third place ribbon.

"I thought I lost this recipe," Kennedy said, looking at the swirly writing on the adjacent page. She'd also forgotten how excited she'd felt when she'd won that ribbon. It was as if she'd finally found some kind of tangible proof that maybe she was special.

Kennedy turned the page and a watery smile spread across her face. There was a photo of her grandma dressed like the queen, wearing pearls, white gloves, and a hat fit for a royal wedding.

"I borrowed the pearls from Pastor Cunningham's wife, and the gloves from Mabel," Edna said, nostalgia lacing her voice.

"You made me that dress," Kennedy said. She'd loved that dress, wore it until it went from midi to mini, and Edna said she was giving too much away for free.

"It's still in the attic."

Beneath each photo was the sweet creation that made that moment possible. A three-tier coconut cake, a recipe straight from her grandmother's Southern roots, that she made the following year. It took second place and she won high tea at the Ritz-Carlton in Atlanta.

It was her fourth attempt, though, a perfect Southern apple rhubarb pie with a Georgia pecan crust, that took first place, then took her on a six-week Down Home Sweets journey at the local culinary school, cementing her fascination with small-town living, Southern eats, and a deep love for baking.

Kennedy carefully thumbed through the pages of photos capturing some of the most precious moments of her childhood, the respective recipes that made it all possible. Ignoring the photo of her and Edna cooking snowball cookies in their pajamas on Christmas morning, since that recipe would now forever be connected to that rat-fink *lo-bar* and his pathetic "Uh" in the throes of passion, she stopped when she found what she was looking for. At the back of the journal was an extensive and itemized list she'd assembled, her LIFE'S ICING list, which indexed every recipe she wanted to try, every competition she wanted to enter, and every goal she wanted to accomplish, complete with coordinating check boxes.

Not a single one was marked off.

With a shaky breath, Kennedy flipped the page and scanned each item, stopping midway through when her heart gave a little stir:

39. Make a *Rogel* with *dulce de leche*.

She wasn't sure that she had quite mastered the flair for creating the soft, but crumbly texture of that variation of dulce de leche in the Confections of South America class she took over the summer. Let alone something as intricate as the layers of puff pastry required to make one of Argentina's most treasured desserts. But since Philip had robbed her of checking off the first and most important recipe on her list, a *Five-Tiered Wedding Cake*, she was taking what she could get. Because somewhere along the way she had forgotten that she needed to be in charge of her own destiny.

She remembered it now.

"What I need is a job." One that would allow her to get a new apartment, get back on her feet. Although she had some savings, she needed to make sure her bank account had enough padding so that when she started writing those checks, they didn't bounce.

"Already got you one lined up," Edna said, handing her a printout of a job listing for a pie shop. "It comes with a little frosting, too."

"What's this?"

"Sweetie Pies," Edna said, snatching the paper back and flipping to the next page to display several photos of a quaint brick storefront and their award-winning pies, including the five-pound Deep Dish HumDinger. Between the sixteen Gold Tins hanging in the window and the title of "Best Apple Pie in the Country," the two women in the photo were undoubtedly looking for a true, down-home baker. Kennedy was, sadly, neither.

"My old friend Fiona owns it with her sister-in-law. She e-mailed me that ad."

"You called her? About me?"

"Of course I did."

"When?" Kennedy's life was still shoved in her trunk.

"The second you said you were heading home," Edna tutted. "Picked up the phone to see if she was looking for some help for the harvest season. Even told her that my granddaughter is a college graduate with a fancy degree from a fancy school, and works at Le Cordon Bleu."

Kennedy was the first Sinclair to finish college, something that gave Edna bragging rights on her side of town. Because people who grew up in this neighborhood seldom got out. But Kennedy had, and there was no way she could go back.

"I work in an office at Le Cordon Bleu. Writing checks and balancing payroll, not baking pies," Kennedy reminded her grandmother.

"You bake on the weekends, take classes every chance you get," Edna said. "And still manage to win awards."

"I was a teenager, it was the junior category, at the Georgia State Fair." Kennedy looked at the picture of the shop again. It was exactly what she'd dreamed of working in when she'd been a girl. Charming, welcoming, and looked like a mother's kitchen should look—sweet, warm, and a safe place to land. Then she read the address and her head started to pound. "The shop is in Washington State?"

"Destiny Bay. It's a little town on the southern border of Washington, nestled between the Cascades and the Pacific Ocean. Known for apples and, since Fi started baking, pies. It's the perfect place for you to find a new future."

"Destiny Bay?" It sounded perfect. Even the way it rolled off the lips implied it was the kind of place she could go and forget about her problems at home. Create a new life.

Only running away was a classic Candice move, and Kennedy would rather take dance classes from Gloria than be like her mother. Then again, she didn't really have a home any longer, so it wasn't as though she would be technically running away. "Isn't that where you met Grandpa Harvey?"

"I met him in Seattle, near where I grew up, but followed him all the way to Destiny Bay, where he got down on one knee, right there in the middle of town, with a bouquet of spring posies and his mama's ring." Edna sighed dreamily, as if remembering the day, and Kennedy gave in to the romantic nature of her story. "Met Fiona there, too, she was my maid of honor, my best friend, and the person who took me in when Harvey moved to Tuscaloosa, making it clear it was a journey for one. Fi gave me a job selling apples on her family's plantation so I wouldn't starve to death."

Kennedy sat up and shook all that romantic naïveté right off.

She was a finance girl, not a frivolous girl—and baking pies in the meantime to get over a broken heart only prolonged getting her life back on track. And kept the Sinclair curse alive and well. Which was why she refused the urge to make a life-changing decision because of a man.

"I don't want to spend the last few weeks of my summer baking pies. I need to buckle down and find a new job." Preferably before the new semester started.

"Oh, you wouldn't just be baking, honey." Edna leaned in and lowered her voice as though she was imparting a national secret. "I have it on good word that Fi isn't looking for short-term help, she and her sister-in-law co-own it, and are looking to pass on their legacy. They're looking for a strong-willed, sensible woman, who loves baking and is brave enough to carve out a little slice of life's pie for herself."

"And there aren't any of those in their hometown?"

Edna laughed. "Fi's got herself a slew of nephews, and Paula a son, but not a single female in the family. And Paula's got the arthritis, which is why Fi's still baking pies every day even though she's got more miles on her than my old DeSoto. She's ready to slow down and retire, and Paula needs to give her joints a rest and go on that cruise they've been blabbering on about. They're just waiting for the right owner to come along."

Now it was Kennedy's turn to laugh. "And you think that's me?"

"I think this is one of those opportunities we always talked about, where with a little courage and a lot of hard work, you can change your life."

Kennedy felt her throat tighten. How many times had she sat right there on the porch swing and wished she could change? Her situation, her options... her life.

And she had.

It'd taken years of hard work and perseverance, but Kennedy had created that new life she dreamed of. A posh downtown apartment, a respectable job, and a man who represented everything her childhood and upbringing lacked.

Only as fate would have it, Philip found her lacking, and Kennedy had lost it all.

Nope. Courage wasn't the problem. Neither was hard work. Kennedy hadn't figured out the difference between an option and an opportunity—between loyalty and love.

"We don't know if it would be a change for the better," Kennedy said.

"That's what's so exciting," Edna said, her eyes lit with excitement. "You can either spend the rest of your life like I did, pushing someone else's pencils and dreams and end up right here on this front porch, or you could start making some of your own come true."

A strange lightness filled her belly, warming the parts of her soul that had moments ago felt hallow, because suddenly the ridiculous idea didn't seem so ridiculous.

Kennedy had gone into business because she loved the idea of owning her own company, building something of her own that no one could take from her. And this opportunity seemed to combine her two loves with what she was trained to do. But there was one thing Kennedy couldn't seem to get past.

She rested her head on Edna's shoulder and admitted, "I can't even plan my own life, let alone a business." Especially a pie shop in a small town in Washington.

"Honey, you came out of the womb planning. It's what you do."

A slow panic started to churn in her stomach, moving faster and faster, until she regretted eating three dozen snowballs. Because wasn't that exactly what Philip had said?

"She's willing to sell it to you for a bargain." Edna pulled out a packet from underneath Amos, who let loose a throaty growl, and handed it over. "She almost sold it last year to another buyer, but changed her mind when the woman started talking franchising. Here is the contract she'd had drawn up, told me to have you look it over and give her a call if you were interested."

Kennedy straightened and flipped through the papers. Fi and Edna had both gone through a hassle putting this together so quickly; it was the least she could do.

She took her time, read every word, and decided that it was a standard sales agreement, straightforward and easy to understand. Then she reached the overview of the financials and felt her eyes bulge a little. "Her pie shop made more money last year than Philip did."

"And it was a slow year since they closed up for ten weeks last spring to take one of those senior trips to Alaska," Edna said, sounding wistful.

Kennedy looked over at the woman who had raised her and felt her heart turn over. The dreamy look on her face over the idea of a vacation was a painful reminder of just how much Edna had sacrificed. She spent some of her best years raising Kennedy, and most of her retirement savings sending Kennedy to Georgia Tech. Kennedy was diligent about paying her grandmother back, but with her student loans and bills, it was slow coming. Owning this business could change all of that.

"How much is she asking?"

Her grandmother rattled off a number.

"That's it?" Not that it wasn't a lot of money. It was. In fact, it would nearly wipe out Kennedy's entire life savings. But based on the shop's financials, the price seemed extremely low. Which meant either that Edna needed to get her hearing aid checked, or Fi wasn't being honest about the profits.

"Oh, that's the down payment, honey. But since Fi owned the property outright, she's willing to carry the note so you can pay her in monthly installments, with a small balloon payment due at the end of every fiscal year.

She also said she'll sell you a few acres' worth of her special apples at cost for the lifetime of the shop and let you stay in her caretaker's house for six months rent-free, so you can get the apartment above the shop cleaned up."

"It comes with an apartment?" This deal couldn't get any sweeter. Having an apartment would allow her to save up enough money for a down payment on her own home someday—one that didn't have a live-in heartbreak waiting to happen.

One that belonged to her.

"The store, the apartment, her recipes, supplies, and name are all yours if you say yes." Edna smiled. "Did I mention Fi's apple pie is a sixteen-time Gold Tin winner?"

Kennedy gasped. Only the highest honor any pie could receive, and it explained the incredible numbers. It was too good to be true, which in Kennedy's world meant it was.

"What's the catch?" Kennedy asked, her eyes narrowing. "And what happens if I can't pull it off? Or I can't make a balloon payment?"

"No catch. But if you default on the payments, the shop passes back to Fi," Edna said as if the word *default* were no big deal. As if it didn't cause perspiration to break out on Kennedy's hands and her stomach to roll with unease. After a lifetime of being passed back and forth, only to eventually be passed over by the people who were supposed to love her forever, it was terrifying.

And sure, money would be filtering in for her half of the condo she and Philip had shared. But she had no idea when he could make that happen or how much it would even be worth—details she wasn't ready to face. And money she couldn't rely on.

"Look at you, already planning yourself right out of an opportunity," Edna said softly, taking Kennedy's hand in her frail one, and giving a pat that connected with every insecurity Kennedy tried so desperately to control. "The worst that can happen is that it doesn't work out, you check a few things off your list, get a chance to live in a new and exciting place, and have memories that will last a lifetime."

In true Sinclair fashion, Edna completely overlooked that she'd also wind up broke and homeless. Then again, Kennedy was already the latter, and she'd spent most of her life being the former. But she'd never been a failure—until now.

She felt the familiar crushing disappointment close in, but refused to let it take hold. Because, while the setbacks caused from her chaotic childhood were out of her control, she'd chosen the path with Philip.

And she could choose a new path, a path of her own, she told herself, because more than her fear of failing was the fear that she'd be sidelined for the rest of her life. Spend her career behind a desk, managing other people's dreams and never stepping out to go after something of her own.

Maybe this was her chance. Sure, it didn't come in the package that Kennedy expected, but sometimes the best opportunities presented themselves in the most unexpected ways. And hadn't she just been wishing for some excitement in her simple life?

Kennedy pulled her phone from her sweatshirt pocket, and swallowing down all the *what-ifs* that would normally have her wearing her cream ballet flats, she clicked on the selfie mode of her camera and said, “Smile, Grandma. I need a new photo to go next to my snowball cookies.”

“Of you covered in crumbs and crying?”

“Nope, of me going after a little icing.” And Kennedy snapped the photo.

Fall in Love with Forever Romance

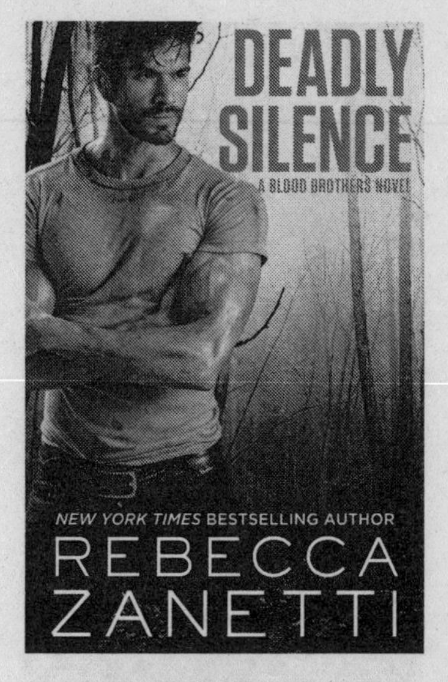

DEADLY SILENCE
By Rebecca Zanetti

Fans of Maya Banks, Shannon McKenna, and Lisa Jackson will love this sexy, suspenseful romance from *New York Times* bestselling author Rebecca Zanetti. Paralegal Zara Remington wants to keep things casual with private investigator Ryker Jones. But when a secret military organization starts to hunt them down, her true feelings for him surface—just as their lives are being threatened.

Fall in Love with Forever Romance

TOO HARD TO FORGET
By Tessa Bailey

The "Queen of Dirty Talk" is back with the third book in the Romancing the Clarksons series! Peggy Clarkson is returning to her college alma mater with one goal in mind: confront Elliott Brooks, the man who ruined her for all others, and prove she's over him for good. But she's in for a surprise when this time Elliott has no intention of letting her walk away.

Fall in Love with Forever Romance

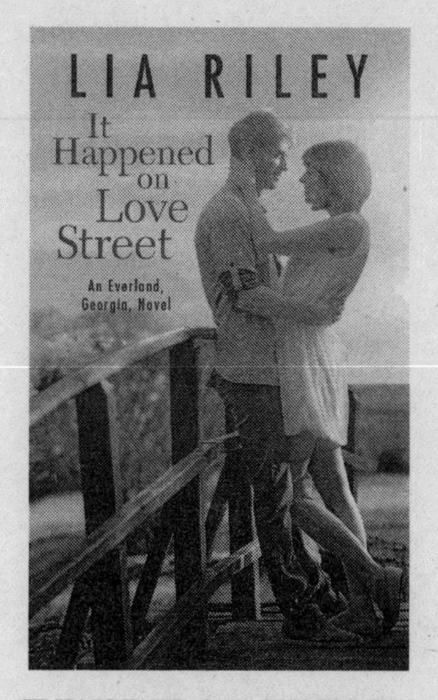

IT HAPPENED ON LOVE STREET
By Lia Riley

Lawyer Pepper Knight finds herself stranded and unemployed in Everland, Georgia, and she turns to the sexy town vet, Rhett Valentine, for help. But when she starts to fall for him, she has to decide: Will she be able to give up her big city dreams for love in a small town? For fans of Kristan Higgins, Jill Shalvis, and Marina Adair.

Fall in Love with Forever Romance

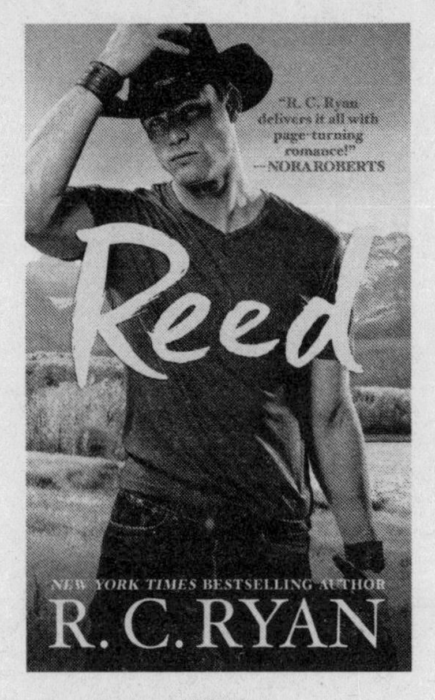

REED
By R.C. Ryan

In the tradition of Linda Lael Miller and Diana Palmer comes the latest from R.C. Ryan. Cowboy Reed Malloy is Glacier Ridge's resident ladies' man and now his sights are set on the beautiful Allison Shaw. But a secret feud between their families threatens their love—and their lives. The heartwarming conclusion to R.C. Ryan's Western romance series, the Malloys of Montana.